Fall Winter Collections

Fall Winter Collections

Koral Dasgupta

NIYOGI BOOKS

Published by
NIYOGI BOOKS
D-78, Okhla Industrial Area, Phase-I
New Delhi-110 020, INDIA
Tel: 91-11-26816301, 49327000
Fax: 91-11-26810483, 26813830
email: niyogibooks@gmail.com
website: www.niyogibooksindia.com

Editor: Gita Rajan
Cover Design: Dsgn Unplugged
Layout: Shashi Bhushan Prasad

ISBN: 978-93-83098-84-2
Publication: 2015

This is a work of fiction. The names, characters and incidents portrayed in it are the work of the authors' imagination. Any resemblance to actual persons, living or dead, events or localities, is entirely coincidental.

Printed at: Niyogi Offset Pvt. Ltd., New Delhi, India

To my son Neev Tanish;

And those endless moments in Santiniketan when life felt as perfect as its bounteous Nature ...

There is something common between us. We both appreciate beauty. Cosmic beauty, beauty of external appearances and internal devotions, beauty of language and art, of articulation and expression, of each enlightened day fading into dark, and the beauty of life-where people come close and drift apart by shrewd interplay of destiny and yet, nothing stops because almost everything or everyone has a time-relevant substitute. Only difference between the sculptor and the professor is that the sculptor wants to capture his object of beauty, the professor lets go.

Fall Winter Collections

Sanghamitra Banerjee
Santiniketan

It's quite happening and crowded here during this part of the year. The first few days of the *Poush Mela* are usually so hectic that we hardly get time to breathe. 23rd December or the 7th day of *Poush* as per Bengali calendar celebrates Debendranath Tagore's birthday at Santiniketan. The evening before, everyone gathers at Gour Prangan for *Baitalik*, which is basically going around the campus in a procession while singing Tagore's compositions. This formally starts the annual festival. The procession repeats itself on 23rd dawn, with fewer participants for obvious reasons. Every year I get up at 4:00 am to take a bath and prepare to attend this occasion at 5:00. I love being here. After *Baitalik* is over, I never return home. Instead I go for long walks. I stop only when I can walk no more. The soil is red in this part of the country. And it has a specific texture. In spite of the *developments* catching up to give it a *city* status, the flora, fauna and landscape here is too stubborn to let go of its originality.

Many known faces and acquaintances come into view when I stop at Ratan Pally for morning tea. Women who belong to this place or those who have spent a considerable part of their lives in Santiniketan, can be distinctly identified. They might be loud or subtle, as per their character and occupation. But they sport a style statement unique to this place. They wear a sari with aplomb and carry it effortlessly; they can even ride a bicycle wearing the sari without getting it entangled in the spokes. I find that quite an achievement! Often they have long hair, sport huge bindis, adorn themselves with terracotta or white metal jewellery … the more fashionable and affluent ones do up their eyes with great care and effort. Casually, they are smart in jeans and trousers, often coupled with a batik *kurti* and a scarf thrown carelessly. Whatever be the dress code, women here never give up that feminine Santiniketan style, which can't be exactly defined. At tea stalls, at the Central Library of Viswa Bharati, on the way while walking the cycle, they discuss music and literature and other intellectual stuff and argue over critical decisions in politics and history. And in between furious debates if their *kurti* shifts places, much to their neighbour's delight, they are cool about it.

Men are no less at being *branded* with the place. Long kurta, stubble, glasses and sling bags–the ever popular Bengali *jhola*–hanging down their shoulders are stamped as credentials. Those who can play a musical instrument or can sing (many claim mastery but very few actually can) score high with the opposite sex. But somehow, here I miss the madness of a man! Often men here seem to lack ambition; they tend to seem adrift, to lead an aimless, dreamer's life. They are not exactly interested in sports. Rather, the so-called intellectuals would love to spend an evening in the library, putting to risk their already damaged eyesight, have *meaningful conversations* whatever that means and convert their intellectual outbursts to smoke at every given opportunity. I don't see passion; I don't see them growing; they're so damn rigid. They may have memorised every word of Tagore including the punctuations, but many of them dismiss Shakespeare and Tennyson as peanuts without even bothering to read them. These people explain their bitter failures with such philosophical pronouncements that it sounds like sacrifice; sadly it doesn't hide their frustration! Even ideals seem passé and they survive on an arm-chair state of mind! Men here are just too calm, too *thanda*, too cold … lacking the vigour and vitality that essentially defines masculinity.

No I am not a man-hater, but here I do miss *real* men who challenge themselves and break barriers. My father, who had contributed thirty years of his life as a cancer specialist and fought the dreaded disease before he succumbed to it himself, had probably created an invincible benchmark that refuses to leave me alone.

My eyes wander in search of someone interesting, as I lean against the wall of Sukumar da's stall sipping the brown liquid. I consume it more because Sukumar da calls it *chai* than its aesthetic or nutritional value. I am disappointed in my search, but am nevertheless amused. Off and on, the postman-fruit vendor-barber-cobbler greets me with a *Namoshkaar didimoni*. Instead of returning the *Namoshkar*, I raise the glass in my hand like a toast and smile. That's what I am. A *didimoni* or professor of Economics, with a diverse social circle. There are some students who swear by me and trust me more than the text books; some colleagues with whom I share love-hate relationships; some uncomplicated friends; a bicycle I have named Pushpak; and a small house with two rooms that grant me peace whenever I desire. And there are also some lesser known people like these … the postman, cobbler, barber, etc. from Ratan Pally market, who never cease to surprise me. On hot summer afternoons they'll suddenly appear from nowhere and offer to shelter me with their tattered umbrella to save my more expensive and educated self from the scorching heat; if I refuse, they'll insist. They claim to be better off in the sun because they are born here and are used to it, but swear I'll dehydrate through lack of protection! It's difficult to ignore this expression of love. Not that they do this expecting any return. They'll not accept a penny unless there's a valid transaction, so strong is their sense of self-respect. Yet they are protective and gentle, with rough exteriors suggesting life-altering experiences that they may have gone through. Absent-mindedly I had kept the finished cup to be taken away; Sukumar da has refilled it when I was not watching. He does take advantage of my absentmindedness often; I don't object. Rana, the guy from the next shop, is taking down the bamboo sticks that he uses to close the shop every night. He tells me, '*Didimoni*, did you realise, it rained last night?' The girl washing plates at Sukumar da's yells back, 'What rain? This fool must have been dreaming! Rains during *Poush*!! And you are trying to fool our *didimoni* with your nonsense!' The two start arguing fiercely. I half-follow their conversation and decide, there must be something going on between them. There's a sparkle in both their eyes. Rana may have targeted the statement at her; he just addressed it to me.

Their fight continues, though it is much more milder now and they are pulling each other's leg. Its 8:30 in the morning; winter winds are more efficient than my sweater and shawl. I can see some known faces advancing. Head of Department of English Literature, Prof. Ganguly. She is nicknamed Cleopatra for her oomph, short hair and foreign accent. I straighten up to show respect. She smiles, greets me and moves on. I feast my eyes on her for a while ... lovely sari! The Ratan Pally area is comparatively less crowded now. The crowd is participating in the functions of 7th *Poush*; I can hear the music. As I gather myself to pay the customary visit to Chatim Tala (where the remains of Maharshi Debendranath Tagore rest in peace), I spot Anusua Lahiri taking gigantic steps forward. In fact I am being really polite in not mentioning that she is running! She is one of the saddest souls here. Santiniketan was not her destination, she repeats often with a philosophical sigh, looking skywards. She deserves to marry a French musician and settle in Las Vegas! Poor thing is stuck here as a Professor of Graphics in Kala Bhavan, because of *shrewd interplay of destiny*, as she puts it. The amply-endowed lady huffs and puffs as she reaches me. 'Sukumar da, chai,' she orders. 'Hey, do you have change?' Well, that's my cue. Without wasting words I place a note on Sukumar da's table and share a quiet smile with him. She behaves like this when there's something spicy to share and you have to understand that you are paying for the spice. 'Spill,' I command. Her eyes wide, she lowers her voice. 'A *chikna* is joining us in sculpture,' she gushes, 'second week of Jan.' 'French?' I ask with a smile that invites scorn. 'He's a big name in his field. A PhD from Harvard, M.F.A. from Yale; specialises in capturing human emotions on black stone. In fact he works on the female anatomy. His list of credentials is long, with national and international recognition. Everyone within the department is busy betting that this guy, who's not even a Bengali, would be a misfit in our traditional pedagogy. But the fact is, he's too dishy given his qualifications. Huh! Sukumar da, two more biscuits please!' Alright, so that's the spice. The typical gossips for and against a qualified newcomer. As Anusua pours out more, and subsequently moves on to different topics, we get up and walk towards the ground where the *Poush Mela* has been declared open just a while ago.

The huge field looks action-packed. Literary, food and garments stalls are scattered randomly with small scale, unorganised vendors selling artificial jewellery, paintings, toys, bags, batiks, musk, etc. sitting on the ground. The stage is set for Baul performances in the evening. Many of them have already arrived; smoking ganja, their *ektaras* fallen beside them on the ground. We come across some known and unknown faces. Anusua introduces me to a few; I return the compliment. Stalls cajole us to buy their wares; some of them invite us to sit there and help out. We find the sari-clad, vermillion-stained Sia, a half-Mexican Indian, at the stall put up by the department of English Literature. Her partner, Shayan, is busy helping out at the store; she is bored and wants to go out for a smoke. The three of us move away from there and walk ahead towards an *on duty* Swagata Sanyal trying to collect bytes for reporting *Poush Mela* to 'What's New/s' for a television channel. We call him Stuart (Little), alluding to his height. Stuart and I had been batchmates in college. Both of us did our Masters in Economics and then picked up different professions as per our interests. He owns a house in Prantik, the railway station next to Bolpur, and comes here often. Stuart and Sia share a smoke, when we spot Shayan coming hurriedly, looking all tensed up. Sia throws the cigarette on the ground and stubs it out with her shoe, arousing Stuart's disgust. We realise, while walking off we had not mentioned our departure to Shayan and the poor thing was probably tensed up that his wife was lost. To cover up, the moment he reaches us, we shout in unison blaming him for disappearing from the stall. Sia was so upset, we add. Taken aback by our joint attack, Shayan is rendered speechless. We control our laughter and move on for lunch.

The evening is mine. I had spent the day chatting around with friends and socialising. After lunch, we had spent some time sitting at Purano Melar Matth, the smaller ground where the fair was held earlier in front of Upasana Griha and gorging on oranges while the winter sun blessed us with its pleasant warmth. My house at Simanta Pally is a little in the interior. I have done it up as per my taste. Every inch talks about me. Houses at Santiniketan have a typical look. Usually pillared exteriors, uncomplicated interiors, windows with straight grills, doors with bars, floor usually red, etc. In such a traditional get up, I have contrasted the décor with pearl white walls and double curtains in windows–a transparent orange inside and white cotton printed with golden outside. Two walls have floor level sitting arrangements facing each other. These can be joined at night to make a bed. Both of these have reading lamps fitted on the adjoining walls, and a huge lamp in between. The wall facing the lamp at the other end has a huge, round mirror. Right at the entrance to the house, there is a brass Saraswati supported by the wall. I offer flowers to the deity every day, not because I am religious but because I respect what she symbolises–education! That's the base of my faith all through my personal and professional existence. The two rooms of the house are my study and bedroom. The study has books of my choice, not necessarily Economics. The make-shift bed accommodates me on days when I fall asleep while reading at night and feel too tired to transport myself to the bedroom. The bedroom, along with a master bed, has photographs of my closest family on the adjoining table. I believe that it is important to see and remember your near and dear ones, last thing in the day and first thing in the morning, because it makes you feel loved and protected. There's a lot of open space in my house which allows uninterrupted vision. I can't live in packed areas. I have a small veranda as well where I like to sit in the early mornings and late evenings, sipping black tea. The tea I consume comes in the form of leafs, not granules, sourced from Darjeeling. While boiling water I add some mint leaves, ginger and a pinch of spices; once the water is boiling I add the tea leafs and soak them for long. The aroma fills my mind. I watch TV, read books, prepare for my lectures, cook, think, write … all uninterrupted and at peace, whenever I am home.

Hey wait … What would he be like? Anusua's *chikna*! Typical creative types? Ponytail and tattoos? A sling bag and glasses? Achievers in niche specialisations are usually arrogant. It would be fun if he is. Such intellectuals make great subjects during our gossip sessions! What is the name of the *chikna*?? Did Anusua mention? Well, what's in a name??

What's in a Name??

Dr Aniruddh Jain Solanki
Kolkata

This part of the country seems to love its woollens! I found Delhi romancing the winters with fashion and creative celebrations. Kolkata, that recorded much higher temperatures, is capped and covered as if it were snowing. My friend's father, Krishnendu Patra, or Krishna Uncle, as I call him, was even wearing gloves and a muffler when he came to receive me at the airport at 8:00 pm! I heard that this is the best time in the city, to have fun, given the benevolence of the weather. During the last few days in Kolkata, I visited the Victoria Memorial, Birla Planetarium, Birla Mandir, Rabindra Sadan and Nandan, etc. Krishna Uncle had offered to take me to the famous Alipore Zoo as well, which I politely declined. I visited many times the Academy of Fine Arts, which is a place of special significance for my professional pursuits; I heard this is the Mecca for art lovers in Bengal.

During one early morning jog I encountered a gentleman in tracks and pullovers, smoking a *Classic* and sipping tea. He greeted me with a good morning and lectured on Bengali culture for almost fifteen minutes. It was only later that he realised I did not exactly understand his language and sadly his fast-track delivery did not allow me a chance to declare the fact! He was undoubtedly disappointed and tried to replicate the performance in English, but the translation did not carry half the fire as the original and had to stop midway. Back home I tried to share the joke with Krishna Uncle. His attention was wholly mine as I narrated; but at the end I was not treated to the laughter and smiles I expected. Instead there was a heavy-throat 'Rubbish!' He explained why he hated the kind of people who are so closed and culturally conservative that they can't look beyond Bengal and experience learning from other parts of the world! He spoke in English for half an hour. Phew!!

With the kind of characters I came across during my first few days in Bengal, I realise that there are three types of Bengalis–the 'Britz,' the '*desis*' and the 'comrades!' The Britz are either foreign returned or foreign educated or have too much of *London* in them. They ooze Shakespeare and Wordsworth, discuss high profile political and economic models, smoke on pipes, retain inherited gramophones for their antique value, speak Bengali-accented fluent English loaded with words imported from the Oxford dictionary. Their conversations are regularly punctuated with, 'When we were in States/London/Greece/Athens/etc. Krishna Uncle belongs to this category!

The *desis* are true to their culture, proud to belong to the land of Rabindranath Tagore, Sharatchandra Chattopadhyay, Netaji Subhash Chandra Bose, Satyajit Ray, etc. They seem to be completely distanced from the present state of Bengal, residing in an ideal zone of pride and perfection, well crafted within their own minds. They listen to old Bengali songs every morning, raving about a glorious past. Descending from that past is an achievement bigger than the shame associated with messing it all up in the present! Their habits, food, attire, choices–all strictly adhere to the codes of pure *Bengali culture*.

And then, the Comrades. They are the politically aroused, often Marxist, youth (or those who are no longer young but retain the same burning passion). They may or may not be academically aware of the history or policies that have led to the present situation, neither do they have a practical solution towards change ... but they do have an opinion. A robust, loud, uncompromising opinion. Comrades are emotionally led by a cause, which they themselves are often not very clear about. Yet they can give food or sleep or any other personal motive a miss to selflessly stand in support of someone who they believe is wronged. They can easily part with their monthly salary for a greater agenda instead of bothering about future securities. They believe they are dedicated to the welfare of the society and are prominently active in college unions. There's no bar on drinks and smoke (bidi or cigarette according to the size of the pocket). Then one fine day their parents or families get hold of them by their collars and get them married. They are thus domesticated, but in their views and opinions they still remain Comrades.

Thankfully I have not been befriended by a Comrade till date, but I see them hanging around at tea-cigarette outlets in neighbourhoods or conducting political *bhashan* for a locality or leading a rally or doing some other social service! Apologies for being blunt but according to me these are purposeless idealists.

Over the last few days I've gathered that Bengali men usually bond over politics, cricket, cigarette and *mishti*! They are passionate about all four and these are their ice-breakers with new acquaintances. One of these, if not all, is bound to work between people who have just met and need to initiate an action or conversation. Needless to mention that smoke and *mishti* is the action, politics and cricket the conversation! Krishna Uncle's wife has a long name starting with K. I found it difficult to decipher, let alone pronounce, though she repeated it many times. So I stuck to calling her just Aunty. On our first meeting she had heaped a plateful of sweets in front of me, demanding I demolish it all and don't leave a morsel behind! The family was quite unhappy at my being a vegetarian. Not because they didn't approve of my food habits, but because I was depriving them of the pleasure of feeding me exotic Bengali dishes prepared with fish or meat Once she even asked me if

I would like to sample some, given that my family was not watching! She lamented that my health was not as good as it should be because I have remained under-fed–only on a veggies diet with no one to look after–during all those years spent abroad. The next question to follow was about my plans for marriage! 'You need someone to look after you!' I dodged these without much hassle because Krishna Uncle's sophistication did not permit interference beyond a point and I am usually known to be soft spoken. The questions or statements were not put forward with expectations of well worded answers. Aunty accepted my smiles as the perfect response of an ideal, eligible bachelor.

Though I didn't have answers to most of her queries, I don't find Aunty suffocating. She is innocent and affectionate. A retired school teacher, well aware of the latest news and academic updates, yet tradition-bound in her presentation and in running her house, I have a lot of respect for her. More than interference I sense concern in her approach; a concern that I hardly experience these days. And she is unconditionally loving. She taught me some weird words in Bengali. *Dur chhai* is an expression of disgust, *jachchole* is equivalent to O No! *Chuloijaak* is go to hell, *okhaddo* is bad, *bidghute* is horrible, *arre bbabba* is an exclamation of happiness or fear–as per context, *kaan-chappati* is a particular way of hitting below the ear, *gondo-desh* is cheek, etc. Most of these words and expressions have a specific tone of pronouncing. If the tone goes wrong then the word loses its relevance. Aunty would tutor me on the tone and pronunciation and would laugh out loud every time I spoke out the words. I quite enjoy her open laughter and simple ways of having fun!

Around 8:00 pm I get a call from home. I am informed that my second cousin is getting married in a few months and preparations are about to start. As usual all members have been allotted jobs. I am reminded of my duties as an elder brother. I hold back from saying that I am one of the chief catalysts for this marriage, though others may not know about it. I was the one to whom the bride-to-be had confided her feelings for the would-be-groom one stormy evening and post that I had played some tricks to bring the two together and unite them as a couple. Rather, I want to ask whether someone has bothered to think about my future, given that I am thirty-seven; but restrain. Zero expectations, less conversation and more observation offer perfect health and pure peace in life!

My life has followed an unpredictable pattern, which I was least prepared for. Stone-willed and sincere to the best of my spirits, I have approached every goal with reasonable preparation; destiny has been by my side handholding through all my wishes. I really didn't expect myself to be so lucky. We are a family of diamond merchants based out of Jaipur, Rajasthan. A huge clan of uncles, aunties and cousins stay together under the same roof, which in local dialect is called the haveli. Our house is actually huge, with lots of open spaces, carefully maintained gardens and orchards, temples and an old fashioned pond which our generation calls the pool. I and all my cousins, were born to affluence. Our business was started by my grandfather and it has flourished with time and expanded in product lines, thanks to the business acumen of his sons and grandsons. Every male at home is supposed to grow up breathing and dreaming diamonds; joining the business is an achievement; an elaborate puja where the entire family comes together to pray for success and prosperity of the new entrant is an auspicious prelude to the joining. And thus starts an endless journey where every mistake is ripped apart and every success celebrated. Big families like ours have their own cultures of kitchen politics, envies and futile power equations; yet the business keeps us together. All women of the household prepare food together and the entire family still comes together for the morning puja, breakfast and dinner in deference to a non-negotiable rule. I happened to be a special favourite of my grandmother. They say that the goddess of prosperity showered special blessings during my birth and business multiplied immediately after. My birth *lakshans* were perfectly crafted by the goddess! As I grew up, a lot of my demands were treated with special favour, drawing prolonged arguments and comparisons in the kitchen. However, my grandmother believed that I am blessed by Lakshmi-Narayan and settled all debates with a 'let him be!' After school Dad expected me to study metallurgy; I said if at all I have to continue with academics then it will be Mathematics from Delhi University. All wars that continued for weeks behind closed doors initially and with the participation of a greater audience later, were settled with a 'let him be.' No one knew that the worst was yet to come.

My favourite occupation as a child happened to be breathing life into clay and mud, while others played around the pond at our haveli. With great patience I would remove the rocky particles, smoothen the clay with hand, dampen it so that it wouldn't crack, grind some of the rocky particles with hammer or use sand and mix it all with the clay to give it elasticity, gather hay and grass to build the base and then apply my mixture over it to replicate faces of those I liked in the family. Mostly these were modelled on my Kaki-sa (wife of my father's younger brother), not because I was especially fond of her but because she was exceptionally beautiful. Each of her expressions had a language, dipped in pride and rich in sophistication. She was my favourite *subject* and it was a self imposed challenge to capture her moods. Our pool-side thus had many sculptures, most of them representing Parul Aditya Solanki. At nineteen, when boys usually elope with girlfriends, I eloped from Delhi to Baroda with a desire and decision to pursue a career in Fine Arts; and not Mathematics. After five years my clan was expecting a MSc. mark sheet; I posted to my address the certificate of withdrawal issued by Delhi University. My cousin reported to me, stealthily and with promises of his name not being disclosed as the source, that there was huge civil war at home and everyone blamed my mother. Out of guilt, I promised myself that one day I'll have massive achievements to my credit, which I'll dedicate to Mrs Meena Arjun Solanki. I engrossed myself in learning the craft with utmost sincerity, as success had become a *do or die situation* for me! I had to justify my act to the rest of the family. The clan had already disowned me; other than two cousins, no one was in touch with the traitor. And then there was an unexpected mishap in the business. Three workers were injured fatally in one of the factories. The media was immediately active pointing out loopholes in our safety measures reporting it as a 'cost cutting strategy at the expense of the lives of poor labourers.' Labourers stopped work demanding compensation and better facilities at work. Two huge orders got cancelled, thanks to this furore! The family faced its first major setback and it was the question of sustaining goodwill in the market. Everyone seemed to question everything. When conditions were bizarre, my grandmother, after her morning puja, suddenly cried aloud that her Lakshmi-Narayan had been violated and hence this misfortune. 'Bring him back immediately and LET HIM BE!!!!' I entered the haveli once again in style, like a Hindi film hero, in slow motion, not for special effects but scared that others might shoot me down. But I trusted since then … I must be blessed by destiny. The family had accepted my choice of profession. Now I just had to prove myself.

Fifteen years hence, I have experienced massive heights in my career. I have studied in the best colleges, researched under the best guides, exhibited my work across the world, received unconditional acknowledgements that adorn my CV. I am adored as a professional and have to my credit some lavish projects in Europe. I have been awarded an MFA in sculpture from Yale University, and I have been a Fellow at the Radcliffe Institute, Harvard University. My sculptures are included in the collections of the Nevada Museum of Art, Portland Museum of Art, Farnsworth Art Museum, Harn Museum of Art, Jackson Laboratories, Bar Harbor, Maine, Runnymede Sculpture Farm, Woodside, California, Emory University in Atlanta, and in private collections in Maine, Boston, New York, Miami, and Santa Barbara. I have kept my promise. Yet my happiness is hampered by a realisation– my family doesn't care! My craft doesn't hold any meaning for them. During heated exchanges I am still referred to as the guy who ran away, my mother is still blamed for bearing a son who ditched the ancestral business. Ironically even my parents never try to defend or support me citing that I am living a successful, self-made life of honour. They suffer the insensitivity of their selfish son quietly. The only person who cared has been silenced years ago and no longer the voice orders, 'Let Him Be.' All my struggles and hard work that led to my success hence feel no less than a huge loss. I realise that before rebelling I should have detached myself completely from everyone who didn't find meaning in my pursuit of creative passion. It hurts. But in the last few years I have more or less made peace with the situation and have distanced myself from Jaipur. I am mainly connected to them through Facebook and get to learn their updates from the social networking sites. Phone calls are short, curt and rare. Yet, what surprises me is that consciously or subconsciously, I still call it home!

Tomorrow I head for my new *Karma-bhoomi*, Santiniketan! Before landing in Kolkata, I had had long chats with the Kala Bhavan, Head of Department, Dr Shyamal Bhowmik, over phone and Skype. Most of the times he would drift away from professional conversation and discuss aspirations, ideals, philosophies and literature. His range of interests and source of knowledge is vast. In one such telephonic exchange he claimed that mine is a very popular Bengali name. Aniruddh is supposed to be Krishna's grandson. The word means 'uncontrolled', 'unrestrained' or 'without obstacles.' I just told him that Krishna, I guess, had charmed Rajasthanis as much as he did the Bengalis; so the name of his descendants stands to be a common interest! Dr Bhowmik though loved adding an extra 'a' at the end of my first name every time he pronounced it with a thorough Bengali accent.

I am not sure whether I did the right thing choosing Kala Bhavan. I took it up on an instinct. One of the sacred places in the history of Indian art and crafts, I have heard and read a lot about this institution and the contributions of its founder, Rabindranath Tagore. Many warned that not much is left about the place and petty local politics have ruined a lot. Yet, there was an inner call that defied justification or logic. I experienced similar emotions when I started my journey as an aspirant sculptor. I have heard funny and nasty remarks about creative people being crack-pots. To a large extent I agree because I have experienced unexplained turmoil within my soul at awkward moments that has made me do things that were unpremeditated and impulsive, quite unlike me. Otherwise, I would like to call myself quite organised, both in thought and action. Perhaps a book of photography, that covered the people and landscape of Birbhum district in West Bengal acted as a catalyst. Or perhaps the fact that this was the place where the great poet found peace. He and his father sat here for meditations. I am looking for peace and isolation too, to finish an incomplete task that doesn't allow me to rest! From the translated literature that I have read, I have a feeling that Tagore's work had rubbed on to most of his contemporaries; some imitated him while others protested against his style by doing diametrically opposite. But no one could manage to remain uninfluenced. And his art ... it was as sensuous as his poetry! A presumption haunts me like a presentiment. It tells me that this place will stir up my creativity like never before and my CV will thank me for this decision.

Hence, a journey begins!

The Journey Begins...

Sanghamitra Banerjee
Santiniketan

I was born in the midst of a Bengali summer. Since both parents were out at work during the day, I spent considerable time alone at home during my growing up days. Compared to my contemporaries who were escorted to and from school, I often travelled alone since third standard. That was real fun. Baba gave me some money to buy bus tickets. I walked the distance and saved the amount for something I wanted to buy. Usually I borrowed books from the local library by getting into a hush-hush understanding with the librarian; I was under-age for membership! All my days when I was dependent on my parents, I never knew what pocket money was. Baba never agreed to that concept. He always gave me the money that I required for commuting. But he did play games with me at times. Often he would leave coins in some part of the house and go to work. If I found them, they were mine. If I didn't, I lost the chance.

I grew up in a traditional Bengali household typified as impulsive, passionate and laid back. These qualities are still a part of Kolkata, in fact the whole of Bengal and of Bengalis who are born and brought up there. Morning starts early in that part of the world; at 5:30 am the earth shines, roadside grocery sellers start washing their corners and extend the charity a bit to clean the adjacent part of the roads, customers are out with a jute bag in their hands. We stayed in a rented apartment right in the middle of the marketplace; hence these memories are just so intense. I and my parents resided in a two-bedroom house on the third floor of a building which Baba occupied during his bachelor days; it was old but generous with natural light and air. It had a balcony as well. Red flowers from the gulmohar tree, *krishnachura* in Bengali, outside the balcony, often reached our railings. Cuckoos and parrots flocked in between the reds and greens of the gulmohar. I was told, when Baba started staying there with some of his friends, the flat did not even have windows and doors. Only after his marriage did the house get its due.

When I was a kid, my cousins often came over for lunch or dinner. Ma cooked all the goodies herself and my entire clan swore by what came out of Ma's kitchen. A traditional Bengali love is expressed at the dining table. The loved one suffers heaps of food, especially non-vegetarian, cooked in mustard oil with loads of spices; and varieties of sweets served as dessert post that. The lover makes sure that the loved one eats each and everything piled on his plate! Bengali men are proud of their rimless or fat-framed glasses and smoking habits. Glasses are a sign of intelligence, sophistication, richness and sincerity; smoke signifies pure intellectualism. Women are delighted with their collection of saris, most of which are treated as family heirlooms and are passed on from one generation to the next. In the building that we stayed, the second floor was occupied by two families staying in two separate apartments. Our doors were forever open and we kids sneaked into each others' doors as if we were entering another room in our own apartment. The men had a strange chemistry among themselves. Every Sunday when they were home, Baba would stop at second floor while coming back from the local market and start comparing the prices and quality of fish and vegetables. Three men would get together examining each other's collection of the day and qualitatively analyse how well had been the day's shopping and where it could have gained them a better deal. The topic of discussion eventually shifted to politics or cricket. Ma would have to yell from upstairs demanding the groceries as they needed to be processed and cooked! Baba would call the girl from second floor and ask her to carry it upstairs to Ma while he carried on with his stimulatingly intellectual discussion. The poor girl would stretch the heavy bag up the stairs; none of her parents would be annoyed at my dad for asking her to do that. It seemed natural for all of us to be thus ordered by any set of parents.

My maternal relatives played an intense role in all my growing up years. They are my *masis*, *mausas*, *mamis* and *mamas*; and of course my cousins. Most of them are settled in Calcutta, some are outside as well. I am extremely close to all of them. Ma was the youngest in a family of six daughters and two sons; I enjoyed the pampering of being the only child of the youngest daughter of the family. Ma's *kaka* and his three sons also share a close bonding with us. So I had five *masis* and five *mamas*, all included, we Banerjees are a huge brood.

Looking at the bedside photographs in my bedroom at Santiniketan reminds me of them and much more! I am haunted not only by some adorable personalities who shaped my character, but also a city that resonates in my brain with a host of childhood memories. Kolkata two decades ago, the old house which all the resident families abandoned one by one, the scary cracks that showed up on its walls, the insecurities that grew after Baba left, the vendors down the market, a half-broken tape recorder that had to be spanked to get it working–everything conspires to create a lullaby that puts me to rest for the day.

This morning as I am busy working on some papers, a rickshaw pulled some heavy trunks with enormous effort. Even on a winter morning the poor guy was sweating and panting! Seeing my window open, he stopped for a while. I ask from inside whether some water would help. He smiles in affirmation. While he gulps the liquid down his throat, my eyes inquisitively wander around the huge boxes. The puller looks at them and remarks, these belong to a *pagla sahib*! 'You call him crazy because he made you pull these?' I ask. 'Na *didimoni*,' he responds, 'they are heavy, so I asked him, what do they contain. He said these boxes are full of magic slates that can change form and become living creatures!' I am amused and curious, but decide not to spend more time with the rickshaw puller on this. I turn to get back to the house. The boy calls back, '*Didimoni*, he is shifting to Mridangam in a day or so! Soon he will say that all of you were his black slates and he gave this neighbourhood its existing life. Be careful, all of you, times are really bad.' He guffaws, and huffs and puffs again to resume his onward journey.

I watch him struggle with the load and remember some stories I heard from my grandpa, when they shifted to India from Bangladesh. The sketches he wove in my brain through his tales were something similar to the rickshaw puller taking his difficult steps ahead–companionless, uncertain and insecure, yet strongly connected to the humour of life!

During partition, my maternal grandpa shifted to West Bengal and we were one of the first families to settle in the refugee camp of DumDum area. Later Dadu built his own home and accommodated everyone. Slowly his family grew and multiplied. My *mamas* got politically connected and involved more severely with the place. Till date I am known as the niece and grand-daughter of my maternal family in Kolkata. Wherever I travel in the city, someone who knows the greater family emerges and reports that I was seen at so-and-so place, at so-and-so time, with so-and-so! It irritates me at times, but I also feel very proud to be associated with those lovely people, many of whom are no more today. Somehow they have outlived the number that counts the years of their existence on the planet!

I left Calcutta after completing school, in search of an independent life which does not connect me back to my family by trespassers at different parts of the day! I wanted to experience the hostel; I wanted to spend my hours unprompted; I wanted to strike my own balance with discipline and bohemianism. After graduating from Lucknow University with Economics Honours, I however came back to Jadavpur University for post-graduation. Later I travelled to Mumbai for a job but got disillusioned soon after! Corporate job felt rigorous and did not allow me time to breathe in peace. I wanted time for reading, music, painting, plays and travel! Though I was too insecure to shift without an alternate plan, I started offering myself loopholes. I worked hard, till one day I felt stuck in a purposeless existence and left the job to go back to Calcutta. Four times in seven years I just went back to Ma without caring for 'what next!' I would just roam around in the hills for two to three months and then suddenly I would bounce back just the way I disappeared. I did get a job as well. I may have lost quite a bit with this bohemianism, but it allowed me the freedom to *live* my life my way. So what if one girl out of millions is not as ambitious! Eventually, I started working on my PhD. I had grown so accustomed to studies that it felt unnatural not to sit with books in the mornings and evenings. Soon after, I realised that academics was where my call lay and I would not like to let go of it! A few competitive exams later I was employed at Viswa Bharati, Santiniketan.

As evening falls, I lie on my make-shift bed and travel through the pages of a Jane Austen novel. The country tale on British romance interweaves through uncomplicated style and comic potshots present language at its playful best. I put the book down and try to relax. Somehow I remember the words I heard in the morning. 'Magic slates that can change form and become living creatures!' Did the boxes belong to the sculptor Anusua was speaking about? She did mention that he specialises working on stone. I don't remember though which rock he chose for his work. Certainly it is the sculptor's job to carve life into lifeless objects, I wonder. If it is actually the recent talk-of-the-town who is shifting into this neighbourhood, then he must be equipped with good humour. I smile remembering how the rickshaw-puller called him *pagla sahib*! I almost hallucinate an ill-kempt man with careless growth all over the face and neck; his clothes half dirty and hair longer than usual. His shabby hands handle complicated tools with professional ease. Bespectacled eyes are keen to achieve perfection and he dangerously climbs a ladder to reach at the top of his sculpture and hangs on there drilling a curve that apparently seems to be unimportant!

I get up to prepare tea. I am embarrassed realising that I have been thinking of a person I know nothing about. I fret at Anusua for sharing unnecessary details. Also I realise, the person I was thinking about was not necessarily the sculptor that Anusua raves about. I was thinking of some old, poor, talented souls who sculpt the huge images of the Durga family every year during Durga puja. Their address is not something as stylish as Mridangam and their work affiliation is not as prestigious as Kala Bhavan; rather they hide their talents in dirty tents to protect the deity from trespassers or untimely rains. I take my tea out and sit on the veranda. The old couple of Mridangam is returning after an evening walk. Twilight sets in as they stop in response to my smiles. Before leaving, they confirm that the new tenant in their top floor is a 'nice boy who was a sculptor in some other country!'

Twilight

Dr Aniruddh Jain Solanki
Santiniketan

Astrologers predicted that my life would start at 35! That would actually be my ARRIVAL on the planet, when I would be blessed with divine possessions that could be more soulful than materialistic. I found it disappointing. I felt, what would remain to achieve in that weird age, when white hair would conspire to make its entry, when looks would start waning, when I would be burdened with forty odd responsibilities, and when each day would be a to-do list. Today, at thirty-seven, I somehow remember the forecast, probably because certain things have been happening. I can sense a change within. A peaceful restlessness or a calm whirlwind! I have been through a transition where I have started realising the meaning of my existence; all that I ever wanted to tell myself and the world are coming back to me in explicit expressions. And it's worth mentioning, that till date the white hairs are not so prominent, I still look presentable and I do live life on my own terms!

Santiniketan gives me enough space for myself. I find this place peaceful even if growth opportunities are limited. I have not come here for growth, that's for sure! I have had enough of growth in my career. I came here looking for some meaning that I myself am not too sure of!

The first day I joined, I understood two ground rules about this place. One, a bicycle would serve better than my luxury car. And two, this place thrives more on relationships and less on strict professional exchange. You have to strike a rapport with whoever you have something to share. Students and teachers have an active 'outside classroom' interaction and it is that 'time spent over tea' that nails a teacher's relevance with his target audience. It is threatening for me that I don't consume tea! Moreover, I don't speak their language. I'll surely have to pick up more than *jachchole* and *dur chhai*!! First day at Kala Bhavan, when I was exchanging pleasantries with Dr Bhowmik, I could sense that students following our conversation were amused and were exchanging sarcastic looks. Other than Dr Bhowmik, the other professors seemed to be restrained in expressing warmth towards a new colleague. Two of them, Anusua Lahiri and Pritam Sen acted friendly enough, but I did not find them as innocent as they claimed to be. Thus, the first impression was less than impressive with the people over here. However, these don't dampen my spirits any longer. My family has offered enough experiences that made me immune to such non-acceptance and indifference. I don't blame them though. My qualifications are bigger than my age and are at times intimidating. Think of the old professor Prasoon Adhikary I met the other day. It is unnerving for people like him to accept that at around half his age I have achieved three times his CV! I had travelled, learnt and equipped myself with opportunities that he may have been deprived of. Or, maybe he did not lose as much as I have, to gain my equivalence. I believe that life is a balancing act. To gain big, you have to lose big. There is nothing called accumulation or deprivation. I risked and lost my family, my support, my home, my sheltered existence. There were days when I barely could manage food and survived on water, because I had to save up for house rent and college fees. In the process, I gained name, fame, money. When I was introduced to Prof. Adhikary, he extended a cordial *namaskar*. But each of his exchanges was sarcastic for the next few minutes that he spent with me. He could not fundamentally accept the truth of my achievements. He stood there with his wife and son; they had similar looks of disdain. I realised that they were together. They must have discussed me behind closed doors and happily concluded that my certificates were fudged and fixed! He was incapacitated, compared to me, on his professional deliverables. But even his incapacities were lovingly supported by his family. They believed that what he said and felt were true. That's something I'll never have!

They put me up in a guest house initially. Soon after, I shifted to a space of my choice. It is a paying guest arrangement but I am floored by the look of it. The house is at Simanta Pally. A huge gate with beautiful creepers growing on it opens onto a pebbled path that leads to a huge bungalow. Engraved outside was its name, Mridangam, along with the names of the owners, in Bengali script. The entrance has a tulsi stand. The bungalow belongs to an army Major. His retired parents are residing here with two full time servants. The interiors are tastefully done; but more attractive than that are the inviting smiles of the residents who greet me in. They lead me to the first floor that is connected to an external door and marble staircase. This meant I would not have to disturb the old couple if I had to leave early or return late on some days. The first floor has one bedroom and a small study with minimum furniture; the bedroom door on the rear end opens on to an extended terrace. There is also a small kitchen and I am allowed to use it but I'll have to source the oven myself. The lady offered to cook for me as she does for the rest of the household, so that I don't have to 'burn my hands' every day. Heaven, absolute heaven! I shifted immediately and the couple helped me settle in.

It is evening and I walked aimlessly to explore the place. Santiniketan is very green and close to nature. As I walked, I could hear a tanpura and *mridang* playing afar. My footsteps followed the music driven by a natural instinct. But though the audibility grew with my advances, I didn't seem to reach the destination. It was difficult to locate the direction beyond a point and I stopped to rest. The sun had set and it would be dark soon. I looked around for help. A girl with a long braid and sari walked her cycle, not too far away. My loud 'excuse me' shatters the melancholic silence but did not seem to affect her. I ran and reached closer; in broken Bengali uttered, I need help. She looked and I froze. Parul Aunty, my first model! As she turned, I shrieked in horror! Half of her was the original human face and the other half was my sculpted clay-work!!

I woke up in sweat. This was my first night, or nightmare, at Mridangam. As I poured gallons of water down my throat, I was struck by the beauty of a winter morning outside, unfolding itself to sunshine. It was foggy at 5:35 am and visibility was restrained. In the next five minutes I brushed, changed, wrapped a shawl around myself and stepped out. The pebbles below my feet were moist with dew. I opened the main gate and walked on aimlessly, trying to acquaint myself with the roads. I crossed the gate to walk past the Upasana Griha and tried to take a closer look from the locked exteriors. It is a hall with white walls sculpted gracefully with coloured glasses adorning the arches and marble floors. I stood there for quite some time, trying to imagine the poet and his disciples praying and chanting here. And then turned homewards.

A few steps away from my residence, I stopped at something unusual. This house was standing abruptly on the road, unlike the other constructions that had a garden as a prelude. There was a coconut tree on the roadside and a small path connected it to the veranda that accommodated the main door. And on the outer wall of the entrance, there was a huge brass Saraswati, sensuously holding her veena. Her clean architecture and the flowers near her feet suggest that she is worshipped and cleaned regularly. But I had never known a Hindu household that keeps a god outside their home! The windows were open but my view was blocked by curtains. If windows were open so early on a winter morning then the occupant would surely not be sleeping. I had a strong urge to knock and ask the occupant why is your god seated outside. It was a cultural shock to me, having grown up in an environment where pujas are a compulsory ritual and gods are treated with absolute respect and importance. Should I knock, I asked myself. No, a voice said, it's none of your business. I moved away.

For quite some days I have been watching this house every time I cross it. I thought for once I will find its occupant lazing outside on the veranda and I'll ask the justification of placing the goddess outside the door. But it didn't quite happen and each time I killed my instinct of knocking the door and going ahead uninvited. But the house makes a statement by itself, which draws my attention and my speed naturally slows down when I am walking past. Today happens to be a rare morning when I am out for a walk yet again. On my return, I turn to look at the brass Saraswati. She has been freshly washed and some flowers, which the locals call *tagor*, are placed in a brass bowl in front of the deity; incense sticks burn beside the bowl. Automatically I stop.

The main door is open. A pretty lady emerges with a cup of tea and a few biscuits. For a moment my focus shifts from the brass woman representing knowledge; wet hair lying carelessly all over claims my attention. She is not conventionally beautiful, but there's a dignified elegance about her being. Oblivious of my presence, she sits on the veranda leaning on a pillar. Her right side faces the road where I stand, she takes a sip from her tea, and starts playing with her hair making an effort to dry it. I have seen my mother do the same after bath to smoothen the tangles and dry the hair faster. I want to move away noiselessly, but end up making a sound as if I am clearing my throat. She jerks to attention, but composes herself fast and asks in polite Bengali, what exactly I want and why I am standing at her doorstep! In English

I convey that I don't speak her language. Briefly I introduce myself and add that without meaning to intrude or be rude, I am curious to know why she has placed the goddess outside her house! She smiles and responds, 'I want my home to represent knowledge. I see myself as a carrier of knowledge. So she welcomes my visitors and hints at what they can expect if they choose to enter!'

'Why don't you place your books outside too, then? You care for your possessions and not the deity who symbolises it?' I myself am shocked at my immodest articulation, quite a first time for me.

'I don't believe in gods and goddesses; am some kind of an atheist. My life revolves around my work. Books are fundamental to my existence and I need to protect my ownership. Studying is a part of the air I breathe in. For you, Saraswati is a goddess and you are shocked that I have placed her outside my door. For me, she is a representation. A symbol. Just like a name-plate. It represents the person residing, but it is not the person herself.'

Oh atheist, did she say? I have come across many of those smart, modern people who form their opinions before knowing enough about things. She must have prayed to God asking for something; when the wish was not fulfilled she picked up the goddess and placed her outside and decided that God is nothing but a religious symbol! She looks amused at my disgust, but her reactions are not nasty. My eyes rest automatically on her name-plate. It doesn't read her name. It reads Mrigaya! Her eyes are smiling, having judged the next question that has come to me. 'It means travelling to the forest to hunt wild animals, especially deer.'

'I know Hindi and a bit of Sanskrit. So the word is not new to me. But may I know the relevance?'

'I loved the word and hence named my house after it.'

'It seems you attach more importance to your house than yourself. That plate deserved your name as much as that of the house.'

'Sanghamitra Banerjee!'

'Sorry … come again please.'

'What's so difficult? It's Sanghamitra Banerjee.' Her voice is suddenly harsher and she sounds annoyed!

'Nothing actually. Sorry, I got it.' I take two steps away from her. 'And before I leave, may I share a thought with your esteemed intellectual wisdom? There is nothing called atheism, let me tell you. God is a faith. And there is no one among the silly, simple human beings who can exist without a faith. It might be your relations, profession, a material possession, or anything on the planet that you trust and worship. From this limited interaction with you, madam, I gather that you worship your books and everything that is a source of knowledge. That's your faith, and that's god for you. So please don't call yourself an atheist! Have a good day.' I turn to leave without waiting for her reaction. Pseudo-intellectual, I tell myself!

'Wait,' she calls out from behind, definitely not happy with my words. I turn and find her walking towards me. She stands in front and I am enveloped by her sandalwood fragrance.

'So Mr Philosopher is an ardent and orthodox follower of God, is it?' That's a direct attack. She is agitated. I want to calm her down and remind her about the tea losing its warmth. But she has more to pour. 'Then what about those stone-studded rings on your fingers?'

Now where does that come from? At various times of uncertainty I had knocked the doors of astrology to make my journey smoother. Soon after my fingers adorned a yellow sapphire, an emerald, a pearl and a solitaire. I wear the diamond and emerald on the same finger. I look at them, totally confused! She continues sarcastically, 'So you believe in God and worship God with all your being. You also care to be ritualistically and culturally appropriate … such is the passion of your faith. Then why on earth did you need those stones? If you trust god then why not just accept his decisions as though He knows best what is right for you? Why do you need to correct him with astrology!' She has poured her venom out and I stand there astounded. I have never thought on these lines. She is correct in some sense and her words echo even after she stops. With the same aggression she continues, 'It's easy to worship God and difficult to trust! You know why? Because most of us are not sure that he actually exists or not. So through astrology and other means we keep a second option open so that if God is not there for us, something else can take over and offer the security that we wanted God to provide! Agreed, there's nothing called atheist; but there is hardly anyone who is a true believer either!'

I am completely taken off-guard and my facial muscles must have disclosed everything about my state of mind! Are these words flowing out of her impromptu or has she actually thought in-depth to logically acquire a stand on her choices? Her eyes are smiling again looking at my bewilderment. I nod a semi-assured goodbye and turn to move. 'Dr Jain,' she interrupts with a calm voice, 'I do believe in a supernatural presence guiding us. That's not about Shiva or Durga or Lakshmi. It's just a force. It is Omni-present and by placing a symbol outside my home, I am not respecting her less. She's represented inside in the form of books, a tanpura, CDs, etc. as much as she's outside.' She smiles pleasantly. 'I didn't say these to disturb your practices. I just want to do my things my way. My way is not too different from others, yet people get unnecessarily judgmental. I didn't exactly mean to be rude but you seem to be quite upset.'

I smile back at her. She has jolted me enough and I didn't wish to wait. I thank her politely and walk off to start the day. But her words do not leave me so soon.

I try to fix my schedule and plan workshops to take the students through the standard Introductory programme of modelling, carving, casting and assembling; enlightening them on how representational sculpture is achieved in predictable stages through construction, combination, and measurement of simple geometric forms; and the time to be allocated to each session. 'The initial parts of your specialisation will focus on understanding the characteristics of stone as a material, and you will be introduced to the work of many sculptors, both contemporary and historical. We will then spend time making several small maquettes (small models) in an easily-carvable material, i.e., clay or plasticene, before embarking on a piece in stone. Along with techniques of chiselling, you will also learn the possibilities for splitting and bolting stone and incorporating other materials or objects. These techniques will be taught and explored as your carving progresses …'. Oft-repeated and rehearsed, my first interaction with students goes as expected. Initially, they seemed to be more interested in learning about me, rather than learning from me! They chuckle at my Rajasthan-meets-England accent. At the end of the two hours I spent with them, we feel connected by a purpose. They've grown more attentive and cooperative. All day I have to make special efforts to brush off the early morning experience and concentrate on my job, but her words erupt at regular intervals.

This part of the world doesn't value the difference between formal and casual dressing. While I am formally dressed for my class, the students are casual in jeans-T-shirts and even kurta-pyjamas. This is the accepted norm of the place and I should keep away from challenging or trying to change it. I spend considerable time in the library. Some smart students come forward and try to be friendly. I extend all my warmth. They linger along, offer tea which I politely decline, chat for a while, and then leave. On the way back I stop to take a peek at the local bookstore, Subarnarekha. It is dark, when I enter Simanta Pally. My steps slow down as I walk past the coconut tree, which stands guarding her house. There is a lantern hanging from the ceiling of the veranda. The softly illuminated exterior and trembling shadows makes the house look even more haunted! There's a long drawn monotonous sound of the night that makes the silence and solitude much more prominent. It might be the frogs or the crickets. My pg-owners did analyse the sounds and their sources for me last evening, but I have confused my senses on that. I drag myself forward delaying each step as I walk. 'She stays here all alone?' I ask myself; no one answers. 'What does she do on dark evenings like this? Is this kind of an accommodation safe for a young lady? Where are her people? Is she as abandoned as I am?' I cross the pebbled road of Mridangam and climb up the stairs. As I unlock my door, I realise that the moon is shining beautifully bright. It has entered my apartment through the open door and windows. There's a power cut here. Before bolting my door I look back at Mrigaya; it is clearly visible from my first floor entrance! And I am shocked once again. The lady is sitting on the terrace with her hair left loose and flowing all around. She's looking scarily isolated. The half visibility offered by a soft and majestic moonlight made a mystic sight out of it. 'It is inauspicious for women to sit in the open, after sunset, with hairs unkempt,' my grandmother's voice reprimanding my cousin sister plays in my brain. Similarly, out of an instinct, I wish to warn her. Of course I don't. I go ahead to wash myself. By the time I return to my window, the lights are back. I steal a look at the adjoining terrace and she is gone. The ground floor is illuminated from the inside of curtained windows, drawn perfectly to block all views!

It is Inauspicious for Women...

Sanghamitra Banerjee
Santiniketan

I went to a missionary school in Calcutta. Sometimes ma dropped me an hour before school started, to match her office timings. I sat on the stairs of our church. When the church was not closed, I would peep in through the big window. One day the Father called me in to join his audience as he read out from the Old Testament. And then I was directly exposed to the rituals of Christianity. Hindu rites and rituals are practised as though they are celebrating God. The religious music, smell of camphor, pomp, lamps of aarti, chants, etc. are no less than a celebration. Whereas Christians perceive God in peace. For them, procedures of worshipping are extremely serene and self absorbing. Soon I was the only non-Catholic girl who was allowed to sing for Church choir; I participated in Church services as well; got emotionally involved with the people there; helped the orphans who were taken care of by the church; played Virgin Mary in Christmas celebrations for six years; led Christmas carols; read The Bible … even narrated some of the stories to the orphan kids; just stayed away from the uniform. When I was in Class Ten, Father asked me, 'Why don't you convert to Christianity!' That was a shock! I said, 'Father, I didn't know that I am not a part of it already … and if these are not mine then I don't wish to own them today. I have inherited a faith and I won't disown my inheritance.' I did not think before I said these. I pondered over the words much later. Somewhere, it makes me proud, though I probably hadn't understood their weight while speaking. Till date I don't have a religious bias; I am a Hindu by birth and worship a supreme existence which is more powerful and pure than I am. Beyond that, I have some people in life who I feel are godsends. They have selflessly and unconditionally done good to me, even when I have had nothing to offer! Mythologically, Shiva fascinates me.

There had been times when I have prayed for something I dearly wanted. I have received those, and later realised that they didn't do me any good; I would have been happier, had my prayers not been answered. Consciously I decided that I would stay away from praying with pre-decided expectations. There were no further agenda-based visits to temples, or any other holy places. I helped myself to trust that there is a supreme force that pulls the threads; I would much rather have faith on this force and let go of my personal ambitions to control my life! Since then, it has been easier to sustain. I agree with all my senses that I have been at the receiving end of much blessings. There's some force which has the power to give what I can never think of demanding! Then why make a mockery by asking!

This, in short, is my religious status!

When Dr Aniruddh expressed concern that morning, I was quite taken aback. I am used to people's curiosity regarding me and can handle that with ease. Usually they are never as abrupt or intrusive as he was. Either they try to fish out information from me via conversation or they garner the details from my colleagues, friends, and people with whom I constantly interact. The more curious ones do both of these and judge me from the sourced knowledge. Hence, it was a shock when Dr Aniruddh intruded so innocently. He didn't try to hide or gloss over the fact that my lifestyle didn't match his experiences and hence he wanted to know more! After the battling interaction that morning I said to myself, this man will struggle here for sure; he is too open, too candid, too pure in his expressions!

That morning I had said, I am almost an atheist. That's certainly not correct. The way the sculptor had charged me for keeping Saraswati outside, I was simply amused and wanted to irritate him. And it was fun watching him erupt and recoil thereafter. Challenging the practices of a rigidly pious person always gets him defensive. Such people look at the world through a cylinder and happily believe that nothing exists outside the hollow. I deliberately wanted to be a mismatch to the sculptor's cylinder and contradict his version of religious orthodox! He must be thinking that I am loud, arrogant, mirror-cracking feminist; one of those who are desperate to prove that a man is always wrong and can take their opinions to any extent driven by an acute superiority complex! He was almost running away after making that 'no one is an atheist' statement; and after I attacked his astrological strengths, the poor thing stood speechless! Atheist, I am not, certainly. It's just that we differ fundamentally in our approach and understanding of God. Maybe, he is God-fearing; I trust God! I am spiritual; he is religious! He is conservative in his submissions to the Almighty; I am liberated and have agreed to comprehend the Power my way.

I saw Dr Aniruddh again on a Wednesday. Viswa Bharati observes it's weekly off on Wednesday and not Sunday. At 7:30 am I was there at the Upasana Griha to attend the prayer services. From afar, I could see him in blue jeans and a white shirt, looking upwards, studying almost everything about the place. The soft sun of a winter morning reflected on his glasses. In the stream of whites, that happens to be the dress code of all attendees, his blue looked conspicuous and made him particularly visible. Hidden among the streams of people, I had the liberty of stealing glances at him without being noticed. He looks simple. Short hair, lean body, clean shaven ... nothing like the so-called creative types. He doesn't even have an air of superiority even though his accomplishments are such that few would dare to dream. There's a huge solitaire in one of his fingers. Girlfriend? What's the brand of the watch he wears? Looks quite expensive! I swallow a chuckle and look at him again. He is sitting on a bench outside the temple and has befriended some Patha Bhavan (junior school) girls. They are showing him some dance mudras. We disappear in our respective worlds after the prayer services are over.

A few days later we bump into each other again at Ratan Pally. Anusua and I are shopping for veggies and groceries, and I have piled upon myself a bit too much. Kalidasi, a lady of Santal origin, runs a dhaba for breakfast, lunch and dinner for students, just next to the vegetable vendor. She yells at us, 'No need to cook today *didimoni*, come I'll feed you!' I smile at her and continue shopping without a word. She repeats the request and runs me through the menu to kindle my appetite. After a while I instruct her to pack something. She chuckles. 'How much do you think you have the capacity to hold, thin woman?' I turn to smile back at her, but before the facial muscles form a curve, I almost slip over a stone and all my shopping threatens to fall off the hand. In a split second this happens and somehow I manage to guard myself from falling down. But soon I realise that I restored balance because strong hands have off-loaded my burden suddenly and my hands were free to grab the nearest available support. The sculptor is now holding everything I had purchased. I am shocked, not sure of how to respond to this! 'Are you ok?' He says, then looks at the stuff I purchased, which rests within the folds of his hands now. 'Er ... mmmm ... may I ... I mean, I am helping you!' A sheepish grin emerges at the corner of his lips. I try to hide my embarrassment. Meekly I utter thanks, and mention that it's not required and I can manage, I am used to doing these things by myself. The sculptor shows no sign of returning the baggage and gestures that they are better off with him. Anusua looks back and her face registers a barely concealed grin. She continues picking up the *bhindis* one by one, holding them up towards the bulb of the vendor as if they are transparent and the light would make their insides visible. The vendor tries to resist. 'Who purchases vegetables like this *didi*?' She doesn't answer and looks away. A little disgusted with the forced affinity, and embarrassed even more, I try to smile and start rehearsing an apt line that would firmly deny this favour.

'You don't feel scared staying there alone?' Another abrupt question!

'Where? OK I mean, no! Not really. Who should I be scared of? Not everyone has the time to question my religious instincts at 6:30 in the morning!' I am partly amused, partly confused, mainly I want to get rid of him. He doesn't seem to understand my mental status. He's smiling.

'I know I am not too polite in my approach each time. You certainly don't appreciate it. But you lead a very unusual existence. Secluded, but you don't look unhappy. Will you be my subject?'

Is he on drugs? I wonder! Anusua, is not watching, but listening for sure. Never in her life has she been so silently concentrating on something. Those veggies are not her object of concentration, I bet.

'Of course,' I utter, 'As soon as you return my bags!'

Thankfully he understands the sarcasm and clarifies. 'People like you are my subjects. You lead a humdrum life, but in your own way you are challenging the norms of conventional living every single day. You must have had to answer people; your relatives if not others. Living alone may not have been an easy and welcome decision. You think differently, which must be inviting resistance. It seems you are enjoying the challenge. I need to know more and understand better. That helps in carving the mind along with the body ... rather face. Once I set the equation right, another black limestone is destroyed.' I begin saying that I am not interested but he's not finished yet. 'That does not necessarily mean being a model. It's different. I intend to learn from you about you and put that to use later. No further unwarranted interest. No offence meant.'

Frankly I am embarrassed and I wish to say, leave me alone! But his credentials are too big to be rude. I am searching for some firm but polite words; pat comes a statement in a very deep voice. 'I am not trying to be smart, Ms Banerjee. You can trust that, I have no wrong intentions.'

Finally Anusua intervenes. 'Sorry to interrupt, guys. Allow me to offer you a lift you till your destination.' I look at her, conveying deep gratitude. She understands and gestures reassuringly. I know her maturity won't last and she'll read more into this interaction and give it romantic overtones. But she'll do that behind closed doors, not in public. I feel a strange disturbance. What's wrong with me? Why can't I just stop him straight away? He is sitting beside the driver in silence now, answering pleasantly to things that Anusua is asking. Ten minutes of car ride and I'm ready with my answer. I decide it's better to come out clean and straight-forward with this weirdo. We descend from the car and Anusua bids adieu, not before winking at me.

'Dr Jain, there's no doubt that your credentials interest me. Your abruptness even fascinates me. But I can't encourage intruders in my life. My life is too personal.'

'Don't you miss home? Your parents? Relatives? Siblings?'

'No, I don't have any of them! Can I take your leave now, please?' I'm fairly disgusted. We are standing in front of our house.

'Last word of the day. Tell me one fascinating thing about being here, living in this lonely house all alone, and yet feeling happy. Just one, and I'm off.'

'Look up.'

'Whoaaahh!' He makes a face, unable to understand what I mean. I point skywards with my hand and he looks up. Our vision meets the trunk of the coconut tree, from where the branches have made their way out. Millions of fireflies have flocked in there and it looks like a galaxy. The sculptor looks bewildered. He stares at that for long, and then turns. 'I know as per my promise, I must leave. Thanks for sharing something so beautiful.' He smiles and walks backwards for a few steps before he turns and faces away.

'Dr Jain,' I surprise myself by calling him from behind.

'In Santiniketan everyone knows everyone. Simanta Pally is a dark lane with less people travelling to and fro at 8:00 in the night. I don't want to be seen with a man, walking in at this hour. Already there's enough speculation about my relationship status. I have lived a scandal-free life all this while. This is a small, closed area and people form opinions too fast. You will be at peace if you are not too brave with your public interactions. Good night!' I add a smile to soften the words.

He reciprocates, but waits for a while hesitantly. 'Ma'm, you constantly noted my movements at the Brahma temple last Wednesday, but never cared to come up and say hello! I can understand this but can't practise it myself. I consider my behaviour this evening more honourable and straight-forward. A place acquires the character of its inhabitants. I don't mean this to be rude, but can't people be more open, more honest with each other? As long as it doesn't hurt, of course …! Your hello wouldn't have meant that you were interested; it would just have suggested that you acknowledge our acquaintance! Not everything or every action needs to be interpreted beyond the obvious. No?' He leaves.

For quite some time I don't find the strength to move. I'm feeling insulted. Something is burning inside. But deep down I know he is right! And that's why it probably disturbs so much.

Next morning I start my usual routine. There's a slight headache, which I tend to ignore. A bath and I'm feeling refreshed. Mechanically, driven by routine, I pour water to wash my Saraswati first thing in the morning. As I walk back in, my eyes spot a piece of paper, folded twice, lying at her feet, soaked in water. Carefully I pick it up and open it. The ink is half washed, but I guess I found it just before the words became illegible. 'I guess, I owe you an apology.' No addressee, neither any signature.

He uses fountain pens! Classy? Or stylish?

The moment I enter my class, I am rejuvenated. Teachers are usually never biased, but all teachers have their favourites. Some faces, which light up on seeing me, make me feel happy and wanted. My classes are usually not a one-dimensional flow of knowledge. Each topic is covered in a set of two lectures. First session, I teach the basics of approaching the topic, with ample reference to real life examples. Next class, the students teach me back, with pre-approved case studies sourced from various geographies, following the guidelines that I had shared in the earlier class. The knowledge sourced on each topic is thus varied, visionary and creative. Classroom sessions are also punctuated at regular intervals by debates and newspaper article analysis. Initially when I joined Viswa Bharati, they attended my class because they feasted their eyes on a pretty young professor. Slowly they found meaning and substance in my deliverables and warmed up to me as well as the subject I taught. I can say this, because not only has the attendance in my class improved, but the grades are higher as well. I can sense the seriousness and sincerity of the students in the questions they ask or the quality of assignments they submit

Outside class, I am very friendly with my students. However, I never encourage anyone to come home. I crack jokes, laugh with them, discuss career prospects, etc. but somewhere I have always maintained a distance. Over-enthusiastic students are put to rest by a firm, cold stare. Mentor-protégé is the most romantic relationship, they say. When I was a student, I had almost made a mentor suffer my romantic outbursts. He was Dr Samarjeet Sengupta, a scholar from the University of California! I lost my tongue whenever he was around. A particularly funny incident I remember from my college days. Mathematics is something that I feel I am born to kill ... that's what I believed. So, all through the year I ignored the papers of Mathematical Economics, with the faith that the moment I open the book, all numbers would explain themselves to me smooth as honey. Just a week before the end term exams I tried to rekindle my finesse. To my utter shock, everything seemed lost. I couldn't decipher a bit of it! Next day at campus, we got to know that the lady who taught the paper was going on maternity leave. The subject would henceforth be handled by Prof. Sengupta. Horror had never spread itself so miserably over me. I would rather die than flunk in Prof. Sengupta's paper! Anusree, a kind classmate, offered help. Next few days we were glued to each other, me learning and she teaching the theorems. This however, was no preparation for the Mathematical Economics paper. Sengupta would never give direct theorems and all his questions would be application-based. I didn't have time for consulting test papers for such questions. Hell! And I knew that I am entering troubled waters soon! On the day of the examination, I felt blank. Anusree wished me luck as we took our seats. We were seated in adjacent rows, sitting parallel to each other. The format of the question paper was such that there would be six questions out of which we had to solve three. As soon as I got the paper, I turned to read the last question, which was supposed to be a maxima-minima problem. I knew that I could crack it. I turned to question five. It was a twisted tale, but I could decipher what exactly was asked. Question four looked terrible. Question three again was friendly, though it did not ask for something too simple. God, I love you! With full concentration towards my answer paper I solved it all. Till the time I was solving the Maths, I had no clue what was happening around. When I finished, with relief and satisfaction, I raised my head. It was shocking to find the rest of the class red-eyed with anger, restless with helplessness. Even Anusree was a part of this bewildered team! I couldn't believe my eyes and immediately started revising. After my revision, I was sure that I had solved my paper perfectly. Anusree requested help and I shared almost half my paper with her!!

Later, I realised that everyone had started reading the paper from question one. When questions one and two seemed difficult, their confidence hit an all time low and they were no longer in a state to understand that three was not so difficult after all. They wanted to score and I wanted to pass! Hence, my approach of reading the question paper was different from that of the others. And that's what worked. I scored a 97 per cent, the highest in class.

Such has been my relationship with Mathematics. Even if I am not prepared, my brain seems to work faster in its favour. I read numbers easier and better than anything else.

My crush in college thus tickled my ego and developed within me a desperation to score. I can see some of my students sharing the same desperation, thankfully unaffected by any romantic awe. But they trust that I am the best teacher. This soft worship is very fulfilling. I realise, as much as they love me in person, they are equally attracted to my subject. Hence, I am very true to my job and faithful to my students.

Today's class is dedicated to consumption curves. I draw the diagram on board and discuss how things change for normal goods, inferior goods, complimentary goods and the substitutes. The class listens in silence. No other subject, I feel, is so driven by logic as Economics is.

After class, I am back to my seat in the teacher's section. There are some assignments waiting for the red ink. The headache has persisted. I decide to step out and take in some fresh air. The winter sun is soft enough to accommodate a late-in-the-day stroll. Through twists and turns I reach the main road and then walk straight ahead. Walking aimlessly without a destination in mind is quite liberating. This place is too small for anyone to discover any spectacular area that has not been explored before. Yet, seldom does one have the freedom to follow the mind. I have reached Shonajhuri Forest, popularly called Khoai due to the soil erosion. A thin stream of water flows through the eroded bottom; broken rocky surfaces dangerously maintain themselves at both sides of the stream. It is fun for everyone here to venture through these rocks and reach the bottom. I too would have done it, had I not been wearing a sari. I sit at the edge, and loosen my hair leaving it open. It is still damp! A chai-wala appears suddenly and offers tea. God bless him! Before leaving, he says, '*Didimoni* came here alone?' I smile. He adds, 'I am a commoner, maybe talking out of turn. Yet, ladies should not come to such isolated places all alone!' He leaves. His warning had been well-intentioned. But I am too tired of hearing this. People here can't seem to accept that I am single. I mean single status has to come with a sad face here. They can't understand that I am single and I am happy! Does everything always have to follow a format? A format for life; a format for happiness; a format for reputed existence! Why is my non-interfering existence always intruded into by expectations of pretence? Can't I just be the open-minded person that I am, and be left alone happily ever after?

I did have my share of relationships in college and one after I joined my first job. Only one was sincere and serious. Others didn't last. Because, in my heart of hearts I knew, that I had not loved. I never missed anyone, hardly ever did something special, didn't in my distant dreams see a future together and I detested their bad habits more than appreciating their genius. The relationship status with them was something like, 'I'm fine with you for a while!' Very soon I knew that this arrangement of convenience is not working out. Much against the wishes of my mother, I declared that marriage is not happening! Probably I am in love with the freedom that comes with being single. It is not dangerous living like this, if you can conduct yourself correctly and if you really enjoy being by yourself. There are some natural dos and don'ts that come with it. You can't be provocative in word, thought or gesture. You have to stay away from nuisance creating elements. You have to control your tongue more often than not and keep people in good humour, so that you are in everyone's good books and can seek help when genuinely required. You have to be back home in time and the locks need to be strong. You have to be in great terms with your neighbours; they often become bigger supports than any blood relations. A phone needs to be handy and you have to be extremely alert. Santiniketan finds my theories inappropriate, but it is affectionate towards me. That is because I have never ever tried to meddle with the rules of the place. I haven't tried to prove that I am capable of going beyond it. My personal space is designed very much within the boundaries it had offered. I have not fuelled any controversy with any kind of ambitious indifference to whatever it expects its inhabitants to adhere to. But that does not mean that I am living a life of compromises. I am enjoying every bit of it.

So here I am, on an inauspicious, forbidden journey, pledged to walk on it as long as I don't start believing that I am wrong in deciding the course of my life. Many had warned, it'll be too late by the time I realise. I am ready to take the risk, rather than giving in to other's beliefs. Today, right here, right now, I am happy. Nor I, neither others know what's in store tomorrow. Why then follow the format?

My thoughts are interrupted by a sound from behind. I turn and freeze.

The Forbidden

Dr Aniruddh Jain Solanki
Santiniketan

Seasons show upright here in Santiniketan. Winter is marked with the abundance of *kanchan*, *rudra-palash* and *shimool*, the fire-red blooms that set the world ablaze. Winter winds cut through pullovers. I have experienced worse winters, so the temperature and its effect don't bother me. Rather, I'm enjoying the winter. My relations with colleagues and students have improved. Colleagues have understood that I am not a threat to their lives and are rather cordial now. Students, the other day, proposed an outdoor session. It would be work and fun. The idea was harmless; getting an approval from the HOD was no big deal. With tools packed in bags, we set off for Shonajhuri. Students treaded in their bicycles. I could not convince myself to go for it; purchased a bike instead. So I reached there before the others did. And I was in for a surprise.

I spotted her from a distance. Sanghamitra Banerjee. She was sitting with knees folded towards herself, as if hesitant of occupying too much space in this vast land. Hair open, spread all over her back. She was looking away, holding a cup of tea with both hands. Looked like she was enjoying the warmth that the clay cup had offered. She seemed deeply engrossed in thought. I stopped the bike afar, not to disturb her with its roar. There is something about her. She is not that perfect or loud in the beauty department. But there's a thrust. She looks so much a part of the place where she dwells at any given time; a part of nature actually. Even her silence has eloquence, has language. She speaks more with her eyes and expressions, rather than misusing the vocal chords. And at the same time she is by no definition, a soft spoken person. Her disapproval comes through a cold stare, which can silence the smartest intruder. Yet, I have seen the same eyes sending out mischievous smiles. I can't say that she is breathtakingly beautiful; but she's capable of attracting attention without any conscious effort from her end. That morning too she looked like a work of art, embedded there, as if she was a part of this landscape, this vast expanse. If she moved away, the place wouldn't remain the same! It was wonderful to watch her from a distance.

Hey wait! Didn't I throw her way some not-so-pleasant words on this, an evening ago? This watching from a distance? And then I was doing the same myself. Her eyes spilled venom at my words and I had literally fled after sharing my mind. I usually avoid being too pleasant or unpleasant with anyone, but this woman makes me talk, makes me do things strangely out of character. A bit too much at times, just the same way as she has captured my attention right now. She's fair and tall and slim. Waist-length hair and small gold things in her ears. She was wearing a yellow sari and contrasted it with a blue blouse. Those colours looked good on her. I started walking towards her to make my presence felt. The students would be there any moment. Before they came I needed to settle anything unpleasant that was left over from the evening before. I left an apology at her doorstep that morning but that might just not have been enough. I cleared my throat loudly. She turned and sprang up to her feet, as if on fire. I stood, arms folded, in front of her. She stared for a while, composed herself, then put a clip to control her unruly hair. Sure, I was her unwanted intruder. I broke the silence. 'I came here on a special request from students for an outdoor class; please don't read this as an attempt to bother you, Ma'm.' She didn't object to the 'Ma'm.' Just responded, 'This time probably, I am at the wrong place, at the wrong time,' and prepared to leave.

'Is our score settled then?'

She stopped and looked at me. She seemed tired. 'What score?'

I reminded her of my offence. She didn't allow me to complete my sentence. 'What you said was not entirely wrong. And what you did might make you suffer some gossips. I am an old hand here. They'll take some time to catch up with me.' She smiled conclusively and left. I watched her walk away as long as she was visible. Not for once did she turn. Her slender body has rhythm. With expressions and language, she invites me constantly to know more about her, and yet maintains a distance whenever I try to get friendly. The place looked vacant without her. I closed my eyes and in the mind sculpted an image of the lady, sitting alone and sipping tea! I couldn't do this for long though. The students had arrived and one of them, sweet chap, rode my bike to park it in the same place as their cycles.

I started my lecture. Rehearsed and read umpteen times, history of world sculpture is smooth sailing for me. Whenever I am talking about them, I feel I'm romancing Egypt and Greece and Rome. I touched upon Rodin and Maillol; the modifications introduced by Renaissance artists, and subsequently the surrealists post the World War, finally discussing modern sculpture. 'Sculpture, as a category of visual three-dimensional art form, is not just about replication of an expression. The sculptor initiates and translates a non-verbal communication through his inspiration. It is an intellectually challenging exercise which accommodates observation, vision and perception, all at the same time. The sense organs of a sculptor, hence, are more acute and visibly different than many others. He tends to see and perceive such things about his objects of interest, which others may not. The vision of work is often influenced by the sculptor's personal upbringing, motivation, personal beliefs, likes and dislikes. The finesse of his art comes from his imagination and creativity.'

I explain the usage of symbols in sculpting, to drive home an idea, which is prevalent since pre-historic age. 'The Egyptians for example, believe in a life after death. The body of the Egyptian ruler or pharaoh, was carefully preserved, and goods were buried with him to provide for his needs forever. The Egyptians often combined features from various creatures to symbolise ideas. The human head of the pharaoh Khafre was added to the crouching figure of a lion to form the Great Sphinx, suggesting the combination of human intelligence and animal strength.

'Around 600 BC, Greece developed one of the greatest civilisations in the history of the world. Sculpture became one of the most important forms of expression. The Greek belief that "man is the measure of all things" is clearly shown in Greek sculpture. The human figure was the principal subject of all Greek art. Beginning in the late 7th century BC, sculptors in Greece constantly sought better ways to represent the human figure. The Greeks developed a standing figure of a nude male, called the Kouros or Apollo. The Kouros served to depict gods and heroes. The Kore, or standing figure of a draped female, was more graceful and was used to portray maidens and goddesses. The winged female figure, or Nike, became the personification of victory. The most important function of Greek sculpture was to honour gods and goddesses. Statues were placed in temples or were carved as part of a temple. Greek temples were shrines created to preserve the images of the gods. Greek sculpture changed with Greek civilisation. Praxiteles' Hermes is slimmer and more elegant than the strong, vigorous Spear Bearer, by Polycleitus. Figures by Skopas from the Mausoleum at Halicarnassus are harsher and more dramatic than the quiet, controlled figures by Phideas. Hellenistic sculptors emphasised the human figure. They reflected the great changes in their world when they treated in new ways, subjects traditionally favoured by earlier

Greek sculptors. A new interest developed in the phases of life, from childhood to extreme old age.

I feel as if I have travelled through the past, while I pronounce these. My monologue is punctuated by the visuals that aid me on my laptop and the chirping of birds here in the open. At the end of the session, I exhibited some of the ancient sculptures from world art and invited comments. Some of the responses were exciting. I made a mental note of the faces and the names of those who had thought beyond the obvious.

After the session we halted for tea on the way back. I ordered hot chocolate for myself. The students were curious to know about me, my life. I settled their queries with best elaborations. They wanted to know the scope of sculpture as a profession and how to make money out of it. I told them, there's no definite answer to their questions. But I'd try to help them. For creative satisfaction, they would have to derive their own calling and put into that job all their heart and soul. Sadly however, this emotion may not be able to bring them bread. So, they'll also have to stretch their work preferences into such commercial propositions that may or may not be creatively fulfilling. When it comes to a primitive art form like sculpting, the craft and its creators would constantly be challenged by technology. The world has less time to understand the beauty, romance and sensitivity of manually carved designs. The market is catching up with a different kind of art practice where it is purely the ideas of the artists, not the hand, which counts. New technologies and ways of working offer fresh prospects and possibilities. This includes the option of outsourcing many of the processes that you don't want to or can't do, and spending the time focused on ideas. But they might get frustrated or feel like a fraud if the sculptor's presence doesn't hold importance when the work is created.

Sagnik, one of the more ambitious students, asked for suggestions that would help them to grow. I asked him, what do you wish to achieve from your life? 'Name, fame, money and power,' he shrugged with a smile. I smiled back but felt sad at his response. As a teacher, I would have been happy had he said Art. Practically though, I don't blame him. His hunger might help him sustain. There are also strong chances that he'll get drowned in arrogance and that will take him nowhere. I have observed an acute superiority complex in him, when it comes to his batchmates. He is too good at his work. Actually it's not only the craft that he is good at. He is sincere and attentive and non-distractive. I have observed his behaviour during workshops. He learns and practises the skills as if that's his soul. Sagnik spends more time with the professors than with the students. I revealed to him the importance of PR, public relations, that might make or break anyone in our times and our line of work. It is important to keep auction houses, exhibition organisers and art collectors in good humour. His reaction to this told me that I am making sense. I advised the students to intern with celebrated houses at the beginning of their career, involve themselves with renowned architectural firms and interior designers.

We dispersed.

This morning I had yet another rigorous theoretical class with the students elaborating on the Greco-Roman influence on art and sculpture. 'The Greeks were defeated by the Romans, but the Hellenistic style lasted for centuries. Greek sculpture survived because the Romans were greatly impressed by Greek art. From the early days of the republic, Romans imported examples of Greek art, ordered copies of famous Greek works, and commissioned Greek sculptors to do Roman subjects. Rome profited from the double artistic inheritance of Greek and Etruscan sculpture. The inventiveness of Roman sculptors added to this heritage. The most important contributions of the Roman sculptors were portraits. The development of Roman sculpture was the reverse of that of Greek sculpture. Instead of progressing from fairly simple, abstract forms to more natural and realistic statues, Roman sculpture, once realistic, became far more simple and abstract ...'

At the end, everyone is loaded with too much information and walk towards the cafeteria discussing the content I had just injected in their brain. I am about to ride off, when I realise that Sagnik is standing behind me. 'You want to talk?' I ask.

'Don't you wish to know why I want to be rich and famous?'

'Wine, women, wealth ... one or all, I guess!'

He pauses, doesn't answer immediately. The handsome brat seems lost for words. When he opens his mouth, I am dumbfounded.

'I am in love with Prof. Sanghamitra! Someday I wish to share my life with her.' He leans against a lamp post, in no hurry to go!

For a while we are both quiet. I am not sure what should be my reaction. This infatuated kid is smitten by the gorgeous lady and unfortunately, I am the chosen one to receive his confession! The general practice here in Santiniketan is to address professors as *dada* and *didi*. I am Aniruddh da. Sagnik had made some efforts to not call her *Sanghamitra di*. After a while I get my humour back.

'Does she know about your noble wish?'

'She does, but not through me. I'll have to achieve enough before I tell her myself.'

'How do you know her?'

'Who doesn't know her here? She is a beauty. Everyone has a crush on her. She is Anusua di's friend and often comes to Kala Bhavan to see us working. She has an interest in sculpture.'

Now that's news to me. I have never seen her anywhere near my department. She has never expressed any interest in my job, though, with all humility, I can claim that I am the best in the craft here. She keeps a distance, rather. My thoughts must have translated to my face. Sagnik said, 'She often doesn't express in words.'

Again my humour catches up. 'What language does she apply to express herself to you, your highness?'

He doesn't react to the sarcasm, but tries to retort. 'If your senses are strong, you would know what she means. I do. I know who or what she's looking for the moment she enters the house.'

Unmindfully a question pops aloud from within me and I regret the moment I pronounce it. 'What more do you know about Sanghamitra?'

His eyes glow as he talks about her. 'She loves tea, can gulp it in gallons if you can capture her in an interesting conversation. But more often than not, she's not listening to you though she's with you. I have seen her do this with Anusua di and Stuart da. She doesn't like visitors at home. She worships books and loves music. In fact, she's trained in Indian classical music. She's also into yoga. Her opinions are strong and logic-bound. She's not closed to an argument though. She's fiercely independent. And she is fascinated with Shiva.'

A statement comes out once again, before I control my tongue. 'She is not the religious type.'

'Show her a composition on Shiva, Aniruddh da, and see her reaction.' He smiles and reflects, 'You should see her during rains. That is the time she sheds all masks. A headstrong woman otherwise, unarms herself of the tough shield and comes out in raw sensuality. Just that you have to be lucky enough to spot her walking in the rains unguarded, and you'll know what I mean. She looks like poetry then.'

The problem with men is that, when they see something like what Sagnik has detailed out, they appreciate the aesthetics of it. But when they hear, they experience the deprivation of not seeing, and start visualising. I have started visualising the back of a woman walking in the rains, draped in sari which she doesn't try to discipline. The cloth clings on to her body, as does her wet hair. She's walking aimlessly, as if her journey matters more than the destination. She looks up to face the sky, and the rains, with eyes closed, asking for more. Water droplets sensuously flow down her neck. She expresses a thirst that might not be quenched by this downpour, but she smiles in satisfaction, happy with less, because it gives her the scope of repeated consumption. I am not sure whether the woman I saw is Sanghamitra; but she was a part of the rain-washed greenery, as much as the Economics professor was a part of Khoai the other day.

I jerk back realising that I had been doing something inappropriate. I am visualising sensuality out of a dignified lady, who has not given me any reason to do so. Not yet.

I look at Sagnik, he's been watching me. There's something in his eyes that makes me feel uneasy. 'You just saw her, right?'

Dangerously outspoken this guy is, I decide in haste and start my bike. But he is not finished yet. 'I saw her talking to you that morning in Khoai.'

I frown at him. 'So?'

'You're interested in her, aren't you?'

I almost choke. 'Are you insane?' is what I managed to utter. Is this what Sanghamitra had tried to warn me about?

The guy is not alarmed by the sudden rise in my decibels. 'I saw a glitter in her eyes while she was talking to you. I watched you guys from behind the banyan tree there. Hardly have I ever seen her lighting up to anyone. There was something meaningful about what was shared between the two of you.'

This doesn't seem to be a harmless infatuation any longer. The kid might be treading a dangerous zone. He can mean trouble if not helped out in time. In fact, it's already quite late. His outburst may strip the lady of her honour. An evil thought crosses my mind simultaneously. Is she actually a lady of honour? What if she is well aware of his devotion and indulging his passion to grow? Nevertheless, that's not for me to judge. I have learnt in life to protect and respect women. I would try and talk this boy out of his madness, I tell myself. Somehow I could not bring myself to believe that Sanghamitra is deliberately fuelling Sagnik's infatuation; she's too sophisticated for that.

I compose myself and manage to say, rather calmly, 'Sagnik, what you did was not something decent. I understand your fondness for her, but I don't understand why you have to hide and watch two people talking. Grow up, boy! And no, I have no interest in her the way you mean. We're neighbours. So it is but obvious that if we meet somewhere, we'll exchange pleasantries. You don't have competition from me. Are you happy now? Then do exactly what you are doing. Don't take yourself any further till you deserve to be with her. You're a bright boy and I'm there to guide you.' What I don't tell him is that the lady has managed to throw some questions at my being too. It happens with almost everyone who has ever inspired my work as a sculptor. Till I get them on my tray and replicate their truth on rock, they keep questioning my contribution to the art and I feel vastly incomplete with my deliverables. Often this takes peace out of my system and puts me in an intense zone of desperation, which many might misunderstand. For the first time in all these years, I have stopped on a young, beautiful face. I didn't choose her, she chose me. Her expressions, I mean. Indeed, she would be a great study. She's real, yet enigmatically mysterious. I remembered her sitting on the terrace, bathed in moonlight. With all her presence she has convinced me that there's something I'll achieve if I get to work on her. However, Sanghamitra was right; I have to be careful here. I am not dying to take her to my table tomorrow; I am ready to wait and give her time to understand my passion and not feel threatened.

For some odd reason, Sagnik's confession has put me in an uncomfortable space. I'm not too sure why! I want to warn Sanghamitra about this. There are a thousand reasons as to why I should not get involved and walk my own separate way. Yet, I wish to know what she thinks of it. Has Sagnik managed to touch a fraction of her mind with his desperate devotion? Or it is just his one-sided glory? And why did he confront me with something I felt was a helpless jealousy? He said Sanghamitra's eyes were shining as she spoke to me! Was this true? Or it was just his hallucination? What was it, if at all it was there? Strange thoughts disturb my routine, and repeatedly I force myself back to work! She appears again, challenging my intentions to carry her to my carving room with a hopeless indifference. I tell myself, there's no hurry. But in my mind I know that I am restless and her aloofness is not doing kind things to my ego. And more shockingly, I never knew that I can get this impatient with anything!

That evening I return home late. I slow down automatically when I am crossing Mrigaya. Soft tanpura plays inside, accompanying a *thumri* on Raga Misra Khamaj. I stand there leaning against the coconut tree, as her voice flawlessly caresses the notes and spends time on every word, exploring and rediscovering the beauty of the evening raga. Melodiously she intones *Kaun Gali Gayo Shyam*! I wait till she finishes. On the curtain of the window, her shadow stands and moves ahead to keep the tanpura in its place; then disappears. Sanghamitra would shoot me down if she learns that I had been standing outside her home, in the open, allowing the passersby to witness my unjustified, whimsical obsession over God knows what! Thankfully it is dark here and no one is looking this way with too much attention!

Kaun Gali Gayo Shyam...

Sanghamitra Banerjee
Santiniketan

I ideally wanted to learn Sitar. My parents had introduced me to vocal classical music at a very young age. Today I am sufficiently out of touch. As work pressures and responsibilities caught up, time for hobbies naturally went down. The background that I came from was liberated enough to accept anything I chose as my career. After my graduation in music fetched a distinction, ma asked me whether I would be pursuing the art more seriously. Any kind of classical music, vocal or instrumental, needs unconditional commitment. I deliberated over it and decided that it would be far easier to earn my bread through academics. So I focused on Economics instead. Music remained with me, in all its melodies, as a pastime. Hardly anyone knows that I hold a degree in music. Whoever knows comes up with weird requests of unfolding my vocal genius in public gatherings, much to my embarrassment. I detest that kind of attention or affectation. So, I maintain a low profile on this aspect of my being, as I do about a lot others. If ever I feel like revisiting the notes, I string the tanpura late in the night when the world is asleep. These days I mostly listen. My home is temple to a huge collection of instrumental classical music, captured in CDs. I protect them fiercely from borrowers. After my regularity with the art ceased, I sheltered myself in the instrumental version of what I had learned so sincerely for fifteen years. I indulge myself with the flute, santoor and sitar. In moments of exhaustion, energy-deprived both mentally and physically, the Indian flute is extremely therapeutic. It's best to hear in isolation. The instrument is designed to end turbulence and usher in peace! Sitar is good for mood elevation. Each and every composition, whatever the raga, starts slow on the *vilambit*; and as it progresses, both the player and the listener are on a fresh journey of discovery. By the time it catches up on *drut*, notes are released in quick succession to create short or long compositions without harassing the grammar of the raga; creation and absorption, both offer ultimate fulfilment. There's excitement here, as also some kind of celebration. Santoor makes me feel romantic. Rather, when I am in a romantic mood, I listen to the santoor. The aqua music brings to life a playful, mischievous soul that knows it is hiding something. It is like a restless woman's anklet, which rings every time she walks stealthily to play a harmless prank. It is also like a shy lover, waiting anxiously to experience the moment of extreme unrestricted indulgence that unshackles his deepest and purest desires.

The other evening Anusua had invited me to Kala Bhavan for a musical evening. She sings Tagore's songs and is very good at it. Often Stuart joins her with an unconventionally coarse voice. It is a treat to watch Shayan play the guitar and Anusua joining him with her vocal chords activated to life. They are a great musical pair. Both of them have been here almost all their lives. They've studied here from schooldays; later they joined their respective departments as professors. Hence, their relevance is very prominent all across the place, irrespective of the subject they teach or the discipline they serve. It is easy to accompany them. Access and acceptance to important groups and communities here come handy because of the endorsement they offer to their friends and acquaintances. Impromptu on some evenings they sit at Kala Bhavan campus and do a musical bonfire. And there's no one around who would want or choose to avoid or ignore it. Known or unknown, visitors or passersby, all would join in to absorb the experience.

Just as they were arranging the mats on the ground, I heard a familiar voice humming *Kaun Gali Gayo Sham*! It stopped abruptly as I turned to face the sculptor walking behind, probably unaware of my presence because he too halted unceremoniously to prevent us colliding against each other and within that moment of unanticipated shock, the tune in his lips was gone. It might be a coincidence that I had been singing the same *thumri* just a night before, but it was also too difficult to be brushed off as a non-significant serendipity. I tried to get my answers from his reactions, but his face registered nothing and he walked off as if I was just one among the crowd and nothing more. Rest of the evening he was nowhere to be found. While Anusua took us through the choicest notes, my eyes wandered around. Each time my vision hit the corner room of the teacher's section, which was the only place which had its lights on. Rest of the professors were enjoying the music outside! What kind of person is closed to this kind of an experience? Does he feel disconnected because he doesn't understand the language? Or he keeps a distance from his office unless it is strictly professional. Anusua did tell me about his eccentric behaviour in the department. But how did he pick up on the *thumri*? Did he hear me singing it? The question refuses to grant me peace. My mind creates imageries where I walk into his room and ask him the source of that tune. My body sits tight and moves only when the evening is over and Anusua is ready to drop me. Till the end, the sculptor doesn't show up even for a single second!

Music and art is in the air, here. And there is Nature. This is the only place I've seen which has a spring and an autumn. Nature unfolds with all its blooms, greenery and weather, creating a sensation such that every soul responds to the difference. It's February and the air is already humming songs of spring. Mornings and evenings are cool now, days pleasant. I have plans to visit the book fair in Kolkata in a day or two.

I go to the Book Fair out of a habit that refuses to die out. As a child, my mother would give me a budget and encourage me to prepare a wish-list within that budget. I would go up and down the journals to examine the charm of that season and note down everything that I wanted to lay my hands on; along with the respective prices. Later I would sit with my friends in school and compare our lists. The common ones would be crossed out because they can be borrowed. At times I shrewdly convinced my friends to buy the more expensive ones. From the rest, I would evaluate the options through a cost-benefit analysis and finally decide what all I am buying. More often than not, I saved for an ice-cream from the budget.

This year Jadavpur University Press has invited some of the ex-students of the university to man their stall in the Fair. I will have to be present for the last four days. Stuart has informed our batchmates and we have agreed to a re-union of sorts on the campus. I'll reach Kolkata two days in advance.

One of these days Stuart met Dr Aniruddh. We were sitting at Sukumar da's in Ratan Pally celebrating Shayan's paper being honoured at an International Conference in London. Over soft drinks and food, we were at our hilarious best, pulling each other into pranks and making fun of all achievements that any of us would boast of. 'We' means, I-Shayan-Sia-Stuart. Anusua is about to join us after a class. We spot her walking with lazy steps, accompanied by Dr Aniruddh. Scarlet T-shirt and cargoes, hands tucked in pockets; not bad, I wonder. They're discussing something. Immediately the group leaves everything else and starts a gossip.

'Is he interested?'

'May be, they look engrossed.'

'No friends, I've heard this guy is hell of an arrogant. He'll not fall so fast.'

'He's polite but, manages to smile.'

'Hunk he is, no?'

'What hunk man? If you have a fair complexion, any colour would suit you.'

'And if you don't have a pot-belly like Stuart, any shape would fit you.'

'Hey, how does he smell?'

'Go try him yourself baby!'

'I thought creative types always sported a ponytail and a beard.'

'He wears a small diamond in his ear.'

'Rich eh? What do you think would be his bank balance?'

'Running in losses. God knows why he has come here, moron, leaving all riches and prosperity that the West was giving him!'

Silently I listen to their conversation. True he looks stylish and handsome, a dish for any woman looking out. But a man looks more like a man in his formals. The way I saw my father carrying himself. I tried to imagine how the sculptor would look in a white shirt unbuttoned at the top to bare his chest, and beige fitted trousers. Sleeves folded, dark brown belt and formal shoes matching the belt. A sure shot boundary!!! I know a wicked grin has crossed my eyes. Of course the sculptor doesn't know he is being watched and discussed; his face is engaged with workaholic expressions.

'I think they're discussing the next porn film they'll watch together ... ha ha ha,' that's Stuart of course, in his unabashed, shameless way.

Shayan blurts out, 'Or maybe they're discussing how cushioned would it feel to kick your butt!'

I hold both their heads and get them to collide with each other. They utter a sharp cry of pain; Sia laughs out. They've reached us. Just outside Sukumar da's dhaba, they stand and continue their conversation.

I expect Anusua to join us after they are done; the sculptor will go his way. I wait for this to happen, when our eyes meet. He sends across a half smile, acknowledging my presence. Restless Shayan gets up and walks towards them. 'Hi Anu, hi dude. Please come, join us. Otherwise you make me feel really jealous.' Both of them look at him, unsure of what he's talking about. He smiles, 'I get jealous when Anu speaks to hunks,' he tries to lean on her shoulder. She moves away. 'Don't worry bro, we are talking shop, about course curriculum in fact.' Dr Aniruddh is all smiles, tries to reason. Shayan catches hold of his arms and drags him to our table. 'We all would love to be honoured by your esteemed presence, Sir!' He makes him sit by pressing against his shoulders. That's something special about Shayan. He doesn't waste time in judging people. He just makes friends. He says, it's better to be fooled by trusting people than being fooled by not trusting them. He can get close to anyone in a jiffy, and people share their saddest secrets with him. He is loyal enough, not to ever divulge them. People love him for obvious reasons. He seems to be approaching the world with huge space in his heart, ready to extend himself in support of their pains and happiness. From the fruit vendor to his HOD, he is preferred company to one and all. Shayan strikes the same magic with the 'hunk.' The sculptor looks at me again, as if asking permission. I utter, 'Would Mr Sculptor enjoy it here? We are everything that he is not. He may not approve of the sinful things we do and say here. See, Stuart is lighting a cigarette! We're an awful lot, I tell you!' The retort that comes from six-feet above the ground catches me off-guard. 'How do you know I don't smoke, Ma'm Economics?'

'Well … er … I haven't seen you smoking.'

'Do you see me very often?' He's teasing me on that temple issue, again.

'Tea, coffee or cold drink?'

'None!'

'Good. None of them are available anyway, right now. Coconut water?'

'Yes please, if that's available,' he smiles. So do the others.

I lift myself, relieved, and walk towards Sukumar da to place the order. I know he doesn't smoke. I have observed his lips. Too pink for a man, and too unpigmented for ever having accommodated the white stick! There's a hand on my back and I jerk back shocked. It's Anusua. She frowns. 'Are you ok?' I am gasping, 'You scared me!' I can see from the corner of my eyes, a gaze has followed me. I turn to face Sukumar da.

We place our orders and come back to the table. The introductions and pleasantries are over. Everyone is engaged in some discussion now. Dr Aniruddh and Sia are subtle in their expressions. Stuart is loud. He has been instructed by Shayan to turn away from the table each time he exhales the smoke. He is not quite happy about the extra work. Once again I can't but help appreciate Shayan. Not only has he taken care to comfort the new person here, but he has also led a very normal exchange of conversation without dwelling on his accomplishments so that the sculptor is not embarrassed and the others don't feel inferior. Stuart has raised a topic.

'But why are you so strict about the vegetarian diet, Doc?' They've nicknamed him already.

'Why should I not be, Swagata? What's the fun in killing animals for your diet?' For a moment we look around to understand who's Swagata. Soon we realise and settle down.

'Its survival of the fittest everywhere, dude! And the dishes are all so tasty!'

'Is that enough reason to slaughter? Human beings are supposed to have an evolved brain. You can afford to prepare tasty dishes without killing living creatures. Yet, you are ready to commit the crime to merely satisfy your taste buds.'

'Hang on Sir. Aren't you killing living creatures for your diet as well? The plants that you feed on also carry life. You veggies are not doing anything noble! In fact, by consuming only one category of life, you are only disturbing the ecological balance of the universe, leading to environmental evils like global warming!'

This is getting sensitive. I can see that the sculptor is uncomfortable with the last comment. He's a Rajasthani with conservative rituals and food habits that he has practised all his life. It's not appropriate to challenge personal choices and beliefs with logic. Not in public at least. Probably Stuart understands that as well. The sculptor puts forward his last argument meekly. 'How would you like it if anyone wants to feed on you, Swagata?'

Stuart quips, 'Like a lamb. My boss does that everyday! So does my wife!'

So woebegone is his expression, everyone laughs.

Our pranks and laughter continue till dinner. All of us de-stress ourselves in such gatherings. All the while, they didn't allow Doc to move away. Twice in between he wanted to take leave. Stuart and Shayan blocked such chances and ordered customised dishes for him. Our fish was served on a separate table so that he is not discomforted. I can say he's loving the attention. He's getting friendly with every passing exchange. With him facing me, I can't emote freely. I'm conscious that he is watching. Every time I am laughing out loud or venting out scorn, he is intently observing the expressions on my face.

We disperse around 9:30. It is quite 'late night' here. Shayan and Sia would drop Anusua on the way. Stuart has his bike. I am left with the obvious choice; my neighbour after all. Just before leaving, Stuart calls, 'Sam, I'll call you the day after and meet somewhere. Pritha would join us after office. Safe journey.' No prize for guessing that Pritha is Mrs Stuart and our batchmate. In college my name was shortened to Sam and Stuart still calls me that. The 'safe journey' is to wish me before I depart for Kolkata the following day.

I start walking; a pair of shoes matches my footsteps from behind. Sweet melody of a flute impairs any conversation that either of us would have started to kill the silence. I know the source of this music.

As we reach the start of Ratan Pally, Dr Aniruddh is startled as much as I had been, when it was my first time. A rickshaw-puller is playing a wooden flute, sitting on his vehicle. His name is Karim-bhai. All day he earns his bread. In the evenings, he earns his peace. It is fascinating that a rickshaw-puller, homeless and abandoned by family, who goes through myriad struggles throughout the day, has the capacity to surrender and drown himself in sublime music at night. What better way to challenge and worship life, both at the same time? The sculptor looks at me with disbelief, trying to confirm the sight in front. I pass an assuring smile. We walk silently till the music is no longer audible. Then he says something with his usual abruptness. 'There's something special about us!' Unsure of what he's getting at, I flash the question through my eyes. He doesn't notice, kind of lost in himself. 'There are certain things I have experienced here, which will remain with me for life. These experiences are not commercially important. But had I not been a part of it, I wouldn't have valued my presence in this corner of the world as much as I do today. And more often than not, these moments happen when you are around! I feel alert, attentive and alive to life like never before!' He pauses, and continues, 'It may have been a coincidence that you are a part of the same geographical circumference, when my senses are being activated to new learning and realisations. But as much as it is an unplanned predestined conspiracy, equally is it a fact! And I can't choose to hide how much I appreciate taking in these experiences with you. Your presence enriches them with appropriate expressions, be it silence, scorn or smiles. It is beautiful that we are here, together, appreciating some divine moments in peace.'

For a moment, I am lost for words. I am flattered, of course, but I am not telling him that. 'Aren't you reading too much into it all?' He doesn't look at me, but smiles, and remains calm. The silence kills me though!

'Doc, may I just …!'

'Please!' I am interrupted by his soft rudeness.

'What?'

'Don't call me that. I have a name. If you use it, I'll respond better.' He's smiling and flirting now.

'You are too senior for me to use your first name. I don't share the American ease while addressing seniors.' I say grimly.

He sounds amused. The romantic intellectualism has disappeared as if it was never there. 'Really! What's your age, may I ask, though I know it's a rude question!'

'Seniority is not defined by age alone. It can also be defined by achievements. In response to your rude query, I am thirty-one.'

For a few moments we walk in silence. And once again, when I am absorbed in the uninterrupted calm of the night, he intrudes with a deep voice, jerking my senses to the unanticipated change. He doesn't notice the difference though.

'Where are you headed Ma'm, to deserve a safe journey wish from your friends?'

'You can call me by my name. I am leaving for Kolkata tomorrow to attend the Book Fair.'

'I hope I don't sound like a stalker when I say, I am headed for the city tomorrow to launch Partha Banerjee's book on bronze sculpting. O no, he signs as Bandopadhyay, not Banerjee. Tell me, why do Bengali surnames have alternatives? Bandopadhyay and Banerjee, Gangopadhyay and Ganguly..!'

I interrupt before he gets any further. 'Same reason as to why a Solanki becomes Jain, and Jain becomes Jain Solanki. It is simply the wish of the individual!' Dr Aniruddh had mentioned to Shayan that their ancestral surname is Solanki and he's a Rajput Agnivanshi, whatever that means! Jain is the religious title which his great-grandfather acquired, and his grandmother dismissed. Though many people in his family have dropped it, he did choose to have both of them behind his first name. Caught unaware the sculptor laughs out loud, shattering the quiet of the night. 'Softly,' I chide him, but enjoy the spontaneity and freedom in his expression. He composes himself. 'Can we go together?' he asks.

I ask, 'Are you going to the Book Fair only with that agenda? Or do you have something else in mind?' He runs his fingers through his hair. 'Crowds suffocate me. I want to go to Dakshineshwar and Belur Matth to detox myself.'

'You are quite a religious fanatic, no?' I ask with a smile. 'By your standards, yes,' he utters, 'I love visiting places with religious significance and believe in the mythological history associated with it. I have grown up learning that a morning puja is the first thing you do after an early bath. It runs in my blood, too late to disconnect from the practice!' I remain quiet. The sculptor continues, 'My grandmother worshipped Lakshmi-Narayan. She was a superstitious but practical woman who knew that all through her mortal existence Lakshmi-Narayan would give her the materialistic pleasure that Shiva, whom our community had patronised for ages, could not. I grew up under strict supervision. My grandmother's Lakshmi-Narayan had dominated over Shiva not only in our household but also in the brains of my family members. Everyone was too scared to practise anything that she did not approve of. In her choice of deity, she had made a strong statement which read: everyone has to contribute and prosper in the money-generating task and that is the sole purpose of the lives of men in the family. No one is supposed to be a recluse; the family did not have the sanction or authority to break or transform any rule or any practice that she had propagated. Shiva was almost wiped out from our system. There was only one space where the lord still resided. In my heart. He still does. I adore his Nataraj form, where he dances to express anger. Has anyone ever perceived anger to be so beautiful? I think of him when I meditate. You know, after I started practising meditation, I can explain a lot of things happening to me. I recognise each of the punishments and rewards I get from life, and even the reasons. Intentionally or unintentionally, my Karma comes back to me in black and white and I can, kind of locate it somewhere!'

He stops as abruptly as he had started. I look at him anticipating more. 'Your grandmother accepted your choice of profession?' I ask. He stops walking and looks down at me. 'Lady, we've reached your home!'

I am visibly embarrassed and turn to go, mumbling a good night. I am surprised realising how much I was captivated by his words. The road that I walk in and out every day had suddenly failed to rekindle its connection with me! He comes ahead and blocks my way.

'Come with me tomorrow,' he demands.

'I am going by train,' I put across conclusively.

'If I have company, I don't mind ditching the car.'

'Good Night, Dr Jain.' He does not repeat the wish after me. I walk past and open the door. I know he's standing there for me to lock the door from inside. Then, slowly, his footsteps fade away.

Nataraj

Dr Aniruddh Jain Solanki
Santiniketan

In a very demurely headstrong way, she knows how to make people value her independence. Otherwise why would someone disagree to a well-spaced car and insist on catching a train that starts at 6:30 in the morning! After working till late, I had been sleep-deprived all night, afraid that I might miss the alarm. What a torture! When I manage to reach her door, I find it locked with a piece of paper entwined through it. It read, 'I'll get the tickets.' I was kind of expecting her to do something of the sort to avoid sitting with me in the same rickshaw.

It took me a while to locate her at Bolpur station. In blue jeans and a faded green T-shirt, hair tied up in a ponytail, she looked no older than a student. I have always seen her in saris and salwar-kameez; so my eyes were not accustomed to this girly look. When I spotted her, she was smiling from a distance. She had been watching me running up and down looking for her, while she was right in front. Anything for your amusement, Ma'm!

She had no luggage with her. Just a small purse hanging down her shoulder, a book titled *The Difficulty of Being Good* by Gurcharan Das in her right hand, balancing a bottle of mineral water in the crook of the elbow; the left hand hanging free! We board the air-conditioned compartment and sit facing each other beside adjoining windows. A vendor comes with tea and she almost gulps down the liquid at one go. They use small clay cups, *kulhar*s, broad at the top, round in the middle and tapered at the bottom. The train is relatively vacant. Our compartment has only twelve people, most of whom have occupied window seats. 'How come you are travelling so light?' I point towards her lack of luggage. 'I have everything I need at my home in Kolkata. I don't need to carry stuff every time I go,' she quips. The morning has done something to her mood. She looks happy and cheerful. She usually wears an invisible shield that reads, I'm closed; but now she seems ready to talk. She knows that I am watching her and distracts me with the mere mention of a subject on which I am ready to bare my soul. 'You were telling me yesterday about your fascination for Shiva.'

My gaze shifts from her and reaches out inwardly to those bronze statues depicting the most passionate dance form in an aureole of flames, lifting the left leg and balancing the right over the demon Apasmara who symbolises avidya, ignorance. Personally, professionally and philosophically, I worship the cosmic dancer, Nataraj, as a depiction of Lord Shiva. Nataraj performs his divine dance, Tandava, to destroy a weary universe and make preparations for Brahma to start the process of fresh creation.. 'Evolve, emerge, or die,' the Nataraj symbolises! Through the violent Tandava, he ruins to rebuild, liberating the world from obsolescence and stagnation. What he emotes in the process is *rudra rup* or anger. Anger, which is born out of desperation, deprivation and repressed urges. This form of emotion is not a weakness, as many might consider, if it can be channelised constructively. It is a passion, an extremely strong one, which can motivate you to achieve the impossible.

A traditional Tamil concept, Shiva was first depicted as Nataraj in the famous Chola bronzes and sculptures. The dance of Shiva in Thillai, the Tamil name for Chidambaram, forms the motif for all the depictions of Shiva as Nataraj. The statues have a cobra uncoiling from the lower right forearm, the crescent moon and a skull on the crest. He performs the Dance of Bliss, ananda tandavam, within an arch of flames. The upper right hand holds a small drum shaped like an hourglass, called *damaru* in Sanskrit. It symbolises the sound of origin or creation; the beat of the drum represents the passage of time. The upper left hand holds *agni* or fire, signifying destruction. The opposing concepts in the upper hands show the counterpoise of creation and destruction. The second right hand depicts the *Abhaya mudra*, offering sanctuary and bestowing protection from evil, ignorance or illusion to those who follow the path of dharma. The second left hand points towards the raised foot which he raises to bring it down with force on the demons and crush them, symbolising upliftment of soul and liberation from ills. The surrounding flames represent the manifest Universe. The snake swirling around his waist is kundalini, the shakti or divine force in the form of a coiled serpent that resides within everything or everyone. This also parallels the sacred thread or *upanayana* worn by Brahmins to represent the second birth. The stoic face of Shiva represents his neutrality, thus being in balance. The Nataraj form is seen as the image of his rhythmic play which is the source of all movement within the universe. This is represented by the circular or elliptical frame surrounding the Lord.

'I have travelled the length and breadth of India, even the world, visiting all temples, recommended or researched, that are known for their Nataraj statues. The Thillai Nataraja Temple, Chidambaram in Tamil Nadu, bears a history of Nataraj architecture by itself. There are mainly five places in Tamil Nadu itself, where the cult of Nataraj is worshipped with great pomp. These are the Pancha Sabhas or Five Halls, where Shiva is purported to have performed the Tandava at the request of devotees–namely the golden hall at Chidambaram, silver hall at Madurai, copper hall at Tirunelveli, hall of gems at Tiruvalangadu and the hall of paintings at Kuttralam. Abroad, the

Richmond Hill Hindu Temple in Canada performs the Arudhra Darshan with strict discipline and adherence to rituals. CERN, Geneva is landmarked by a tall statue of Nataraj, which was a gift from the Indian government on 18 June 2004, to celebrate the research centre's long association with India. Personally I consider the Nataraj sculpture to be the most spiritually ambitious work of art that Indian philosophies have ever produced.'

As I speak, Sanghamitra remains speechless with all attention turned towards me. After I stop, she remains silent for a short while. Then, like a reporter she leans forward and holds a paper folded into hollow cylinder in front of my mouth pretending it to be a microphone. 'So, Mr Sculptor, tell us honestly–did you visit these places for professional or religious interests?'

'Religious.' I don't take time to respond. She throws a sceptical look my way. 'My profession is my religion. I worship my work. So I can't separate the two. As a child when I studied scriptures, the incarnations of Shiva fascinated me more than Lakshmi or Narayan. Think of Pashupati, the Lord of animals, who is meant to kill the animal instincts within us. Or Rudra, who controls passion. Or Neelkanth, who swallowed poison for the good of the world and held it safe in his neck. While my family chanted slokas for Lakshmi-Narayan in our *puja-ghar* at home, I was reading and memorising Shiva Purana and visiting the Shiva temple few kilometres away to offer my puja.'

She sobers down at my explanation and leans back in her seat, gazing outside the window.

'What is your interest in Shiva if I may ask? Or were you simply humouring me all this while, letting me lecture endlessly on my pet topic,' I ask.

'The tranquil that comes camouflaged in terror!' I wonder whether she is answering me or thinking aloud. 'Shiva, the most harmless, peace-loving deity is visualised with snakes, ganja, dust-clad, wearing a tiger skin. These must be making him look so horrible, so frightening. Yet, his eyes are calm and content with an undefined happiness. Some say he's a hermit, a recluse. And again, he is the ultimate form of masculinity, dream husband. How can someone have such diametrically opposite identities?' She turns to me. 'I don't have any religious inclination here. Shiva is a character, for me, a character from our ancient scriptures, who confirms the law of opposites. This law of opposites is a personal philosophy.' She smiles and continues, 'The law of opposites holds when twin existences or philosophies merge as one. In such cases the characters suffer or enjoy dual personalities, both being radically different from each other. Shiva from mythology fascinates me as much as Shah Jahan surprises me in the pages of history. A man who killed his brothers to attain the throne got the seventh wonder built to express his love for his wife! How can a human being nurse extreme love and absolute hatred side by side within his being? How could the same person appreciate blood and the white architecture simultaneously? Come to think of it, it is the law of opposites that balances the world. Mathematically speaking, the positives have to be together with an equal degree of negatives to nullify all forces and bring the world back to neutrality. This neutrality is denoted by zero! Meaning "nothing." Had this not been the cosmic rule, the earth would have lost its balance.'

This woman thinks a bit too deep, I wonder. Here she is, sitting in front of me, looking out of the window. She's a young, pretty girl. Why does she complicate herself so much? She might belong to the fourth class of Bengalis, who I didn't meet before. The Complicated! My grin makes her turn, but her gaze doesn't stop at me. Two other people have caught her attention. One guy, with a harmonium is singing Tagore's songs, standing inside the compartment. With my limited knowledge I can say that he's singing quite well. After he finishes, she gets up and reaches out to him, exchanges pleasantries and hands over a note. The other is a woman vendor, selling hot loafs of breads. She purchases from her and immediately extends a piece of the loaf in my direction.

With a spontaneous grimace I remark, 'Is this healthy?' She laughs aloud and remarks, 'Forgive me, Mr NRI, for serving you unhygienic, native bread. Oh what an unpardonable sin I have committed!!' She pulls her hand back.

Few moments of silence, and then she resumes. 'Why do they appreciate your art so much?'

'Probably because I sculpt the mind, not just the body. If I sculpt you, my work will speak much more than you do on any mundane day. Moreover, my concept and finishing is worth dying for!' Did I sound conceited, arrogant? Maybe I did, but no regrets. I've worked very hard to deserve this arrogance. 'Why do you usually talk so less?'

'I don't have much to share with the world. Most of the times I don't feel like interacting. I live a private life. Who on earth would be interested in what I have to say or mean? Many might listen to me but very few would have the time and patience to absorb. I am misusing myself if I forcefully wish to make myself heard. Often in between arguments I fall silent because I lack the energy to continue. People think that I have agreed to their impositions. But the truth is, I don't feel like protesting. My perspective though, remains indisputably close to my logic, irrespective of any kind of external support.'

I look at her, not sure of how to react to this! Is she a loner? She looks at me and smiles. Her smile puts language back to my mouth. I ask, a bit sarcastically, 'I heard you love watching sculptures, Sagnik told me,'I could have bitten my tongue. One look at her and I sincerely wished I could take back the words.The smile fades away and she seems to be searching something with intense eyes digging into me. She responds after a while, 'The first guy who shouted for me from rooftops was a seven year old kid, when I was seventeen! One day he saw me exchanging physics homework with a male classmate sitting on the same bench of a vacant classroom and cried banging his head on the wall! The first proposal for marriage came at nineteen, from a man of forty-three! He was a self-proclaimed bachelor, engineer at US, changed his mind after seeing me at a family function! Those days I was fat and ugly! In college the guy who gathered courage to propose to me was three years junior. In Jadavpur University Professor Ujjwal Ghosh was actively into theatres. I volunteered in their group for some time, helping them with the Bengali adaptation of Anton Chekhov's plays. He started writing ballads!!! Must be at least twenty years my senior! In the building that I stay in Kolkata, there is this kid whose eyes light up the moment I enter the gate! During Christmas, Diwali, etc. they make tableaux and put them up on display; I make sure to find out his work beforehand and appreciate it more than others; otherwise he sulks! So either older uncles or kids fall for me, Mr Sculptor. Pray, don't try to search for my contribution or participation in this. And what is it to you anyway!' She counters for a good measure after the barrage.

I laugh out loud; she too grins, sharing my amusement. I thought this question would scandalise and throw her off balance! Tough girl! After a while I insist that she gives me a rather specific response. 'Doesn't this disturb you Sanghamitra? I found him quite desperate. Otherwise who confronts a professor after seeing him exchange a word with another?'

'Dr Jain, I believe every relation is transactional by a strange act of barter. If I don't have anything to give, he'll not have anything to take either. Things have to be reciprocal, to sustain. At best, he can try and embarrass me, like he has, by baring his heart to you. But I genuinely have nothing to give in return, either to him or to the gossips that this might have raised.'

Her statement and exposed sincerity to each word she uttered irritates me for some strange, unknown reason. 'Every relation is transactional? A mother–son relation, relation between lovers, between friends and siblings, all transactional? Are you serious?'

'I am talking about personal opinions, Dr Jain, my personal opinion to be precise. I am not making a generalised or sweeping statement.

A mother can't be a mother unless she has a son and vice versa. Deliverables of a mother is reciprocal to the deliverables of a son. A mother derives satisfaction in pampering her son; the son derives care from his mother. In my life I don't believe in unnecessary sacrifices for anything or anyone. If I walk a step, I expect returns. Otherwise I'd better not walk. I don't believe love is the other name of sacrifice or sacrificing. Anything that doesn't reciprocate frustrates, after a time.' Her voice is cold and calm. I feel a bit depressed, probably because I am able to see the underlying truth in her words. I would like to believe that the relationship between parents and progeny is the purest of all relations, blessed by unconditional acceptance of each other. But hasn't my relationship with my parents suffered beyond repair because I chose differently? Hasn't my mother disowned me at least outwardly? More importantly, haven't I reciprocated by distancing myself further when my family expressed anger and indifference to my choice? Her truth is bitter and unfathomable to my theoretical learning and upbringing. But it is the stark, naked truth, untarnished or unvarnished; the truth that stares at you when you remove those rose-tinted spectacles. I remain quiet. She is patient, silent, indulges me with the time I require to absorb her thoughts, debating their appropriateness in my brain.

The train runs between meadows of yellow and green. Travelling a few miles away from the city unfolds the beautiful countryside. This part of the land is full of water bodies that frequent the farming grounds and plantations. Sanghamitra has undone the ponytail, let her hair loose and is running her fingers through it to get rid of the clinging wetness; gazing outside. This girl should have been happily married by now; her eyes should have had ambitions or dreams or both; she should have gone on foreign holidays rather than the Book Fair; she should have been in someone's arms instead of sitting alone in the window seat of the train and spouting philosophy. But she has chosen a life of isolation. Why? I wonder. I have noticed that she accepts or rejects things only after she has known enough about them and finds logic in investing or not investing her time or trust. Her criticisms are never based on half knowledge. That's fascinating.

The silence between us is suffocating. I stare at her for a while and our eyes meet. 'You asked me a while back, why my art works better than the others. I gave you a half response,' I state. 'The truth is, along with my finesse, I have been fortunate enough to meet some influential people in the same or related trade, who paved my way to help me reach where I am now. My success is not totally self-made or because of my talents alone. It required a team of expert contributors to build my brand. I would say it is a judicious mix of my innate talent and a clever showcasing of it for the world at large that has contributed equally to my success, my name and fame.' She's smiling mischievously. 'What makes you confess this, Sculptor?' She has started calling me thus when she is in playful mood. 'Before the journey ends I should be repaying all debts,' I utter enigmatically as the train enters Howrah station.

'What debt?'

'I am indebted to the beautiful time I've spent with you and some honest truths I have confronted. In return, I owe you my truth.' I smile back.

In the next few minutes we are rushing through an ocean of people in Howrah station, and fighting through them to reach a comparatively non-happening place where we bid adieu to each other. We'll probably meet once in the Book Fair. Before we disperse, I end up saying something totally weird. 'Would you like to come out with me one day? Like on a date?' She is rendered speechless for a moment and says softly but with a definite coldness in her voice and eyes, 'Did I hear you correctly?' Anyone would have backed out after hearing her cold voice and strict freezing stare. Yet I persist surprising myself. 'I am not trying to be smart, Sanghamitra. I don't intend giving you red roses or a candlelit dinner. But if you come with me, I would like to introduce you to a slice of my life. You can rest assured that I will not cause you any embarrassment or make unwanted demands.' I pause. 'Moreover, no one is judging you here. Kolkata is busier than Santiniketan. Though, I am more than sure that you don't care what others have to say about you. You used that I'm being judged dialogue to keep me away.' Her expression says that I have disturbed her. I try to put her at ease. 'I don't have much experience in charming girls. Creative people are introverts by nature devoid of social graces; and often our words hurt more than they satisfy. I now feel, I should have probably gradually built up a friendship with you before asking you out or uttering that I am tempted to spend more time with you. But my impulse worked faster than my logical brain. Sincere apologies.' I walk back a few steps. She hesitates before saying, 'Can I have your number?'

We exchange numbers and disperse.

Our meeting at the Book Fair was brief. She was crowded by her collegemates and seemed totally occupied with duty and fun. We exchanged a few pleasantries and got busy with our own jobs. From afar I saw her laughing openly and soulfully, something that she doesn't do often. Before I left, I couldn't even reach out to say goodbye.

I met her again yesterday. Last evening was one of the most fulfilling times I have spent in many years. I still feel that I am in a trance, a dream I never want to wake up from.

On the way back I take a train again, trying to relive the magic and experience of the onward journey. Sanghamitra was staying back in Kolkata for a while. The journey seemed long and unending. I met the guy with the harmonium, singing songs in nice, slow tunes; I don't understand the lyrics though. Unmindfully I purchased a hot loaf from the bread vendor and gobbled it up. I smile within myself remembering how she made fun of me when I questioned the hygiene of the bread. Each of her expressions and reactions keep coming back. I spend the time outlining in my mind a look of the sculpture that would be inspired by Sanghamitra. Initially it was a concept; it has now started taking concrete dimensions and structure.

I am on an ambitious journey of sculpting Krishna's Women, a series of six statues comprising Radha, Rukmini, Kalindi, Satyabhama, Draupadi and Meera. I have almost completed work on five of them, each of which are derived from our mythological past, but have strong connections with some real life women I had come across. My sculptures are not portraits or facial replications of my inspirations. They just capture the spirit of the women who have been my subjects. Each time I have met these women, I have surprised myself with the dedication and commitment I have essayed in understanding them and expressing their philosophy in my art. I have employed tremendous force to break all barriers that lay between me and them. I look forward to a lavish exhibition, once my series is complete. For that, however, I need the calmness of body and mind. Hence, I have planned this self-imposed exile at Santiniketan!

Radha, Krishna's most legitimate companion, never married him. Yet, their union was so sublime that the connection is compared to that of mind and soul. My Radha was inspired by a lady in Canada, who never married but was raising her lover's sons like her own, after their parents died in a road accident. They were childhood sweethearts who separated after college; when she came back, he was already reduced to a photograph on the wall. She is a cheerful lady, living and enjoying life, with the social status of a widow. My probing into her story revealed that marriage had just been a word of social acceptance for them and it had no impact on the bond they shared; however the questions that the world could have raised was rocked into silence because she had returned to enter a life already deserted by him! I have carved my Radha seated alone, legs half spread, hair and attire neatly done up, anticipating the lordly presence any time around the horizon; she plays his flute in peace. Radha, I believe is the only woman who can righteously ignite the same heavenly music, without which Krishna stands incomplete. Or, maybe, Radha herself was Krishna's music.

Meera for me was Giribala Bharadwaj, the famous Odishi dancer who left her married life to pursue dance and was disowned by her paternal family as well, for worshipping and practising her art. She approached her craft with total dedication and became one of the greatest names in the world of Indian classical dance. My Meera sits holding her *tambura* in *nritya mudra*, dressed in the traditional Odishi dance costume; her head is covered by a halo, instead of the cloth she usually wears. Just as Meera's devotion is believed to have relieved her from worldly desires, helping her to attain Moksha, dance did the same to Giribala Bharadwaj by engulfing her world with creative passion, not leaving her free for a moment to lament on what she had lost in the process. For about a year I had watched her closely and spoke to her whenever she allowed me to, unsure of what exactly was my task. By the time I was done, I had become her family.

Draupadi and Krishna were each other's confidantes, as much as they were politically bound in their friendship. Both knew that they were the direct and indirect catalysts to the greatest war in the history of mythological India. Each and every step of Draupadi was hence governed by Krishna with shrewd intervention and calculated absence at relevant points such that all occurrences that otherwise seemed divine and destined, were actually pre-planned and pre-meditated. My relationship with my soul-sister, Diya, profoundly reflects the same exchange that kept Krishna and Draupadi together, sharing the same cause. Though geographically afar, I had manipulated and designed Diya's life as per her own ambitions and rules. Much against the wishes of her family, I helped her to gain admission in

Princeton University for her Masters in Journalism. Today she is the Bureau Chief for a leading daily, and takes charge of the Western zone. Simultaneously she runs an NGO which manufactures hand-made items for home.

Rebel that she is, I knew she would not succumb to the typical family pressures of an early marriage in a Rajasthani household; neither would she give herself to a person whom others choose for her. Right from school her choice was my cousin, Abhimanyu. At one point of time, I was the mediator between her and Abhimanyu, from a distance, so that things could progress between them! My interference, though not appreciated by many, helped crack some tough equations between her family and ours, who had been business rivals for many years. I, by breaking away from the family had spread enough panic for anyone to force anything upon the new-gen youth! Abhimanyu and Diya are soon to get married in an elaborate function in Jaipur. I didn't need to specially spend time with Diya to sculpt Draupadi. My Draupadi stands with hair strewn open, clothes creased and crumpled, body adorned with ornaments, eyes demure, head downcast and one hand holding aloft the conch while the other touches the ground with the sword, prophesying a calm rebel who might spark off destruction.

My brief interaction with Crisanta Dwarf, the film star, was enough for me to find Satyabhama within her. Self-indulging and obsessed, she claimed possession of everything her eyes fancied albeit for a short while. I was one of her many short-term fancies. As long as her fondness for someone is alive and active, she would do anything for the object of her desire. Crisanta was married, and her husband never interfered with her life. Patiently he would accept whatever she had to pour. My conservative Rajasthani upbringing comes to the fore when I see loud and dominating women crossing boundaries of decency. I admit, I have an issue with myself there. Quietly I managed to move out of her shadow, however, not before I had done my job. Satyabhama was blessed with a boon to stay young and beautiful forever. She was known to throw a lot of tantrums, but Krishna affectionately fulfilled all her desires and always kept her happy. Satyabhama is said to have gone through untold penances in her past life, which earned her a life of pleasure with Krishna, and she celebrated it with pride, arrogance and devotion. My Satyabhama stands in style and ecstasy, exuding arrogance from every angle. With her body curved and rounded in the right places, she exhibits raw sensuousness. She wears a peacock feather on her forehead, declaring her right to Krishna's love.

Rukmini, Satyabhama and Kalindi were Krishna's wives. Rukmini (or Rukmani) was the principal wife and queen of Krishna in his city Dwaraka. Krishna heroically eloped with her on the day of her marriage. Of Krishna's 16,108 queens, Rukmini was the first and most prominent. Rukmini is also considered to be an incarnation of Lakshmi, the goddess of fortune. My Rukmini is inspired by a girl I met while travelling to the Herriot Country, Yorkshire. I was guest to a couple who made their living from nurseries and cultivation of orchids. They had huge gardens that the family worked upon and had commercialised the venture considerably. I learnt later that the couple had eloped and they didn't have a penny to start their married life. They developed everything together. Gardening, which was the girl's hobby, gave her initial earnings as she landscaped gardens for houses with expensive interests and money to spare. They'd seen a lot of ups and downs, but one thing that remained unchallenged was their love for each other. My Rukmini, clad in flowers instead of clothes, sits on a cow, Krishna's eternal childhood companion, also symbolising his association with the cowherds, thus communicating her hold on them being his principal queen.

While Krishna and Arjuna strode on the banks of the Yamuna, they saw a beautiful maiden performing penance. Arjuna approached her and came to know that she was Kalindi, the river Yamuna personified and her only intention was to have Vishnu as her husband. Krishna recognised her devotion and married her. Kalindi has another mention in Krishna's life. When the lord was born, Vasudeva stealthily removed the child to Ambadi, crossing river Yamuna also called Kalindi. Due to heavy rains, Kalindi was overflowing and Vasudeva pleaded with her for a passage and the river gave way. Kalindi is one of the seven tributaries of the Ganga; one who drinks its water is believed to be liberated from all sins. I can foresee a character that is as transparent as water, and as forlorn as a devotee, abandoned by kin and clan. She doesn't have a typical form; changes herself as per the situation she represents, just like water takes the shape of the vessel it is contained in. Nothing or no one probably can define her existence. Blessed with aqua qualities, she can restore lives as much as she can destroy. Aggression and grace, she spreads herself equally in both. Sanghamitra is my Kalindi!

Slice of My Life

Sanghamitra Banerjee
Kolkata

There's a charm about coming back home! We shifted here from our rented accommodation when I was twenty-five. Till Baba was there with us we didn't bother about anything. We were not prepared for his sudden demise so early in an active life. Ma was more practical and composed herself sooner than I did to pick up the loose parts. She decided that we need a home immediately for future safety and security. All savings and receivables were calculated and it was almost an immediate decision to invest in a house. Our home was built in two years time, in a decent neighbourhood of Lake Town. It was a difficult decision to shift base from the place where Baba spent all his married life and left the mortal world subsequently. The house was haunted with memories. Ma and I brought up this new place all by ourselves and created new memories. The sixth floor apartment overlooks a pond at the back and is surrounded by greenery. Three years after I moved to Mumbai with a job, Ma retired. Since then she has been involved in Satsang. She is a trainer with Sree Sree Ravi Shankar ji's team in Bangalore, helping people develop the Art of Living. Many a times she had asked me to do short courses with them but I declined. If I have to learn the art of living with external help then

I would come to believe that I am dead! It's *my life* and *the art* would be *mine*. Nevertheless, I did not stop my mother from following her faith; she did not force me to give up mine either.

Bengal is an area of born Communists, inheriting the attitude of a happy-with-less attitude. My family is emotionally Left-oriented. I would like to call myself a nationalist without any political affiliation and less understanding (read interest) of the subject; but in my heart I know that I haven't been able to escape a Left shot! We feel that a nice home, justified money and peaceful family are enough. Often we are not progressive and lack the hunger for more. Most of us intellectualise this in our own way! I was not spared this influence. However, my darling family always made me feel like a queen. For them I was the best of our generation … I looked the best, was most progressive in studies and was most well behaved. They said my life was destined to be spectacular. I'll have a special existence which would be way ahead compared to the others. I grew up listening to this, and believing this! Two forces thus worked simultaneously on me. One, a laid back attitude that was in my blood. It said I didn't need too much of anything and I don't need to work too hard for any so-called materialistic achievement. The other force was a make-believe world that said I was meant for the best. Probably under these two influences, I have grown up to be a combination of extreme opposites. I am rigid and liberal, energetic and calm, selfless and selfish, attached and detached, all at the same time with flawless balance! I knew I have to do something big in life to prove my relatives true. But I do not know how! I never pursue anything with a passion that leads one to reach the pinnacle. My life is compartmentalised. I want everything. There are allotted hours for all that I wish to do and I never violate that. Hence I have become a Jack of all trades and stopped!! But the pressure does have its impact on my mind. I am still a nothing. I don't have a direction. And the world is watching me expecting something big, which I have no clue how to achieve! This probably made me a rebel. Maybe I feel, if I can't be big, at least I'll be different. To achieve this difference I play all sorts of awkward moves, experiment with myself, make unusual friends, leave them beyond a point of time, develop complicated philosophies and an incomplete bohemianism. I call it incomplete because I do not go completely haywire though I do break barriers. Every time when I get tired, I return to Ma. Not that I disclose myself, but in a strange way she understands my restlessness, though she never supports it. At every stage of my unexplained behaviour and rebellious outburst, however big or small, she walks me out of the confusion with poise and firm balance. She had, in her days, experienced the same twilight and can perfectly guess what exactly is bothering me!

I grew up on Mehndi Hassan, Ghulam Ali, Amir Khan, Kishori Amonkar, M.S. Subbalakshmi, Pt. Jasraj, Bhimsen Joshi, Ravi Shankar and Hari Prasad Chaurasia! Early morning I woke up with one of these performing a morning raga, and sat on the floor of the balcony to study in the morning breeze, till it was time for school. Evenings again were meant for books. At times I would hide novels behind History books! Ma introduced me to fairy tales as a kid; and subconsciously I learnt to dream. I still have The Little Match Girl and Ugly Duckling with me. They are beautiful layered stories with lots expressed unspoken. As I grew up, I ran through Ma's book rack, read difficult works in Bengali literature. A less known writer called Subodh Ghosh wrote fat books on travel to different parts of India; the books came in fifteen volumes and were called 'Ramyani Bikshya.' I learnt a lot about ancient India and its evolution from them. By the time the book rack was over, I started borrowing from a paternal grandpa who was a retired Prof. of English Literature in Calcutta University. His home was a library. When I was in the Sixth, he gifted works of Milton, Wordsworth, Shelley and Keats to me. Those are still amongst my most treasured possessions.

Today, as I sit on the balcony sipping my tea, I feel strangely cherished. This house gives me the shelter that Ma would have given, had she been here. Every corner reminds and warns me of her cleanliness, her organised way of living, rigid choices and fetish for home décor by recycling things. Old clothes would become doormats and table covers, used bottles would be coloured and painted into a vase, wood from broken furniture joined together to prepare extra storage, etc. I am not to meddle with any of these. The cable, newspaper and milk delivery services have been disconnected since we don't use them regularly. I am not going to activate any of these for the next few days, I've decided. Electricity bill and other charges are cleared off by my relatives from time to time; we just send them the consolidated amount once in three months. The last few days since my arrival have gone into cleaning in the mornings and rushing off to the Book Fair in the afternoons. Today I wish to relax. The Book Fair duty is over. It was much more fun compared to what I anticipated. Barriers break when old friends meet after a long time. One who was jealous of my grades, one who I disliked because she was more popular, one who had a secret crush on me and had held against me my lack of reciprocation all through our campus years, one who didn't share class notes when I needed it the most, one who was my fiercest competitor, and one with whom I had an ugly fight–all came together and dissolved several pent up issues in the air, mingling like long lost friends. Most of them came with partners and kids. Together we rekindled old memories and created some fresh ones. Some of them whispered in my ears that my decision of remaining single is the best one. I had many admirers in college; I am still in touch with some of them. Old friends laughed at the advances they made to impress me and my friends, to get access to my whereabouts and checked if they still stood a chance! In between, one of the days I met Dr Aniruddh for a short while. He had come for the book inauguration and dropped by to say hello. I attended to him briefly and came to understand that he had been approached by the Lalit Kala Akademi, Delhi, to conduct a workshop for the underprivileged children. He wants to take it up and would leave for Delhi shortly. Also, he plans to return to Santiniketan in another two days time.

During our journey to Kolkata by train, I may have disappointed the sculptor too much. More than once I found him taking serious offence against my opinions and brooding over them. At times I sit back pondering over our apparent differences! His love for Shiva is religious, he says, but his mind favours the Nataraj form which is certainly not a traditionally accepted form for worship as a deity. But Dr Aniruddh refuses to accept that his passion is more professional than religious and that his inclination results from his affiliation to sculpting. Had I pointed it out that morning, he would have sulked even more! He looks at things too much as black and white, and doesn't accept deviations openly. My observations on his conflicting interest also made me face the duality I nourish within myself! Though I haven't ever worshipped Shiva as a God with the devotion that the sculptor exhibits, my admiration emerges from the co-existence of Shiva as the abode of Advaita and Dvaita simultaneously, which is starkly religious!

I laze around my bedside window, watching ducks swim in a row and occasionally bob down their heads to dig up something. The pond is rich with fish and there are two kingfishers. The beautiful blue birds make themselves sparingly visible. But I hear them chirping frequently. A maid comes to clean around 9:00 am. That's when my phone beeps. A text reads, 'Free today evening?' I remember that though I had taken Dr Aniruddh's number, I hadn't saved it. I don't answer immediately. True, I have started enjoying his company. I am also tempted to say a prompt yes. Yet, I wonder, what exactly is this leading to? I didn't like him using the word *date*. What was he trying to get at? Was he trying to be polite, given my single status? I have felt it many times that the sculptor is trying hard to fathom the purpose of my life. Why is it so difficult to accept that I am in complete love with myself and don't feel incomplete being alone. I have chosen this life because I want to live it myself, not because I am constrained to do so! Moreover, I have lost the habit of being at the core of male attention and find this interfering and intrusive. However, I find it difficult to say a strict no! And this is exactly what disturbs me. Somewhere deep inside I have started liking his advances. Something has begun. I am not sure though, whether I'll appreciate the story as it progresses, as much as I am enjoying the beginning. I don't wish to pamper his interest; neither do I feel like asking him to stop, once and for all. In that confused state of mind I type back, 'What's your plan?' Pat comes a reply. '4.00 pm!' No checking on my convenience or consent; just a statement. Once again my wicked brain raises its head. Let's see what's in store. If I lose interest midway, it will be over-and-out for this arrogant half NRI. Nevertheless with the credentials, face and physique like his, it is worth exploring, I decide.

I didn't know then, that the evening would considerably jeopardise my self-esteem and pride.

I hadn't responded to his 4:00 pm SMS. Since he didn't ask questions, I never answered. All morning I was waiting for him to call or text for my address or ask me to meet somewhere. When he didn't, I assumed that his impulse had been overshadowed by his appointments and the plan was called off. At 4:00 pm sharp there was a beep which read, 'Please step down; I am waiting at the gate.' I choked on my tea, but hurriedly changed into jeans and kurta and brushed my hair. In haste I got into the lift that took me downstairs. It felt weird; I have never stepped out so unprepared. He stood there leaning on a BMW, in a red-and-white checked shirt tucked into a pair of jeans, his eyes shaded by dark yellow Ray Ban, his fair skin shining in the evening sun.

He looks hot! I enter his car and we are off. I don't care where he's taking me. With his permission I've rolled down the window-glass. The car is racing on the highway and I am loving the strong spring breeze sweeping through.

'I thought maybe you're not coming.'

'You are quite optimistic about your luck,' he grins.

'But where did you get my address?'

'During the course of our conversation you had mentioned that your building is called Ujaan and you live in Lake Town, near Jaya Cinema. It was not all that difficult to find out.'

'You remembered things from a stray conversation and connected them? Why didn't you ask me for it?'

He looks at me and smiles. 'You have agreed to come out with me. That's enough of what you could have given!'

'Why are you doing this, Dr Aniruddh?' I ask, unsure of what exactly I wanted to know.

'You said all relationships are transactional, remember? If you are right then I would have to give you something in exchange of what I want from you. I need your time, Sanghamitra, and in return, I'll give you some memories.'

'Why do you need my time?'

'To understand which expression or material possession defines you more than anything else. To understand what vibes you emit in your subconscious and what part of your existence makes you most conscious about yourself.'

'Have you understood already?' I conceal laughter and pretend to be serious.

'You are most comfortable in a shielding, expressionless silence, which I can't quite decipher. Easier you make it for me to know you, the earlier you would be rid of my shadow.'

'And if I don't relent?'

'Sooner or later I would find out anyhow!' A long pause, and he utters, 'Sanghamitra means the friend of society! Maybe you should know that I am not a threat to your friendship for your society. But I am Aniruddh for sure, the unstoppable.' He smiles without looking at me.

The car slows down. I look out and am stunned. This crazy man has brought me to Dakshineshwar Temple. Sceptically I look at him.

He comes around and opens the door for me. 'Come for once and share my experience, lady. I am not asking you to drink poison.'

I step out and follow him quietly. He doesn't walk towards the shops selling baskets of offerings. Instead he opens his shoes, washes his feet, and walks straight towards the meditation room. Before entering he whispers in my ear, 'Just try and experience this place, Sanghamitra. If you don't like it, we will move out immediately.'

Dakshineshwar Temple, an 18th century architecture, where once the spiritual Ramakrishna Paramahamsa Dev and Ma Sarada worshipped, is famous for the Kali temple in its premises. Situated on the eastern bank of the Hugli River, the presiding deity of the temple is Bhavatarini, an aspect of Kali, meaning, 'She who liberates her devotees from the cycle of life.' The feisty goddess resides in the main temple; twelve adjoining and identical temples along the river, just opposite the main shrine, each with a Shiva-ling, are dedicated to Lord Shiva. These temples are built facing the east in the typical 'Aat Chala' Bengal architecture and are divided by the river bank, keeping six Shiva temples to the left and the other six to the right on the ghat of Hugli River. Built in the traditional 'Nava-ratna' or nine spires style of Bengal architecture, the three-storeyed, south-facing temple has nine spires distributed in two upper storeys, and stands on a high platform with a flight of stairs. The *garbha griha* (sanctum sanctorum) houses an idol of goddess Kali, known as Bhavatarini, standing on the chest of a prostrate Shiva, and the two idols are placed on a thousand-petalled lotus made of silver. The historical room of Ramakrishna Paramahamsa has been turned into a meditation room for devotees.

Without wasting a word I occupy the space beside the sculptor. The room is too silent; only the inhaling and exhaling of breath by the occupants is audible. For a while I look down and close my eyes. In a jiffy, my entire life seems to roll in, in bits and pieces, as if urging me to retrospect. My old house, me in school uniform, my parents, the sea of Puri, the mall of Darjeeling, my music coaching, almost all of my childhood comes back to me in a second. I open my eyes and return to the present. Dr Aniruddh has been watching me. He gestures that we move and I get up. Once out, he asks me with amusement, 'So, were you meditating?'

'No, I just happened to close my eyes and take in the peace of that room.'

'Sanghamitra, that's exactly why I brought you here. You may not come here for religious interests but you can't deny that it manages to give one a spiritual bliss.'

I dare to say something he was not expecting. 'Your presence does make this evening and this place special, Dr Aniruddh. But I wouldn't need to travel till here for peace. I can source it from the flute that plays in my room during the dark of the night.'

Few minutes of silence. Then he turns to me. 'Where would you take me if you were to plan an evening?'

'Right there,' I point towards the ghat.

We take ourselves down towards the Ganges and sit on the stairs facing the river. Evening bells from the Shiva temples toll from behind. The Howrah Bridge is visible in all its elegance as the streetlights light up the water as much as the setting sun does. And a gentle breeze sweeps through. Small boats are visible afar sailing on the water.

'I am not one of those romantic types, Sanghamitra, who can hold hands and stare. My presence has a purpose.' His voice is deep.

'I am exactly the kind of romantic idiot you are talking about. But I don't necessarily need a companion to share myself. I could have been sitting here for hours, even if you were not there with me.'

'Do you have a goal?'

'No.'

'Tell me the most beautiful moment of your life.'

'My visit to Varanasi during Diwali. Huge lamps decorated the ghats and the pandits were performing the most elaborate pujas. Ma and I hired a boat and viewed the puja while floating on the Ganges.

It was a beautiful sight spread out right in front of us. During Diwali, devotees float small lamps on the river in memory of their dear ones or asking for some favour from the Almighty. So as the evening progressed to night, there were a series of lamps floating down the current and the water seemed lit up. Lines of candles went floating on either side of our boat as well, and the earth had suddenly started looking divine. I have never seen something so natural and so beautiful.'

'I thought you were not a conventionally religious person!'

'I am not. But I am not closed to taking in experiences if they promise something productive. You do things for the core purpose it is meant for; for me I am the purpose! You go to a temple for religious interests; I might go to experience its history and architectural beauty. If I have to worship, my home I believe is good enough for that. In fact you will be surprised to know that I have completed the Char Dham Yatra to Puri-Rameshwaram-Badrinath-Dwaraka with my mother and grandmother. I remember the trip as a beautiful but tough experience through the mountains.'

'Really!' He finds this information difficult to swallow. 'Which one did you love the most?'

'Badrinath. That entire stretch of Yamunotri-Gangotri-Kedarnath-Badrinath was rigorous and enchanting.'

'Tell me more about the best times you've had.'

'There are many actually. My first semester in Lucknow, I would go biking with a friend in the rains. We were like clones, celebrating our rainy expeditions with "pastries shots" and never felt guilty about missing lectures and going for movies, libraries, even the zoo! We both were mad about love stories and referred books to each other! She was a spirited Jatthni and I a headstrong Bengali! From Lucknow I escaped to Jim Corbett, Shillong, Nainital-Ranikhet-Almora-Kasauni, Shimla, whenever holidays happened. I would contact a travel agent who arranged trips only for women's groups; they were responsible enough and I could trust them regarding my safety. Funds were less, nothing extravagant. Yet I hold dear memories of those visits. Have you ever seen a moonlit night in the mountains? When I travelled alone, I planned my trips such that there would be a full moon in between. Jim Corbett, Shillong and Nainital became surreal, can't explain what I had seen! But I have seen the worst of that as well. During Oct 2009 I was at Manali with Ma. We had planned our stay at a tree house which overlooked the apple and pomegranate orchards; snow clad mountain ranges surrounding the valley looked down at us. We travelled to the Zero Point one of the days and due to some military checks, the return was pretty delayed. Around 7:30 pm the moon was shining bright in complete harmony with those peaks and pine forests. And we suddenly realised that we were travelling through a narrow road in a car with the driver and there was no one behind or in front of us!!!! It was terrifying!! Even with such a heavenly scene outside, we were just praying that the journey ended soon. I still escape to Darjeeling when I get sufficient leave. Otherwise some forty-five minutes to an hour's ride from Santiniketan takes me to the tribal Santal villages and to their breathtaking beautiful landscape and handwork. During rains there were often floods in these villages; some of us carry food and clothes for the people there. At such times all communication channels would be lost and phone lines, railways, roadways and the like between Santiniketan and Kolkata would be jammed due to water logging. We spend times helping them reconstruct. These are poor people but extremely clean and organised. Even their darkest complications were also just so simple! Such is my not-so-happening existence.' I pause for a while. 'Enough of me. What's your best time like, Mr Sculptor?'

'What you have for mountains, I have the same love and passion for the sea. Water invites and excites me. I love the vastness of the ocean and the ripples of the lakes, the water sports and sailing in serenity, the ferocity of rivers at their origin and the dullness at the end. I cruised by ship through the islands of Lakshadweep; the evening breeze on the deck surrounded by water on all sides make you postpone any thoughts of returning home. All those days I wished I could be a vagabond with no ambition or address. The under-sea life at the Andamans and the colour of water there can make you go berserk with joy. In that part of India, the colour of the water is influenced by the coral reefs. So you find the sea transparent and the water reflects green, blue, purple and red. A little towards the interiors of Agastyakoodam situated in Trivandrum, Kerala, the backwaters are surrounded by dense forests. They have built a few cottages there for rare tourists, who have a passion for travel and reach there through a reference. This place has no mention in tourism sites. If you haven't seen the rains there, you have missed out on a huge chunk of life. This place has no electricity. Earthen lamps light the cottages and often strong winds blow them off. The drool of constant downpour sends a shiver down your spine in the evening; during the day however you are taken through the best of what your eyes can feast on.'

'You travelled to these places alone?' The question slips out unintended. Or I don't know maybe it was intentional. Maybe I was curious about him, his life, his interests, at least in the subconscious mind.

'No, I went with a group from college.' He smiles. 'My upbringing has a very conservative lineage, Sanghamitra. I don't have a history of escapades with beautiful women, if that is what you wanted to ask.'

Quickly I change the topic, while trying my best to hide the blush spreading across my face. 'You must have seen a lot of exotic foreign beaches as well, Mr Sculptor?'

'Yes, I did. But today we'll keep it to India.' Dr Aniruddh stands up and gestures me to walk with him. We walk towards the jetty and he makes a call. A boat arrives with a long flung sail and he gets inside, extends a hand towards me. Is he kidding? It is illegal to go boating after sunset. I don't say that though, just follow his steps. It is almost dark now. The breeze makes me feel cold. I realise that it is a full moon night, as the satellite shines bright in the eastern sky. It is very silent here once again, only the splash of water slashing against the wood of the boat is audible. The Dakshineshwar Temple is lit up and it looks beautiful from the distance. The moon casts its reflections on the trembling water. I am shivering too, partly out of cold and partly out of anxiety. Why did this man bring me here like this? Before I ask, he starts talking. 'You may have seen a moonlit night on the mountains, Ma'm, but I am sure this experience in your own city has not come to you before. I took quite some pains and moved some contacts to arrange this, to make this evening special for you.' He smiles. I remain quiet, choosing not to disclose that the occasion, rich with an unexpected expedition and his company, made it absolutely wonderful. This moment touches my soul. He leans backwards and lies down on the deck of the boat. His sonorous voice recites slowly and profoundly,

'The fountains mingle with the river
And the rivers with the ocean,
The winds of Heaven mix for ever
With a sweet emotion;
Nothing in the world is single,
All things by a law divine
In one spirit meet and mingle –
Why not I with thine?

See the mountains kiss high Heaven
And the waves clasp one another;
No sister-flower would be forgiven
If it disdained its brother;
And the sunlight clasps the earth,
And the moonbeams kiss the sea ...'

The voice stops abruptly. He may have attempted to dedicate these words to the beauty surrounding us, but they reached me with an aggressive passion. I know the lines of Shelley's that follow, as much as he does!

'What are all these kissings worth
If thou kiss not me?'

I sit like a stone for a while, then lower myself as well. He looks shocked and unprepared for this response, but does not stop me; neither does he change his posture. I feel possessed by the supernatural, as all my guards fall and I lie beside him, distancing myself from all physical contacts, but horribly conscious of his presence very close to my body. His smell, his breath has caught a large part of my senses. It feels like a spell that captures my existence with all its vigour, and I am scattered in a thousand pieces to represent the river, the boat, the breeze, the moon, the man beside me and the dark of the night, all of which come together to create one of the best unexplained experiences of my life. I have never belonged to a moment as much as I do now. I can sense heat within myself. The moon looked big and bright, right above us. Chunks of cloud flow across it time and again. Frequent sound of the row, digging into the water and pushing it away to make way for the boat, add music to the ambience; drops of water splash on us at regular intervals. The night is majestic. For an interminable period we remain there, just like that. Neither of us speak. None of us move a muscle. Nor do either of us cross any boundaries.

In the night I confront myself fiercely. I feel feverish due to prolonged exposure to the moisture laden wind of the river, which I was left exposed to after sunset. After very long, something I thought was lost and buried had kept coming back to me in waves. Desire! A self-engrossing desire! I want to own and be owned. Something inside me wants to take the evening forward and explore what else lies in store. It has been eleven years since I last saw Shekhar, and since then I haven't pampered this part of my being. I have rather taken every possible action to kill the slightest possibility that can fuel my emotions or physicality for another man. After a long time, someone's presence makes me want to look pretty. I feel like spending time once again on the visual sensation I can create with specific aspects of my body and being. It is strange that a woman with desires always wants a man to perceive herself as the ultimate object of beauty. Every other feminist declaration of non-commoditising women falls apart and makes way for the most ancient practices of *shringaar ras*, where women have surrendered since ages to become their man's last fantasy! I know the sculptor is fond of me. But I haven't touched his inner instincts from where the genius originates; neither has he chosen to bare his heart. But there is something lurking inside for sure, which may or may not be romantic. He has something to say. And he has been meaning to express it since long! I didn't care earlier; but tonight I do. His restraint felt insulting. It meant that my sensuousness this evening could not deviate him from his purpose. That's a failure for a woman who had once triumphed about her detachment towards male attention. Had he made some advances when I had dropped all guards, probably my ego would not have been as bruised. But he distinctly maintained himself as an observer, rather than a participant in that divine moment. My eyes burn as I desire to destroy that restraint!

Shringaar

Dr Aniruddh Jain Solanki
Santiniketan

Sleep has eluded me for two nights. I had been working till late, trying to put in place a diagram to frame my Kalindi statue. Three or four ideas are hovering around my brain but I can't yet come to terms on the final look. This period makes me horribly restless and impatient. The state of indecisiveness is close to impotency, which a man experiences after failed attempts at conception! Each time I try to put a diagram on paper and it doesn't seem to justify my excellence, the desperation multiplies. I feel insecure about my abilities rusting out and a much dreaded creative blackout. Logically, I know that this is a passing phase, but at this moment the brain is functioning at irrational speed, trying to nail the problem. The problem will however take its own time to find the best solution.

At 4:00 in the morning I lower myself on the bed. The sight of Sanghamitra on the deck on that moonlit evening hasn't left me yet. She has the capacity of unifying herself with Nature on sudden unexpected occasions. And that evening she was at the height of her grace. She was not wearing any make-up when we met that afternoon. Maybe she was really not expecting me to arrive at her doorstep all by myself; or she did not consider me worth her efforts. The eyes that are otherwise carefully outlined in black were missing their shine; lips looked dry. But that dullness gave her an unadulterated innocence. I could see that she was enjoying my company as much as I was enjoying hers. Yet, she kept it sufficiently concealed. She has an inbuilt quality of enjoying her solitude, while I suffer the same about myself! Like an elegant swan in moonlight, she was enjoying a trance on the riverbed. Her isolation intimidates me. As much as I try to understand her, she manages to keep a large part of her presence beyond my access. I make every effort to explore and gain transparent visibility of her character. Every time we meet and spend some moments with each other, I get to understand new things about her. Sanghamitra nurtures many personalities within herself and keeps challenging me, in her own way, to unfold something that still remains undeciphered. This compels me to design yet another occasion when I can reach out to her depths and explore those undefined virtues that can't be expressed on predictable terms. This last statue of my series won't be easy. The diagrams and ideas I am coming up with are mocking me, pointing out that I have not yet tamed the proud swan in my brain. She exists there as much as she doesn't! Kalindi, true in her form and format, is oblivious of everything that might cause her distraction from the focus of her devotion. That evening, when she lay down on the deck, it felt that she had become a part of the greater universe, apparently disconnected from me. She rested herself beside me with brave, unconvincing ease as if I wasn't there. So beautiful was the sight of her oneness with Nature, I could not gather courage to disrupt the harmony she shared with the moon, the stars, the water and the breeze, though I could sense an inner turmoil within her that begged to be quelled.

Today is International Women's Day. I find this term ridiculous, because no society that I have seen, brings anything different to women on this day. Only that, women are allowed some discounts in urban shopping complexes and attractive schemes are designed in restaurants for the whole week to attract the already spendthrift, shopaholic gender towards all those fanciful things they hardly need! This consumerist occasion does not really celebrate the role of women in lives and society; rather they celebrate the rolling money balls that are equivalent to the collections of Holi and Diwali. Hence, as usual, this International Women's Day does not bear any special meaning for me. Just that, the Women's Day issue of an International Magazine published in Germany, is carrying an interview of mine under the heading 'der Mann vieler Frauen'(Many Women's Man)! The English edition of the magazine has reached me yesterday, as it has reached many other parts of the world. Friends, acquaintances, ex-colleagues and well wishers have poured in their appreciation, regards and blessings. My interview has been illustrated with images of my sculptures, most of which are women projected in various shapes, forms and attitudes that exhibit their most feminine qualities. They had asked me why I chose limestone over bronze or clay which are more popular media, why my interpretations and resultant compositions usually take the form of a woman, my personal and professional journey from student to professional to a stalwart, and the inspirations behind my work. I have tried to use language at my best, which leaves opportunities for soft controversies but won't project me in negative light. Reviews, mails and letters coming from readers across the world will keep the article and me in circulation and discussion for a while. Initially I had an objection to the title and presentation of the interview. They did a photo-shoot with me to bring out a seductive personality that I am definitely not. Out of the fifty odd clicks they had taken in postures pre-decided by the person behind the camera, two pictures in gray-scale have been used for the magazine. In one I sit on a broad wooden chair with legs spread apart; I bend to support one hand on my knees and the other on the chair, look downwards engrossed in deep thought. They made me wear beige cotton pants and a waist-length white kurta with gold prints all over, and a broad slit in the front allowing access to considerable details of my chest! In the other, I fit myself between two parallel walls, such that my back and right foot find vertical support; while the left leg is folded at the knee. I look up to let the intruding sunlight light up my face and neck. They have developed the photographs quite well. I remember how uncooperative I had been to the efforts of the team. The photo-shoot specially seemed a waste of time and I just could not accept that a write-up on me could have such disgraceful title! Dierk Abendroth, a very old friend who had seen me growing and also coincidentally was the Chief Editorial Director of the magazine had spent half a day explaining and convincing me on their vision. 'The world is no saint, my friend. Practise your faith, and let others practise theirs. More than a virtuous gentleman who girls can wed, the audience finds interest in men who are a challenge on bed! Your job is to do good work, which you are doing, and keep your followers guessing. The public persona is as important as your work and they need to find you worth reaching out to. Leave that public image to us, Aniruddh. I am sure you wouldn't find much trouble in trusting me,' he had said. Reluctantly I gave in. Dailies and journals have reported my work before, but for the first time a Page-3 giant have given me such a huge coverage! I owe them a thanks. I start typing my message to Dierk, but before I complete my phone beeps with his. 'Happy Birthday dude. Your gift must be on your table by now.' I am silent for a while. Yes, it is my birthday today. Hardly anyone remembers. I feel horribly forsaken. No one from my family has called or congratulated me on the interview, neither has anyone wished me. I check through the messages and tell myself, maybe someone would call!

My work station is live and functional as usual. No one knows that their professor and his achievements decorate the pages of a renowned international magazine. I smile thinking how much detached a place can be, ruthlessly disconnected from a greater world beyond the peripheries of its railway boundaries. I have a class with the first year students on tools of sculpting. For two hours I am hooked on to my job. It is almost noon when I end my session. The sun has started hinting at the summer heat. I stretch myself and come out of the studio to take a stroll.

Kala Bhavan was founded in 1919. Having come on the crest of the wave of Indian artistic renaissance initiated by Rabindranath Tagore and Abanindranath Tagore, right from the outset the department was planned to be different from a conventional art school. Here art education was visualised not as a programme for imparting technical skills but as an exploration of visual communication; visual arts were not seen in isolation but as part of a larger cultural spectrum, and culture was perceived as a factor enhancing the quality of life, the renewal of which depends on the renewal of creativity. Tagore invited noted painter Nandalal Bose, the founder of Bengal school of art movement and disciple of Abanindranath Tagore, to become the first principal of the institution. In the years to come, stalwarts like Benode Behari Mukherjee, one of the pioneers of Indian modern art with his contribution as a painter and celebrated muralist, and Ramkinkar Baij, the sculptor par excellence, became associated with the college. Their association in due course of time gave a new direction not just to the institution but also to modern Indian art.

I love breathing in the glory and artistry spread around the campus like a casual traditional ritual, and the way they signify the history of this place. The buildings within this part of the campus are differentiated with paintings and murals on the walls. The Kala Bhavan is landmarked by Black House or Kalo Bari, as locals would put it. Kalo Bari is a student hostel on the campus, a building made of mud, designed by eminent artistes like Nandalal Bose, Surendranath Kar and Ramkinkar Baij. The walls of the house are decorated with Mohenjo-daro motifs and that of several folk and classical art forms. Among the students of Kala Bhavan, it is considered a privilege to get a room in Black House and only a select few get this opportunity. Off and on, there are huge trees with sitting arrangements around them to promote academic classes in the open, amidst nature. There is also a small canteen which supplies tea, coffee, samosa and bread-omelette; rest of the listed menu items are usually not available!

The famous sculpture of a Santal family walking to work carrying their meagre possessions stands before the Kala Bhavan. In this larger than life sculpture he represented the tribal peasants of the region, giving the figures iconic presence and dignified grace that was so far limited to the images of gods and rulers. Just across the Santal Family stands another sculpture—Mill Call. It shows a working class family setting off enthusiastically for work on hearing the mill siren. The slender and graceful 'Sujata' stands behind the department. I stop to take a closer look at them. Beginning in the early thirties Ramkinkar Baij filled the campus with magnificent creations, which were innovative in subject matter and personal in style. In a country where all public art-work was undertaken only at the behest of government commissioning and executed in consonance with the taste of conservative ruling elites, this was a radical departure. The use of cement and laterite mortar to work upon the figures combining the skills of a modeller and a carver and the personal vision of Ramkinkar Baij, in which modern western and Indian pre-classical sculptural values were brought together was equally radical. The master's works reflect the life of the poor and dispossessed, and he portrayed them in all their dignity, grace and vigour. These priceless possessions today face an uncertain future because of the fragile medium Baij managed to source with his limited resources. Laterite pebbles and cement make a very unstable combination which cannot last too long. Day-by-day the cement is moving away from the armature and pebbles have started falling off from the sculptures. If not quickly restored, these sculptures may soon be relegated to a passing mention in history textbooks. They need to be cast in bronze immediately to prevent further deterioration. The government as yet sadly sits pondering on its course of action.

I walk back to the studio to acquire the keys to my bike and head home. Most of the classes are over and students are crowding around the canteen or are preparing to leave the premises. I enter the half closed door of the studio, and find my ever favourite student, Sagnik, still working alone. He has a spark, a compelling, almost vengeful desire to achieve, which gives him his focus. He nurtures a fury and madness within his soul, without which a man stands incomplete. I sit beside him, watching his work for a while. He has been selected to participate in an upcoming exhibition to be held in Delhi. He will be submitting three compositions, one of them being what he is working on now. Two pigeons at sunset. One of the pigeons is settled in the nest and the other flying in; a huge sun with haphazard rays on all directions supports the pigeons and keeps the sculpture together. Impressive work and flawless detailing in clay. He looks at me and says, 'Aniruddh da, I want to learn white stone and marble.'

'Are you decided on stone?'

'Yeah.'

'What do you like about it? The colour or the texture?'

'The colour. I want to work on white. A natural one. Why do you work on black?'

'Black explains my creative identity better and my visions transpire perfectly as my work. Working in black was a conscious decision after I had tried my hands in burnt red, yellow ochre and white. No other colour has led me to a natural conclusion like black. My first work with black limestone was the sun bursting out from the prisons of the rain god. I was super-specialising in Harvard then and the work had earned much accolade. It still graces Harvard Library.'

'Where do you source your ideas from?'

'By studying other's works and by activating the power of imagination. The Internet comes handy.' I smile at his innocent awe.

'Aniruddh da, I want to show you something.' I was preparing to leave; his call makes me settle back on the floor. He reaches out for his bag and pulls out some papers; hands them over to me. He has prepared some sketches of a woman walking ahead, holding a pot full of water on her shoulders; water spills from the pot, quenching the thirst of a calf walking behind her. He has visualised it magnificently. The woman, beautifully demure and eyes in front is unaware that a calf, head raised upwards, is drinking the water she has filled in her pot. The cloth that covers her body, also covers her face like a veil. The measurements he has taken seem appropriate for the 3-dimensional form of the design. 'Sometime I wish to do this in white stone.'

'What inspired this Sagnik?' I ask in appreciation.

'I am not sure. Just thought of a woman, one who concealed her inner sufferings from society but blessed many lives, feeding and nurturing them all through her lifetime. Most of the times she is oblivious of the many lives she has influenced, without expecting any returns. That's the traditional definition of Indian women; our mothers and grandmothers maybe.'

I encourage him to keep the drawings safe. He wants to work on that under me, which I don't quite approve. Involvement of a senior professional is often read by the society as more than just guidance. I want him to work hard on that and earn sole credit without my name getting involved anywhere. Maybe I'll help him to gain visibility in due course of time.

I get up to leave. Sagnik raises himself as well, to see me off. We come out of the gate together and walk towards my bike discussing something, when the kid abruptly stops. I follow his gaze and find Sanghamitra walking towards us! Her home was supposed to light up two days ago. I wondered why she didn't return on the day she said she would, but couldn't gather courage to dial her number. She is taking slow steps forward, as if in no hurry to reach me even though I am sitting on my bike and waiting to kick-start it. I steal a glance and find Sagnik watching intently at the lady looking chaste in a milk-white salwar-kurta. She comes forward, passes a smile at her smitten follower and faces me. 'Heartiest congratulations.'

Questions gather up in my mind automatically, and that reflects on my face. She holds up the magazine in her hand and adds, 'While taking the train this morning, a fellow passenger was reading this. I stole it from him.'

'You stole it?'

She giggles like a child. 'There was no chance that I could buy the magazine. So, when he was dozing off, I put it in my bag. By the time he got up, it was time for us to get down and he forgot about it.'

Before I could react Sagnik snatches it from her and turns the pages, awestruck and wide-eyed. He runs away holding it close to his chest and shouts back, 'I am going to show it to our HOD!' Sanghamitra helplessly shouts back, 'I am not done with it yet!' He stops to retort, 'What you stole was never yours Ma'm,' and disappears. There is a funny look of disappointment on her face. She looks at me. 'I haven't finished reading it. Reached this morning, took a class and came here to congratulate you.' I assure that I would give her my copy. 'You are the only person in Santiniketan who congratulated me on this.' I smile.

'No one within your discipline knew about it?' She asks surprised.

'No.'

She opens her mouth to say something but stops as a crowd of people is approaching me. Sagnik has gathered Dr Bhowmik, some senior and fellow colleagues and some students, who heartily extend their warmth at 'another feather to my cap.' Humbly I accept their wishes and promise to fulfil their demands for a treat. My mundane day is suddenly enlightened by their good wishes and kinship. The magazine is travelling from hand to hand, everyone trying to glimpse and gulp down each word printed in the interview. I feel happy. The void that had been haunting me since morning is gone. Every time something good has happened to me or I have achieved some milestone professionally, I have been grounded by the realisation that all rewards can turn meaningless when you don't have anyone to share the joy or benefits. For years I had been cursed with expulsion and isolation. Abroad, people usually don't voice their emotions so explicitly. They are much more polite, which at times seems lifeless. After long I am experiencing these loud expressions of Indian acceptance and shared happiness, which touches my heart. When I was disowned by family, I had lost faith in friendship as well. Some ex-colleagues, college mates, acquaintances have lingered on and kept in touch; but they are not friends. Unexpectedly this detached place has suddenly conspired to celebrate with me. The students lift me on their shoulders and perform a weird dance. I let out a laughter so loud, that I astonish myself. Happiest among the students is Sagnik; he hugs me tight. The group does not allow me to go home. They immediately plan for lunch together. I don't protest; just look around to personally invite Sanghamitra for the lunch. I don't find her.

In between all the chaos she has left!

The students refuse to let me go till evening. Around 8:00 pm I am in front of the house that I had been longing to knock since long. Instead of reaching the door, I call her. Instead of answering the call she opens the door! She looks exhausted after all the cleaning job she has probably being doing. I am invited into her study since the living room is not yet set up for use. She excuses herself for a while. I look around to understand what holds her attention when she is locked inside. Sanghamitra has actually turned her room into a temple of books. Diverse is her taste and interest. She seems to be dusting this huge collection regularly and the library is very well maintained with all books distinctly kept in the alphabetical order of their categories. There is a rack on Economics, where I find some of the Mathematics books I had consulted during my college days. Rest of the racks are books on Philosophy, English and Bengali fiction, History, Travel, Magazines, etc. What effort it might be taking her to be so accurate in organising these, I wonder. She asks from inside whether I would prefer tea or something cold. 'Your kind of tea,' I respond with a smile. She enters in a short while, holding a tray with two cups. She has just had her bath and her hair is wet, tied in a bun with a piece of cloth. She puts the tray down and starts the futile exercise she undertakes to dry her hair. I put my copy of the magazine on her table. 'Why did you disappear?'

'That moment was not mine. I was a misfit among your colleagues.'

'Come on. You were not seeing them for the first time!' I sip on the tea. Though I am not addicted to this liquid, I must accept that it tastes heavenly aromatic.

'I didn't know you were so good with Page-3!' Effortlessly she changes the topic.

I smile. 'You add meaning to a mundane day of my life and disown your contribution so ruthlessly!' She looks at me strangely; doesn't speak. 'What have you prepared for dinner?'

She looks embarrassed. 'Haven't cooked yet. You were meaning to have dinner here?'

'No, I wish to serve you dinner.' I put on the table, the food I have got packed for her on the way back home.

She is surprised; but soon a beautiful smile lights her lips. 'Treat for your interview?'

'No. It is my birthday today. I wanted to celebrate it with you.'

Once again words seem to fail her. She recovers almost instantly and wishes me a delightfully happy birthday. 'Does anyone here even know about this bit of information? Your favourite student?'

'No, not even Sagnik knows. But tell me, had I not brought food tonight what would you be having? Would you start cooking at 9:00 pm?'

'I planned to have just a cup of tea or coffee. I'm too exhausted to cook.'

I find her strangely occupied in her perfect world. She makes and bends her own rules, is available and unavailable at her own judgement, happy with whatever she has or doesn't have in life! I wouldn't have been so unperturbed if I had to go without food at the end of a hard day. The evening however brings to me a triumphant glory. The door, that I have heard remains closed for visitors, has opened for me!

While the lady rises to heat the food, I ask her permission to walk around and see her house. Her house could be a relevant source for me to gather information on how her mind works in solitude. She waits for a split second before nodding a 'yes.' By now she must have started getting less surprised by my impulsive demands. Slowly I usher into her living room first. Her tanpura, the huge mirror on the wall, the lamps, small things hanging from the walls, colourful cushions on the floor-level sofas, everything has a strict planning in them. It probably takes a woman's fantasies to do up the home with such detailing; men most of the times can live buried between work within four barren walls! Sanghamitra's house tells me she loves home! What comes to my mind next is why isn't she married then? Or why doesn't she have a partner somewhere? Quietly I advance towards her bedroom. I stand at the door without entering. A dim light illuminates whatever it can. The walls in this room are comparatively bare; only some paintings adorn the wall on the opposite side of the bed. A reading lamp rests over the bed and she has put some seasonal blooms on a plate on the bedside table near the door.

'You can enter and see whatever you wish to,' her voice rings from behind. I'm not sure when she had come and stood there. She enters the room first and switches on the tube light. I walk inside behind her and my eyes fall on the wooden bedside stand on the rear end where she has accommodated lots of photographs. I pick those and ask about her childhood. She points out at some of the frames and talks about her family, her place and her people. 'I grew up in a nuclear set-up, but my maternal uncles were a big joint family. When I was small, *mama's* home seemed like a palace. It was widespread, with a courtyard at the back and a garden and orchard. It was one of the most prominent houses in the neighbourhood with a nameplate reading Dadu's name in Bengali script. Mornings and evenings Dadu sat on an armchair in the veranda that faced the neighbourhood; many on their way ahead and back would greet him or stop to talk to him. There was something royal about him with huge military moustaches and extreme fluctuations of mood. We got scared every time he called us. In his own way, he was affectionate. The veranda of the house made way to five rooms, one of which was the *puja-ghar*. Shrines, idols and deities that had been with the family for ages, were placed one after the other on shelves of white stone. I specifically loved the *ashtdhaatu moorti* of Gopal, which looked really cute. At the end of the five rooms, there was a back-end veranda that overlooked a huge courtyard. On the right of the courtyard was a garden that stood testimony to Dadu's majestic collection of exotic roses, sunflowers, dalia, rajnigandha and many others. West of the courtyard opened to an orchard that grew brinjals, chillies, cauliflower and such other stuff. '

Sanghamitra fondly looks at a few frames holding the images of early '80's Bengal as she utters these. She seems lost in those and I can see how much meaning they still hold for her. I'm not sure whether the house she elaborates upon so fondly still exists; or it is a multi-storied building now! Or it still stands but in a bad shape, waiting for the obvious fate. Whatever be the status of the house, it still does capture a significant part of the lady's being. I smile at her, as she picks up another frame showing a close up of two men with their hands on each other's shoulder.

'Those days when there were power cuts, we lit lanterns. Those were beautiful things fed in kerosene oil and a small burner that held the fire. I still have one with me.' I had almost blurted out, I know! I have seen it hanging from the ceiling of her veranda on many evenings. I check myself at the last moment and she continues. 'At regular intervals a lantern was kept so that the entire house was illuminated. My father played cricket at district level. He and all the men in my mother's house went crazy about cricket. One evening baba had come there and the radio commentary for some match rooted him to the spot. Gavaskar was out for a duck and everyone was livid. They shouted, thumped on the table with their fists and discussed why Gavaskar should not have played that particular ball. So much was the fury that the evening tea went from hot to warm to cold and no one cared! India lost the match. My elder *mama* sprang up to leave the house in utter disgust and kicked into pieces a lantern that blocked his way! Such was Bengali frustration and anger that only something as important as cricket could trigger.' She smiles and keeps the frame down. 'Long after, when I had grown up, baba was no more, and *mama* had lost his youthful vitality, I remember the after-effects of another match. Due to his participation in a political rally led by the Leftists, he could not watch it on TV. Back home in the evening he asked, hey what happened to the India-Australia match? I said they've won. He asked, who? I blurted, two teams were playing, and one of them won! I was expecting an uproar. But he broke into laughter. I laughed too, but somewhere it felt sad. No one could joke over cricket or his favourite cricketers in front of him in earlier days. With age and time, everything mellows down!' For a moment she looks pensive. I feel she has forgotten that I am standing beside her and she is talking to me. Rather it feels she is talking to herself and I am nowhere! I wish to touch her and bring her back from the past. Of course I can't! Some kind of unexplained anxiety crosses my mind. Why is she still so much caught up with the past, with the things that happened to her once upon a time? Where is the excitement of her present that she can rave about?

As I look at her with undivided attention, I probably get to understand her a little better. This woman has left too much of herself in the days she has left behind. It is too difficult for her to come out of those and take charge of her present. This might just be the reason of her nonchalance towards people who appear around her today. She stays grossly disconnected to them because in her mind she is still living and sharing herself with those who don't exist any longer! For me, today is everything! I left my past behind by choice, and there is no one I can clutch on to for a secure future. My life starts and ends today. Each day is a new life! I wish to hold her shoulders and shake her really hard, so that she stands here with me and not with the ghosts of her past. Something must have transpired to her through the silence we shared for a while; suddenly she looked up at me embarrassed and kept the frame back wherever it was. We both turn to get back to the study, when I stop at her paintings. They are exotic and only a person with thorough understanding of the art would pick these as personal collections. 'Is this the real attraction that brings you to Kala Bhavan? Your interest is certainly not sculpture as you've told some people,' I tell her. She grows pale, I don't know why. With a half-smile she shrugs and walks ahead, hinting at the non-negotiable conclusion of our conversation on her private life!

At night, I am once again left sleep deprived with my sketch book. I scribble lines that mean nothing and the mind wanders haywire. I close my eyes and take a fast recap of the day. I am reminded of Sagnik's sketches and my senses rest on it for a while. Suddenly I jerk up on my seat. Sagnik's elaboration is exactly what I had been trying to conceive. It is a perfect combination of Kalindi's focus and Sanghamitra's detachment. The kid has limited exposure to Sanghamitra and her means, but he has understood and expressed her with an accuracy and precision that I was struggling to comprehend. He did not name his inspiration but I can see through it. Hidden behind the outlines of any other traditional Bengali woman, Sanghamitra's exclusivity sparks on whoever she inspires. Sagnik has visualised and established the creative connect with her much ahead of his mentor!

Lines that Mean Nothing

Sanghamitra Banerjee
Santiniketan

My Hindi belongs to Lucknow. The city of Nawabs had taught me to be civil and polite with the language and to respect a fellow individual, whatever be his status in society. Initially I would goof up on grammar and vocabulary; after struggling with a few lines in Hindi I would switch to English. My friends laughed, but they were patient with me. With time I was quite fluent. Later when I came to Mumbai, it was a culture shock. Lucknow had taught me to 'namastey' all elders; in Mumbai I was *namastey-ing* and hot aunties were returning it with a casual Hi. They looked at me as if I was a weirdo or a rustic country bumpkin!! Lucknow was affectionate and romantic. Exchanges were rich with poetic expressions, derived from a culture supported by the finesse of Urdu and magnificence of the court. People were polite, well-behaved, courteous and warm towards outsiders, considering them to be guests to the city. In Lucknow I experienced for the first time, a deadly interplay of emotions and hormones as my body and mind responded to the call of love!

It was the evening of Antaragni, a cultural festival being hosted by IIM Kanpur which had the participation of colleges across India from diverse disciplines. I was introduced to Shekhar Agnihotri by a common friend. Shekhar was a student of Painting in Lucknow University. He was shy and self absorbed behind a fair handsome face and athletic build. In early mornings when I went out for a walk around the beautiful campus, I would find him returning after a game of football. He knew people there. He and his group had been regular participants in Antaragni and went there during all five years of his B.Fine Arts. That was his first year in M.Fine Arts. The entire day he was busy with events. When he was not participating, I would find him sitting and working on his assignments. I kind of liked his eccentricity. His gaze was indifferent to all living or non-living objects around him that was not meant for his immediate attention. This included me and his cup of tea that the canteen boy left on the bench he sat. At times I stole glances at him. If anything could evoke a response out of him other than his work, it was sports. Celebration cries and shouts coming out of the common room and reaching every corner of the campus crossed all decibel limits, when there was an India–Pakistan cricket match on one of the evenings. We were rehearsing for a play right next door. India won the match and immediately a party was declared in the boys' hostel. All of us gathered there to be a part of the fun and were shocked to find Shekhar among others, booze in hand, grooving madly to music, standing on the reception table that had temporarily converted into a dance floor.

Next day our play was scheduled at 3:00 pm. It was based on the Partition of India when life was changing, values were deteriorating and political unrest led to religious conflicts. I played Swarna, a *tawaif* who was once a celebrated performer, depressed with lack of takers for her art in the period of political and social turmoil. I can't remember long speeches. So I was the obvious choice for this role which used up my expertise in classical music and did not embarrass with never-ending monologues. It was the semi-final round and our play, to our great disappointment, did not make it to the finals. We packed our bags and left the next morning. Few of our batchmates who had made it to the final rounds of classical dance, debate and case-writing competitions had stayed back. They returned with huge excitement, not because they had won, but because they wanted to share a weird information. Shekhar's submissions in the final round of painting were portraits of mine! He had painted me as Swarna, the role I had played. Overnight there were speculations and gossips at scandalous levels which got me paranoid. However, what bothered me more than the enthusiastic intruders was the simple question, did he really notice me for a purpose not related to the competition?

We met again at Varchasva, the IIM Lucknow festival, participating under the same disciplines. I maintained a safe distance because probing eyes were watching us from everywhere. This time we did make it to the finals and stayed till the end. When winners were being declared, Shekhar had done it in painting. To my utter shock and embarrassment, the paintings that he submitted were once again mine; a general, casual look this time. Both my college and his cheered loud as he went up on the stage to receive his award. The microphone was handed over to him to share a few words. His words were, 'To the inspiration of my paintings, I would like to confess, this is the only language I know!' The hall erupted with claps and shouts of glory; even some of the judges on the stage were cheering! I got up and fled. Our play had won the first position as well; but the female lead actor was not available to share the moment.

I can't elaborate what I was feeling. My lips and throat had dried up; October breeze late in the evening was cold. But I shivered with the after-effects of an internal restlessness that had nothing to do with the weather. Never have I been ever put to such turbulence. Girls from my team said that I was lucky to be proposed like that in public; that too by a guy who was one of the most promising students in his discipline. But I didn't know how to react and was feeling extremely shy. Every individual who passed by threw a smile at me; I was suddenly famous. Mandatorily we had to attend a finale party. I went there half scared and half excited. My batchmates disappeared in the middle of the party to leave me alone so that the brave lover could approach me rather easily. We both stood in front of each other, a bit bewildered and hesitant. However, in a short while we were chatting with each other like long lost mates. I gathered that he was not the shy person that he usually came across as. Rather he was a soft-spoken extrovert, who opened up either by choice or for a reason. With the turn of events, we had become a couple already and it did not require my approval any longer. Not that I was disapproving whatever was happening.

Shekhar lived life on the edge. He was good at his work, the professor's choice in college, a hero among friends, and a dream lover for girls. Investing time on creating a future was not his style. He was just creating himself, with or without a goal. My attendance dropped in my college and I was more visible around his campus. Long hours I would spend understanding his work and the passion he put behind it. And often, after my classes were over, I would find him and his bike waiting for me outside our classroom. As I took big steps towards him, the look of envy on the faces of other girls boosted my ego and energy. It felt heavenly to be with him. I didn't realise how much I was distancing from myself and my friends with every passing day to dedicate all my time to a new-found relationship. I didn't exist in isolation any longer. One August afternoon I bunked classes to ride with him through the highway of Raibareilly Road amidst strong winds forecasting rains. Heavy downpour started soon after but Shekhar was in no mood to stop. We must have been biking like that for half an hour with just the two of us on the road and nothing or no one around. I shivered as he locked his bike in the shade of a tea-stall, abandoned by the owner and buyers due to the weather. Water poured down our heads down to the neck, drenching us inside out. He turned towards me, cupped my face, stared for a while and lowered himself for the first kiss of my life. It was long and smooth, soaked in the joy of exploring further the person I wanted all for myself. My palm reached out to his cheek, shoulders, hair, neck and chest, as if to investigate the truth in the moment and feel his presence close to me. When we withdrew, my world had changed. We stood there for long, touching and leaning on each other, making unspoken promises of lifelong companionship. Days that followed were utter madness. I wished to look pretty so that his eyes warmed up to my charm every time we met. He said he wanted to see me first thing in the morning and last thing in the night, and would actually park himself below our hostel balcony late nights and early mornings so that we could wave to each other. He was protective about me and never left me insecure. We were proud to possess and be possessed, and had started discussing our lives together: our ambitions and purpose, our goals and execution. We decided that our parents would know about us when we met them during the summers. One year had passed in between and we were still engrossed in each other as if nothing else mattered. When he came to the Charbagh Station to see me off for summer holidays, little did I know that we were meeting for the last time!

Shekhar suffered a fatal car accident while driving back to Delhi with friends.

With huge support from Ma and my friends, I forced myself to stay in Lucknow till my graduation examinations were over. For post graduations, I came back to the shelter of my hometown and sought admission in Jadavpur University.

Shekhar left his mortal form, but things were not yet over between us. There had not been a formal closure to the promises we made to each other and that did not allow me to let go of him. I did try to involve myself in some affairs, two by self-indulgence and one on Ma's insistence, but none of them lasted beyond a month. Any kind of closeness or male attention depresses me after a point of time. Shekhar still exists in my music, which brought us together. He exists in my love for Nature. During rains I still lose myself to him. I try to reach out, being his, but no one comes to own me in such moments. My interest in art has prolonged even after he was no more. I reach out to that department out of a habit that refuses to die. No one knows that my interest lies not in sculpture; it is the painting department that I want to visit. But I can't bear to stand there. His voice explaining colours and lines, difference between sketches and paintings, echoes in my brain and I seem to go back to the world that no longer holds true. My soul expects him to come back one day, in some form or the other, and put an end to the life he still lives within me.

In all these years, it has been only Dr Aniruddh who has questioned my interest in sculpture. I had sensed the sarcasm when he mentioned that Sagnik had informed him of my fondness for the art. I manipulated my response such that instead of focusing on sculpture the attention shifted to Sagnik. And then that evening when he stood in front of the paintings that hung on the walls of my bedroom and repeated his question! It must be his professional genius and experience that can filter out true passion from fake ones. But that night when I was lying on the boat beside him, for once after a really long time, Shekhar was not there between us.

It is spring again and the land celebrated Holi in its most traditional format. They call it *Basanta Utsav*, translated as the celebration of spring. It starts with an early morning *Baitalik*, where participants sing *Ore Grihobashi*, a song composed by Tagore for this occasion. Soon after little dancers from Patha Bhavan lead a procession dance as they reach out to the main stage. They are followed by seniors from high school and college. Yellow is the colour of the occasion. Boys are usually in yellow kurta and girls in yellow saris. Girls specifically decorate themselves with heavy silver jewellery and apply loud signature bindis on their foreheads. Flowers accessorise their hair-do. The dancers wear a ceremonial scarf called *Uttariya* hanging from both sides of the shoulder, usually sourced from local handlooms with rich batik or *kantha* work, which explains their majestic presence. *Uttariya* is often used by the locals on normal working days. It is meant to represent their honour and elevated position in society. It is a custom here, to remove the *uttariya* every time one meets a senior or someone more respectable than the bearer of the long scarf. It feels nice to find students get down from their cycles or remove their *uttariya*, each time they spot me or any other teacher, as a token of respect. The tradition is a visible and strong medium of expressing regards; the students have followed it and taken the ritual forward through all these years. Ideally sourced from the Buddhist dress code, Tagore encouraged the use of *uttariya* among his followers, which may have resulted from the poet's distinct support for the community and its beliefs.

The dancers take the procession till the main stage and then, students usually from Sangeet Bhavan perform dance-dramas as part of the formal celebrations. When all stage performances are over, the last performers throw coloured powders in the air inviting everyone to soak in the colours of Holi. The festival here is celebrated strictly in the absence of water. It's a dry Holi only. There's fun in being smeared and walking around the campus where students, faculties, staff and visitors form their own respective groups and chat, play music, sing, dance, recite, eat and celebrate in a way that befits them best. Often parents come to visit their kids, who are residential students of the university. Some kids who are otherwise enjoying their adolescence with budding or special friendship with the opposite gender are suddenly rocked back to feigned innocence expressing unchallenged sanctity of their campus presence. It is amusing to watch their sad faces as they steal frequent glances at their friends, unhappy at the parental supervision during the festival of colours which was supposed to be their lover's day!

Only once, since I have joined Viswa Bharati, have I been out in the open experiencing the festivities. Post that, on *Basanta Utsav*, I follow a ritual of my own. I attend the *Baitalik* and roam around for a while to check on the stage performances. Then I return home. Even from home I can hear the songs being played at Gour Prangan and people enjoying their participation amidst peals of laughter and shrill sounds expressing false anger or offence. All my friends buzz around, spending time with each other and moving around the campus. They come to my place for lunch. On my cheek and forehead they put soft marks of the colour to greet me, and I reciprocate. The area outside my home evidences the smear of colours. We sit outside on the veranda with cups of ginger tea. Then one by one they go inside and take their bath. Clean clothes are stocked at my place an evening in advance. Though I don't encourage students to knock my door, on this particular day they come to pay respect. Plates of sweets remain ready for them as a token of my blessings. On this day I cook for my friends. The menu this year is peas kachori, fried rice and kofta; jamuns as dessert. My usual gang is delighted at the spread. After their bath, Sia, Anusua and Pritha, Stuart's wife, start cleaning the floor and lay down the plates. Shayan and Stuart are busy preparing *thandai* with *bhang*. I relax. That is also a ritual. I cook lunch and then sit watching the others work. We finish our meal and *thandai* is served by the boys post that. Each glass has to finish in one go. Stuart and Shayan take the lead in outnumbering each other on the count of glasses. Everyone gathers up into my bedroom and adjust themselves to take some rest; tired and exhausted all sleep off in a while. It feels lazy. The clock has just struck four. I come out to the veranda and put some coconut husk and camphor in a coconut shell and burn them. Once they start emitting smoke I hold the shell by covering the hot area with my dupatta and take it around the house to get rid of mosquitoes. I lower the shell on one corner of the veranda and sit down sipping my tea. The gang is still fast asleep.

Dr Aniruddh is in Delhi for two weeks, to honour his commitment with Lalit Kala Akademi. My visits to Kala Bhavan have been less since he joined, and lesser since he questioned my interest in paintings. Being a part of the population that automatically rises up to gossips, I did not wish to encourage any act that draws attention or raises speculation connecting my visits with the presence of this young, handsome, successful bachelor! Anyway the sculptor doesn't pay heed to such precautions. We meet often though. It is difficult for common faces not to come together in this small town, especially if they are neighbours. At times when we don't get to see each other during the day, he drops by in the evening. His impolite peek into my life, I realise, has jerked up my past and present. True happiness of my being was considerably confined to the days I had once spent with Shekhar. My present life is oblivious of this fact and I have never allowed anyone to gain any information about me. I am not active on the social media because I don't wish to keep in touch. There are a selected few who have access to my mobile number. I don't pick up calls unless I know or approve the caller. My days start and end in their pre-programmed format and my contribution to each passing day is usually limited to a generous presence. Dr Aniruddh's unabashed intrusion shocked me beyond limits and I was forced to take a greater interest in my present and protect the past from being unveiled. I don't ever wish to part with the joy or sorrow that came to me via Shekhar; neither do I want to share it with anyone. I had tried to block the sculptor from entering too much into my life. I had tried to concentrate on the upcoming moments and arrest any weak exchange that clues his interest to the days I have left behind. Result, I ended up concentrating on Dr Aniruddh as well. He was here at my doorstep, few hours before he left for Delhi. He looked restless and unorganised, very much unlike him. I didn't ask anything. This restlessness happens when creative minds can't source their perfect ideas to justify a relentless quest of excellence. I was not experiencing this for the first time. I could not improve his situation, but offered to simply divert his attention. These creative brains need a break at times, to relieve themselves from the overburdened task of invention they take upon their pre-loaded systems. But more often than not, they can't help themselves. They need to be taken care of like a child and their energies have to be channelised towards other fancies. I asked him to shop for Rajasthani dolls for me from Dilli Haat! He was seriously taken aback with my request and didn't know what to say till I erupted into laughter. He composed himself and admitted shyly, no one had ever made such requests before. I had to convince him that it was an attempt to divert him from the melancholic mood he was wearing and I was not serious.

The evening is fading into the dark and houses in the neighbourhood are lighting up. Bengali households play *shankh*, a conch shell during their morning and evening rituals in front of God. The *shankh* as per Hindu scriptures is meant to bring fame, longevity and prosperity; it is the cleanser of sin and the abode of Lakshmi, the goddess of wealth and consort of Vishnu. At dawn and dusk when every household releases that divine sound, an auspicious moment enriched in common faith is automatically established. I switch on the lights of my veranda and walk inside to wake up the sleepy-heads. My phone beeps, 'Back to the pavilion tomorrow!'

Back to the Pavilion

Dr Aniruddh Jain Solanki
Santiniketan

When Sanghamitra asked for Rajasthani dolls that evening, I was lost for words for a while. That was not because she said something out of the blue. But merely that with the mention of those colourful puppets made of cotton and cloth, I was taken back to Jaipur. Girls at my haveli loved working on those. Tirelessly they would sit and make elephants, camels, men, women, drums, etc. in multi-coloured fabric, decorate them with zari and connect those to each other with beads and *parandi* to produce a long chain. They would then hang them on the walls or festoon the doors and windows, or they would pass them on as gifts. Boys in the family often stole those camels and elephants, inviting the girls to shout and chase the life out of them. That was our original rhythm and most accepted sin. Sanghamitra had mentioned that she was trying to divert my mind to something less important and less melancholic, than what had pre-occupied my thoughts. She didn't realise I had travelled back in time and could hear the laughter and tongue-lashings that our house was always abuzz with. I gained composure in a while, though not before I had decided to bring her those dolls, not from Dilli Haat, but from Jaipur. That evening the girl never asked me what was it I was disturbed with; she just tried to soothe my troubled brain. More often than not people demand to know the cause of the trouble. Knowledge and ownership of an innate instinct that belongs to someone else helps them feel rather important and that's when they invest themselves in offering the best solution. Sanghamitra has a natural aversion to asking anything personal. She calls it *unnecessary information overload*! With a strange command over her impertinence, she never bothers to understand what she doesn't need to know. I have seen her cheerful, disgusted, calm and melancholic; but none of these emotions have unguarded her from that strict code of conduct. Unless she considers someone a friend, her body language clearly proclaims that she's not interested, though she addresses all civic and civil duties with finesse. Thankfully, she is not as closed to me as she used to be initially. There's a child in her who reacts to the blessings of Nature; she is also mature enough to appropriate herself as per the demands of the situation. My ego hurts when I realise that there's much more to her than what I or any of her friends have access to. Her eyes tell me that she can be a passionate devotee if she meets her interest. But what would interest her is the question worth a million. It feels as though Sanghamitra is punishing herself with a self-imposed exile, and she is enjoying the punishment!

The Lalit Kala Akademi was a vision of Nehru and his contemporaries, to promote, encourage, teach and exhibit Indian art and culture as our national identity. The institution manages multi-city operations and maintains galleries in key cities across India, which are promising enough for its purpose. Spending time with under-privileged kids was one hell of an experience. While it grounds all pride associated with achievements and materialistic possessions, a bitter truth raises its head. I am what I am because I could afford to name my interest and follow it with passion. These kids, from a very small age, are meant to commercially benefit their families and bring in resources to provide for their daily bread. Most of them were rustic and aggressive. Initially they would fight with each other and make the environment virtually impossible for any kind of training. They found it intrusive when I intervened and requested them to stop. Their system was filled with grudges. Boys specifically would tell the girls to sit at the back; some of the unrelenting girls would yell at them hurling abuses. I had to employ some tricks to bring their attention together and bind them by a common purpose. It took me a while to understand their personal talents and subject the group to a team work, where none of the creations are complete in isolation, unless it passes each table of significant expertise. Once they involved with me and started enjoying the time, some beautiful ideas surfaced. I taught them to use their hands, fingers and nails to carve on clay. By the end of the term, they could not only capture their imagination in tangible terms but also accentuated their work by painting designs on them with poster colour. The whole purpose of this exercise was to encourage the potentials of street children towards art and introduce them to an alternate source of income that is intellectually fulfilling. On the last evening of the session I gave them some gifts and boxes of sweets. They left with tears in their eyes, but came back the day next when I was about to leave Delhi. They offered to carry my bags, polish my shoe, call a cab, etc. all of which had already been taken care of by the Akademi. To them, I represented the key to a different life, with less miseries and better living, which destiny may not allow them to enter. How much ever they know of all alternate paths, these kids would probably whirlwind back to the street-routine, simply because the forces to resist their choice are much more powerful than the forces to support! I bid them farewell, this time with a lump in my throat, trying hard to hide my emotions. The fourteen days that I spent with these kids, day and night, are something I'll treasure in my memory.

The cabbie drives me straight to Jaipur. As the cab enters the city after a few hours, my eyes delight themselves at the sight of the city, each corner of which tells the story of my childhood. This is probably what they call the joy of homecoming! It has been fourteen years since I have last been here. God knows what reception I'll receive at home; but the city definitely seems friendly. As I reach the haveli around evening, clouds of tension hover around me. How would they react to my sudden appearance? From outside the main gate I could see that the house is lit up with lights, declaring and celebrating an upcoming marriage. My cousin, Abhimanyu, is getting married in a day or two. I take slow steps to reach out to the gatekeepers and hesitate to introduce myself. A spectacled, tough-looking guy looks sternly, waiting for me to elaborate my purpose of visit and relation to the family. Once again it feels horribly alienated to accept that I am so disconnected with my own house that I have to go through elaborate entrance formalities to access the interiors. Should I call Diya or Abhimanyu? No, they are busy in the arrangements and I shouldn't drag them into whatever humiliation is waiting for me! For a moment I contemplate whether I should quietly go back without informing anything to anyone. No one is expecting me anyway. As fate would have it, I am spotted by an old book-keeper of my grandfather's times and he blocks my way to understand the origin of the *boy* he could only half recognise. As a child I had played a lot with Munimji, as the family fondly calls him. Quietly I smile down at him, as he scrolls through his memory to locate me. Soon enough his eyes grow wide and tears roll down. He hugs me tight repeating, 'Gora baba' under his breath; that's what he used to call me because of my fair complexion. Soon he is carrying my bags unheeding my violent protests, dragging me inside by the hand and shouting, 'Look who has come, ignorant women; your lost son is back home,' all these much to my embarrassment!

A big crowd gathers in front of the main door; men come out to inspect the reason of further commotion in an already excitable, marriage-prone environment. I can't explain how tensed I feel to face my clan. I wonder whether their disgust would show in public and want the earth to swallow me. For a few seconds there is deadly silence. I am standing in between and everyone from everywhere is watching me, waiting for someone else to react! I try to find a handkerchief to wipe my forehead, but that's nowhere to be found; stupidly I examine all pockets and finally give up. I curse the impromptu decision of coming to Jaipur. For once I remember Sanghamitra, whose open laughter and mischievous demand had provoked my tamed brain to touch the soil of Jaipur. But what happens next is unexpected. Abhimanyu rushes out of the door and hugs me, ignoring everyone else. He laughs, shouts and lifts me up with great joy, puts me back on the ground and extends a prolonged hug again. When I left last time, Abhimanyu was an opinion-suppressed teenager like anyone else in the house at that age. Till I stayed in the haveli, he was one of my most devoted followers and remained with me in everything I did like a shadow. When they disowned me, I was told that he gave up food and sleep! Secretly I would call him up then and speak for long hours to bring him out of the depression. Since then, we have always been in touch via infrequent phone calls and social media. I was the one to encourage his subtle 'friendship' with Diya so that it can develop into a meaningful relationship in due course of time.

Today, he has now grown up to be a muscular, handsome guy. I take a few moments to understand what is happening and then return his gesture with equal warmth. For a while I stand forgetting everything else as we hold each other with a happiness that is exclusive and unconditional to the joint disgrace that the rest of my family might inflict upon me in the next few hours. Soon other cousins join us and now we are all hugging and holding each other, misty eyed and driven by childhood memories. Anish, another cousin who must be nineteen or twenty now, prompts the musicians hired for the occasion to play their *dhol* and everyone around me erupts into an impromptu *bhangra*! Never in my life had I expected to be welcomed back with such warmth and celebration! Only after the women yell from the first floor balcony that I should be allowed inside for refreshments, does their ecstasy reason itself. They hold me from all sides and usher me towards the huge main door. I look around but don't find the two bags I was carrying. Must have been picked up by someone, I decide and move on. Deivi Aunty, the eldest in my clan today, fulfils the welcome formalities with the lights of an earthen lamp, sweets of ghee symbolising prosperity and rice-vermillion tika smeared on my forehead to seek blessings of the lord. I have always seen my grandmother, Gayatri Devi, fulfil this ritual. The verdict of nature so accurately commands role-reversals with time. I can see the dominant old lady who ruled over our brains as much as she decided the course of our lives, in Deivi Aunty today. She has been cast in the same mould as my grandmother; even the body language and mannerisms are the same. She wears an affectionate but stern look, thankfully though not as ferocious as Gayatri Devi, but her presence is graciously intimidating!

From here an old habit takes me to the *puja-ghar*. While I lower myself to the Lakshmi-Narayan of our house, I also mentally note that most of the rules and rituals have remained unaffected in all these years. I move from room to room post this, to meet and greet all elders of the house, starting with my parents. My father, specifically, seems to be really happy to receive me with open arms. *Bhabhu* is more rigid with her expressions. Guests have filled up all rooms; no one was expecting me. I am accommodated in a room that is being shared by other cousins and the groom himself. The moment I came out of the bath, he declares, 'Tonight there is a men's party on the terrace. All arrangements have been made. No one sleeps.' I stand there wondering how he managed to cook this up in so less a time; the answer is very much within me. These guys who are half a generation younger than me are much more smart! An elaborate evening snack follows. I go back to my parents to spend some time with them. My mother plays an important role in the elaborate traditional functions of the Rajput marriage; many of the keys lie trusted and secured with her. She has to leave for her chores, but manages to sit with me and my father for a while.

'We never thought you would come. Work brought you here?' She asks.

Some words slip my tongue and I repent immediately after pronouncing them. '*Bhabhu*, I was never invited, just informed.'

'Family members don't need invitations. That's of course as long as they believe that they are family!'

I don't want an argument to sour up the evening's pleasure. Yet I say, 'All relationships have to be reciprocal. For me to believe that I have a family, you have to treat me like family first.'

'Who started the game my son?'

'You. And everyone else, who did not accept that my happiness was not in your diamond business. Even if I agree that I started the game, then at least understand that you are dragging it on!'

'Look at the way he talks,' she looks at my father. 'He wants us to support his selfish motives and the decision to break away from all of us. That's what we get after years of rearing and caring for him. We were so happy that a boy was born to us; he would set fire to our funeral pyres and take the family forward with offspring. His grandmother, who loved him so much, did not even get to see his face when she breathed her last! Every year we celebrated his birthday with so much pomp, only to realise that his life stands on curses of self-centred greed!'

I feel horrible!.But still manage to say, 'I had much more to give than that misery and sadness resulting from the selfish growth you are talking about; but it is your inability that could not take any more than the curse.'

Before my mother speaks any further, my father intervenes in a firm voice. 'Meena, leave him alone. Please carry on with what you have to do.'

Bhabhu looks at me and then at my father, upset that she is stopped in between. For a while she stares at me, sitting with head held down, face covered with hands to hide the bitterness; then turns to my father. 'Tell him he deserves being like this. Violated, deserted and sorrow-stricken. We have been like this too for many years, before explaining to ourselves that we never had a son.' She turns and leaves. I wipe my face and get up as well.

The moment *Bhabhu* leaves, Abhimanyu enters. He must have been hearing the conversation from outside the room. He looks enraged, but calmly holds my hand and tries to guide me out of the room, when my father touches me from behind and both of us stop. His palm on my arm is kind and assuring, he smiles and gestures me to sit. His tone is not aggressive. 'Don't be sad at what she said. She had been treated like dirt after you left. What is coming out of her is the pent up frustration of not being able to answer the ladies of the house. She had to work day and night, care for your grandmother without any help because your grandmother blamed her for your disappearing act. She cooked and fed the clan waiting to hear a word of praise, when no one cared to even take a second refill on the plate. Once she had been the most loved woman of this house. And then for years no one loved her, no one cared whether she was present, no one asked her for anything and taunted each of her actions. She was the last one to receive gifts or get access to the kitchen. It was not very easy for her to handle. Just give her some time.'

'Don't you ever feel proud of him, Kaka sa?' Abhimanyu could not hold himself back any longer. The fact that I have returned to the haveli after so many years, that too during his marriage, only to hear some rude words from *Bhabhu* did not go down well with him. I try to stop him, but he continues, 'You had the option of doing that. Your son was breaking barriers across the world and engraving his name amongst the best in art! Today he is rich and famous without any support from anyone else; his fame and money doesn't belong to or comes inherited from a family of partners. It's all rigorous self-grilling and hard work. He had worked as a cleaner and waiter to support his living in the early days. Then none of us were anywhere to support him. But today my generation understands and values his achievements. But why are you and Kaki-sa so closed? Why are the two of you being slave to a vain ego that keeps you away from your son! Why does your generation attach so much importance to your seniority that you can't accept that your children can make some choices on their own!?'

Abhimanyu is truly agitated, and for the first time his thoughts locked somewhere in support of his brother were coming out with unconcealed arrogance. Even more surprising was the fact that Jisa was not shutting him off, nor was he showing any signs of anger towards his behaviour. By our family code of conduct, Abhimanyu's backlashing is supposed to be perceived as over-reaction and improper conduct! But Jisa just says, 'Had we not been strict with our vigil, my dear, everyone would have drifted apart and the family wouldn't have been together; and the business we have given our blood to would have shut doors long ago!' He holds both of us with his hands and makes us sit beside him as he places himself in between. Then he looks intensely into my eyes. 'Feel proud of whom, my son? The child who ran away from us? The society was reading it as the biggest failure of parenting! They said that our son had disowned us because we came on his path to success. How could we have been proud of the same success that came at the cost of our separation?'

Astounded I sit there, unable to look into his eyes any longer. I had never thought about it like this. It feels miserable and guilty. Abhimanyu too is quiet.

'You both could have left this society and come to me.' I still try to reason.

My father lets out a deep breath. 'You may not belong to any place, any house or any clan. But we do, Aniruddh. You wouldn't have been you, had we managed to confine you here. We would not live if we were to be uprooted from here!' Few moments of silence and then Jisa continues. 'The world is a strange place, Aniruddh. Everyone here craves for recognition, acceptance and success. Let me tell you something. The farsighted creative vision that drives you to build up a new horizon all by and for yourself is not something you sourced from elsewhere. It's in your blood and genes. We had it very much in our family. My father was like you, ruthless and unrelenting towards anything that came in the way of setting up the diamond business. He made it big enough to make sure that his sons and further descendants can earn their living from his philosophies. He left a wife who never allowed us to part ways and kept the family together. The wife spent forty years to build a dummy of her in her eldest daughter-in-law such that the principles laid down by her husband never cease to exist. My father tried to control his after-generations even when he is no more, such was his pride. You, by taking control of your own life have just repeated his principles in abbreviation, which many of us could not decipher by our myopic standards. It required age and wisdom to understand the trend, which I didn't have before, but now I do. And your ambition? You would be surprised to learn that you inherited it from your mother. Since her marriage at the age of twenty, she had given her best and single-minded devotion to serve this family and gain a position of importance and dictatorship. Hierarchy-wise she knew that she couldn't inherit her mother-in-law's role. So she decided to be the king-maker, where the significance of her advice is non-negotiable. It was not easy to achieve that in our family, complicated with multiple presence, opinions and thoughts. However, she managed to be the most loved and respected woman in this household. And then, you, her most precious possession, failed her! For quite some time she did not know what to mourn. Your conduct or the years of goodwill in the family that was suddenly rendered useless and meaningless! She composed herself to rebuild her position yet again, swimming through the politics of the clan and facing all abuses with silence. Meena never protested. I hadn't recovered from the shock of a betraying son as fast as her. She had a purpose to her life, which she didn't share with anyone. That ambition didn't allow her to suffer losing you for too long. She is much more shrewd a business person than I have ever been. However, as much as she progressed to achieve her goals, she equally blames you for her downfall. You have only achieved my son, but you have not achieved and lost. Allow her the freedom to vent the anger. Only then would she come to terms with it.' Jisa stopped, taking deep breaths after his long speech. I hand him a glass of water and feel blessed to have come here. We have never in my life spoken to each other like this. There was so much for me to hear and for him to say. Softly I just ask, 'And you Jisa? Did you forgive me for leaving home uninformed?'

He frowns at me. 'Did you ever ask for forgiveness, Aniruddh?'

'I ask for it now, Jisa, from the bottom of my heart. Forgive me please. My achievements don't translate into celebrations till the family is as happy as I am.' My eyes are full and there's a lump in the throat. I never knew that I can speak this language!

'Parents can't stay upset with their offspring for too long, son. I had forgiven you long before, but waited for you to come and claim it. One day Meena will forgive you too.'

We hug each other tight. The shehnai that plays to declare the forthcoming occasion feels like originating from heavens, as three of us sit close touching each other and mourning over irreversible time lost in ego, misunderstandings and separation, which we wished we had avoided.

After dinner, the men of the house walk up to the huge terrace. Abhimanyu has created an ambience with red and blue lights that allow visibility but keep it mystic. Shehnai has been replaced by soft piano and guitar. Mattresses are spread out on the floor. Four guys land up holding cardboard boxes carrying beer, wines and whiskey. I look at them wide-eyed. Abhimanyu sits in front of me with his glass and asks what needs to be served. I faintly smile and refuse. He looks astonished and breaks into laughter, shouts out to others. 'Guys, our brother doesn't drink!' Others join the fun. '*Baa*'s favourite grandchild after all,' someone smirked! They didn't force me but.

'The house is no longer strict about its code of conduct and the pious Lakshmi-Narayan?' I ask.

'It is,' he replies. 'That's why we are doing this on the terrace.'

'I wouldn't have dared.'

Abhimanyu remains quite. Anish, another cousin of mine retorts, 'You dared to do something that we wouldn't have dared. But in the process, you taught us life's greatest wisdom. Daring to be different and living up with whatever comes in the package! We admire your courage.'

It's my turn to be astonished once again. 'You do? Why didn't you ever reach out to me then? I was suffering brutal isolation in moments of dejection and joy, which came as a part of my profession!'

'We were scared that you will reject us. We are descendants of the generation that disowned you and kept you away from home. We thought you will disown us back. You don't need us anyway. We were too small when you left, and reconnecting after you have touched the sky seemed very opportunist! But trust me, we were in touch with all your achievements. Every time your name featured in the world reports, all cousins secretly raised toasts and gathered at *Oberoi* to celebrate. I am overjoyed that you have come for this marriage. It couldn't have been more special.'

I look at him in disbelief. Some words emerge from the deepest corners of my heart. I do need you, and everyone else in my family, Anish. Just that I didn't realise I had much in waiting and I had to make myself available to take ownership. I don't spell these out though. Rather I look at Abhimanyu and say, 'You know Abhi, I thought at least you would call me before the marriage and want me to come over and attend it. I thought my presence matters to you.' He looks away, and before he responds, Anish opens his mouth again. 'Bhai sa, you have no idea how incomplete we all felt without you, especially in this marriage. But Abhi did not want to take any chances. He was too scared that if you come over, you might be insulted again and that was not something that any of us wished for you.' A pleasant breeze seems to soothe my aching nerves! We hug each other tight, once again, and allow the music and fun to take over. All of us have much to share about our lives and work. The business has taken lots of twists and turns and there are new terms like 'branding' and 'distribution' and 'boutiques' frequenting it these days. We spend hours laughing and pulling each other's legs and making fun of each other. Some of my cousins smoke and almost everyone drinks. Abhimanyu's bride, Diya, is also the schoolmate of his sister, Ahalya; I quite remember her as a child coming over to our house and lending her expertise in preparing dolls. Diya happens to be his junior in school and kind of a childhood sweetheart and they lived in for five years abroad when Abhi was pursuing his MBA and Diya her Journalism. Of course, the elders in the family don't know this. My cousins don't quite believe that I have led a non-happening, dry existence when it comes to romantic interactions. Abhimanyu makes me talk to Diya over phone and I promise to meet her the next day. Before hanging up she asks, 'What gift do you want from me Bhai-sa?' My tongue slips to say, 'A pair of those Rajasthani dolls you used to make!'

Around 4:30 am, everyone is drunk and is sleeping wherever they found space. I get up and walk down the stairs to reach the third floor of the haveli. Lights are on in the *puja-ghar*. I walk up there and find Deivi-ma, as I call her, preparing for the morning puja. I just sit outside without making a noise. My presence doesn't miss her attention. 'Don't enter,' her voice warns. I know I am not supposed to enter before bath. 'Can I quickly take a bath and come back?' I ask. She turns, 'You still remember these?' I don't answer. She stares at me for a while and says, 'I won't hold back anything for you.' I run to my room, take a quick shower and in ten minutes I am back. The lamps and camphor have been lit, loose flowers are stringed together into garlands, sandalwood paste prepared. But the puja hasn't started. I take permission to enter the room to sit just behind her. A flood of memories rushes back to me. I can sleep-talk through all the rituals she'll follow and mantras she'll recite now, having spent much time observing my grandmother practise these. The entire process takes an hour to complete. In half an hour's time the entire family will gather to perform the *aarti* together. Deivi-ma turns to me. 'Do you still wake up so early in the morning?' Not always. Work often keeps me up till late in the night and my mornings hence are delayed, I am prompted to say. But I respond with a monosyllabic 'yes'. 'And you are the only man in your generation who can recite the mantras with me,' she smiles. I smile back. 'Learnt them from *Baa*.'

'How come you didn't forget these the way you forgot *Baa* and the rest of us!'

I remain quiet but the hurt shows on my face. Deivi-ma lifts my face with her right hand. 'And so you didn't drink last night. You restrained yourself or you are not into it?'

I am shocked at her statement. 'Deivi-ma, you knew that they arranged a party last night?'

'I know everything that happens under this roof. I have to. But I have to be reasonably strict. Our times were different. If I try to stop your generation forcibly, they'll either do the same outside the premises and bring us shame, or they'll run away like you did. So tell me why you didn't drink last night.'

'I don't.' she looks at me trying to judge the truth of my words and then settles back satisfied.

'Do you have a girlfriend?'

'No.'

'When was the last time you were in a relationship?'

'I never had one.'

'Why? You never felt a physical or emotional need?'

'I did, Deivi-ma. But I was too busy establishing myself. Couldn't afford the luxury of dealing with distractions.'

She finally laughs out loud. '*Distractions*? Is that what you call women?'

'Not you.' I have managed to break the ice with her. 'Only those who could come in my way and manage to be a part of my fancies.'

'Your cousins are all very fond of you,' Deivi-ma looks lost in thought. I touch her hand to bring her attention back. When I was a kid, I shared a fun-filled relationship with her. I went to her room, picked her things, demanded food that she was expert at making at odd timings, forced her awake when she was sleeping. She affectionately pampered me all through. 'Even you happened to be very fond of me, Deivi-ma.' She doesn't respond to this, just looks away.

'You so much represent the old lady, the way she used to be.' I try to nudge her more.

She smiles. 'We, the women of this house, have spent more time here than we did in the house we were born in. And we have known our mother-in-law more than our mother. Hence, a natural replication of behaviour happens when I perform her duties. Every moment I think what would she have done, had she been there today. There is no escape. Your *baa* still lives in me with an agenda. Before her death, she had instilled in me the task of seniority! Under my supervision, all members of this house should stay together, bound by our pre-defined culture and purpose. That's a huge responsibility to maintain. At times I have to pull the strings and then I have to let go. Gayatri Devi was flawless at her job till her beloved grandson proved everything wrong. On her death-bed she instructed me to learn from her mistakes.' Once again my head is held down written in guilt, awaiting an emotional outburst. She holds up my face with the inside of her palm. 'There is also something else that I had to inherit from her. I didn't have a choice. That is her forgiveness and endless tolerance towards everything that you do!' I look at her, unsure of what is coming next. Deivi-ma continues, 'Make sure you mend whatever you have ruined in your mother's heart, son. Today you have entered the house because I had some instructions imparted to me. But your mother hasn't yet forgiven you.' I ignore the last part of what she said and ask, 'What instructions, Deivi ma? What are you talking about?' Calmly she puts down the brass plates that she was arranging for the puja. 'On her death bed, your *baa* had instructed me never to send you off if you were to ever stand at our doorstep by your choice! She made me promise that before her mortal form left the world!' For a few moments we both are quiet. I can feel my body trembling and face getting washed with tears. I cover my face with my hands. *Baa*'s love for me has outlived her life, and as much as I wish today, I can't return the gesture to her! Deivi ma bends to touch me; then takes my palm into hers. 'When she passed on this instruction to me, I wasn't happy about it Aniruddh. But today probably I can reason out her fondness for you.' She says softly, 'You know what? Everyone in this house has broken rules in some way or the other. But no one has been as direct and maybe, honest, as you. Yet, you are the only one in your generation who has followed Gayatri Devi's philosophies and principles with austere sincerity even while chasing some personal dreams. You broke away from the family, but didn't do away with the rituals of the family. Maybe you didn't need the family business to stay bound to our culture; rather you have held on to them by choice. Her other grandsons may not have left the business, but they have sufficiently traded with her ideals to find happiness in life. Probably this is why *Baa* could never disown you and found her God within you.' I enjoy the warmth of her palm and we sit for a few moments simply touching each other. She has no idea how much her words mean to me. Both of us wipe our faces and get back to the arrangements of the puja as the rest of the family approaches the *puja-ghar* for the morning ritual.

Later in the day, I go around the house visiting the old corners and filling myself with the changes they have undergone in all these years. They have turned the pond in our backyard into a well-maintained pool with cemented corners and safe stairs. The clay sculptures I had once made around them have been uprooted and kept in a glass house, which serves as some kind of a museum for visitors. Many don't know about me since they are not that updated about the world of art. My cousins however, have taken the initiative to proudly retain my innocence as some of the early advances of my genius. However, they had been strictly instructed not to maintain much contact with me. The originator of this instruction was none other than my mother! I distribute the gifts I had brought for my family, combing the streets of Karol Bagh and South Extension. I have asked Abhimanyu to name the gift he and Diya want from me. Coming from a diamond merchant's family, giving out jewellery would be too repetitive. I had come here for a day, but an extension in the plan is obvious now. I meet Diya one of these evenings with Abhimanyu. She shows me a pair of dolls, dressed as king and queen. Before handing them over to me, she said, 'I'll give these under one condition. You will have to name the person who you are taking them for.' I feel uneasy. I know they'll misinterpret and find romantic possibilities if I use her name. I try to say, 'Actually a colleague who collects … !' Diya interrupts me. 'Just the name

Bhai-sa.' Not left with much option, I take the name. 'Mitra.' Sanghamitra might sound too complicated for them. They exchange meaningful smiles and she gives me the dolls without any further questions.

The marriage happens at Castle Kanota with great pomp. We have a lot of fun enjoying and indulging ourselves. At times in between I have caught Abhi and Diya whispering to each other. They pass weird smiles and I feel they are talking about me! They stop abruptly every time I arrive! I know my questions here won't fetch direct answers. Couples have their secrets. But their giggles get me suspicious! Many a times in between I think of Sanghamitra. I want to thank her from the bottom of my heart. Unknowingly she had triggered in me an urge to visit home. Had I not been emotionally stimulated to visit Jaipur, I wouldn't have known what was waiting for me here and there would not have been a bigger regret. Strange people come into our life, destined with a reason and benefit it from unexpected corners. Today I own a world. I also sense a connection with Sanghamitra, like I have never felt before.

As I reach Santiniketan, I knock on her door even before I have dumped my bags at Mridangam!

King and Queen

Sanghamitra Banerjee
Santiniketan

Today is Bengali New Years Day. Viswa Bharati also celebrates Tagore's birthday today. 25th of the *Baishakh* of Bengali calendar, marks the poet's birth anniversary, which falls between 7th and 9th of May, differing from year to year. The university closes for summer vacation after celebrating the occasion on 14th of April. Every year the college arranges a lavish function to honour the day with recitals, dance shows and musical performances on Tagore's compositions. Every year we gather at Anusua's place in Guru Pally at the end of the programmes. The place is hot at this time of the year and she is rich enough to afford an air conditioner. Along with our usual gathering, there are two added invitees. Dr Bhowmik, HOD of Kala Bhavan, who she considers her mentor and Dr Aniruddh Jain Solanki. Having Dr Bhowmik between us means we are much more sober than usual. Stuart isn't abusing, Shayan is not smoking and Sia has kept her wicked humour in control. Anusua is her hospitable best, each gesture of hers soaked in respect towards the mentor and I am super bored. Dr Bhowmik is talking life and philosophy; how things happened to be during his times and how they have reduced into mere ruins of a glorious past. Sigh! Phew! For forty-five minutes we have been subjected to this torture and I know that this will progress into politics when Stuart will participate violently. For quite some time I look at him pretending deep interest in whatever he has to say; but his endlessness takes my patience. Sia and I step out to sit on the stairs; we close the door behind us. This side of Anusua's house opens to a vast no man's land. Till afar there is no one visible. Sia takes this opportunity to light a cigarette. She offers me one too; I refuse. Instead I take hers and inhale deep. The smoke seems to touch my brain. I keep it inside for a while and release it. I take it once again and return. Strangely this brings on some kind of dizziness; my head spins a bit and instantly I feel tired. This is momentary though. A curt voice calls from behind, 'Since when are you into this?' Dr Aniruddh stands there embarrassed. Before I respond, my semi-Mexican friend chirps in. 'Oh don't be so shocked, Sir. She doesn't smoke regularly. It is only on frustrating evenings that I choose to spoil her.' The sculptor's expressions clearly say that he didn't like the sight of smoke coming out of my nostrils and mouth. He stares for a while, and face downcast retreats. We wait for him to go inside and shut the door. Immediately as the door bangs close we break into noiseless laughter. 'How possessive is our ancient Indian chauvinist,' chuckles Sia. I chide in false scorn and end up smiling. Dr Jain is too rigid himself. True that I don't smoke or drink; but what's wrong if I do? Do I change as a person? Do I kill someone? While I was pursuing my Masters at Jadavpur University I often found stylish, happening women with the white stick in hand. Before I left college, I wanted to take that experience of smoking in public. For three months I was widely visible in the smoking bays and my purse was always loaded. I saw perceptions changing overnight. Some thought that I was too frustrated and needed friends to overcome a *difficult situation*! Some felt that I have been spoilt rotten by bad company and started avoiding me. Many thought I was available and wouldn't mind if they made some advances. And many tried to shower me with advices because they felt it's their moral responsibility to talk me out of the habit. The smokers felt they had got a new addition to their group. Non-smokers regretted that they have lost a *good girl from a good family*! Frankly, I never liked the taste of cigarette. It spoilt a lot inside the mouth with a weird smell. But I liked the show of holding and puffing it in the open. I was into it because of the effect; not the experience. After three months of public speculation, one fine day I just kicked the habit without any announcement. The paan-wala outside the campus would call out asking why I was not buying them from him any longer. I would say, I still have them in my bag. To the *friends* who missed my company over smoke, I would simply say next time. I didn't avoid anyone; I had just given up a habit which was not meant to be mine. But off and on, at times, I feel like taking in that silly poisonous air along with its awkward smell. Today, the temptation coincidentally clashed with the puritan sculptor.

Dr Aniruddh doesn't know much about me. He lives lost in his world of art. Whatever he says usually stems from his work and goes back to it at the end. Only once in all these months did I find him being a different person, doing and saying things that he usually doesn't. The day he returned from Delhi, he brought with himself an uninhibited existence. It was 8:00 in the evening and I received a text, 'open the door.' He was standing right there, in blue jeans and a red check-shirt wearing an infectious smile, with vermillion and sandalwood paste shining on his forehead. Before I could ask anything, he almost pushed me aside, entered uninvited and closed the door behind him. It seemed as if he had suddenly lost his balance or had achieved something that had taken away a large part of his senses making him act so strangely and out of character. Ah that day …

I stood puzzled while he sat down on the ground or rather plonked himself on the floor, his arm resting on a chair close by. I stared at him for a while and went inside to fetch water. When I was back, he was seated in the same position, idly pulling the strings of my tanpura standing to his left. 'It doesn't respond properly to unqualified hands,' I said hiding a smile. He turned to look at me and did the unthinkable. Leaning forward, he reached out to me, held my wrist tight with a strong grip and pulled me forward. Next I realised I am sitting on the chair where the sculptor had rested his arm a while go. My pulse was racing and I was almost gasping for breath. His hand was still holding mine and he sat on the floor looking up at me, his face too close to my knees. The touch was electrifying. I was swamped by his smell and closeness, those large eyes covered by rimless glasses, some gray hairs peeking out of the black, the shirt sufficiently unbuttoned to expose a bare chest, a gold chain across his neck and the diamond stud in his left ear. His polite but firm hold almost ripped me apart. I felt, it's his mercy that my physicality hasn't been explored for so long. If he claimed me right there, I would probably give in without a second thought. I looked at him with all the urges of the soul gathered in my eyes. Dr Aniruddh was oblivious to my longings. In a while, I understood that there's something else. Slowly I suppressed the madness and took my hand off his with tremendous effort of will.

'Are you all right?' I managed to say.

'I went home.' He responded softly.

My immediate reaction was, 'So?' But I curbed that and asked instead, 'You have a home too? You never spoke about it!'

'I thought I had lost it, lost everything to my career. But they did not abandon me for life.'

I sank in sadness as I gathered that the stimulant of the sculptor's behaviour that evening was not me. It actually had nothing to do with me. He wanted to share something. He elaborated on his visit to Delhi and subsequently to Jaipur. His past and present came up all jumbled together as he narrated incidents in explicit detail, not bothering to plan a format which clarifies what happened after what. He was in haste to speak, to say it all; and unfold everything at one go. Seldom had I seen him so excited. I watched the innocently happy face as it had huge details to offer that night, and decided to arrange his stories chronologically in my mind to get the picture accurate. Sentimentally he considered me to be the driving force that steered his sudden visit to Jaipur. He put down on my table some homemade delicacies which his family had packed for him. And he also kept beside it a fancy *batua* bag, with purple and red sequins weaved on gold silk. I picked up the bag and opened it, as he watched. Twin puppets of a king and queen, expertly done up in bright colours sat inside elegantly. I placed the puppets in front of the *tanpura*; they added a spark to that corner with their beautiful finish and shine of the zari. He mentioned that it has been prepared by his sister-in-law, who is apparently an expert at it. She runs an NGO, who prepares home décor items including such dolls, he said. The NGO called Bhoomi started with a group of seven women from backward classes of Jalore, near Jaipur, who originally knew the art. They live in Lakhiya village in Nagaur, which is about three hours drive from Jaipur. Now the number of participants has grown to sixty-seven women who are involved in knitting, stitching and hand-weaving bed covers and home decors and shawls and saris. During her initial days in journalism when she travelled in remote areas of the state looking for socially relevant stories, she had come across the plights of women in backward areas and had promised herself to come back when she would gain successfully her own independent social status. This NGO also produced the colourful Rajasthani dolls, which happened to be one of Diya's favourite hobbies when she was a kid. Under her strict vigil, Bhoomi today was a self sufficient institution that gave its women a reason to live, leaving behind the evils that plagued their lives and come together for each other in times of need. Pride and admiration lit up the sculptor's eyes as he spoke.

'So, did you pay for the dolls?' I asked.

'No,' he replied, 'she had made these herself.'

Dr Aniruddh and I splurged on the spicy Rajasthani food he had carried back. He showed me in his camera, the photographs of a lavish Rajput wedding and the rituals that go with it, a castle which he called home, an empire of flowers that is just the 'garden in front' and the clay sculptures that are restored in a glass house near a pool at the back. Men in their family are blessed with a good physical build and a complexion that can put many pretty damsels to shame. And women are soaked in sophistication with exquisite jewellery and elaborately embroidered outfits draping them. Abhimanyu and Diya look beautiful and happy being a part of the marriage they planned in style and class at one of the best heritage properties of the city. Earlier, the sculptor added, marriages were arranged in the haveli itself; now they avoid it because of the chaos it creates in the insides of the house that are ideally meant to be protected from outsiders. Responsibility of scheduling, planning and executing the marriage is with the core members of the family; others assist and follow instructions. I laugh at the use of the word haveli; he frowns and mentions that this is just local dialect for ancestral property and not a means of flaunting inherited riches.

We discussed about what happened in our lives in the past few days undeterred by time that flows with us, till the huge watch at Gour Prangan struck two with the distinct melody of its bells resounding in the calm of the night. We were sure to be in the thick of a scandal if seen together at that hour. For the first time, Dr Aniruddh seemed concerned. Stealthily he escaped as both of us smiled at the hiding game and once again, I was left alone to battle an unfulfilled desire which the sculptor is totally unaware of.

Why does this man do it? He sure stands apart in behaviour and gesture, and in his impolite intrusion into my life, which shockingly I have started waiting for of late. He claims I bring creative thoughts in his mind, but does he know how he takes with him a part of my emotions every time he appears! Despite his self-proclaimed *conservative* mind and upbringing, he shatters every definition of being a typical Indian male and increasingly I am falling prey to the futile attraction for a person who would probably never be mine!

A spell spent in shines, sultry glamour and wines
And music of thousand souls
To cheer ceremonial pride!
Lurked in the pleasure lies
The vision that blinds, a black that unwinds
A tale to confide
The warring bride!
Dark in her restrained robe,
Withdrawn in design, and sensuous resign
Declines to probe
The pre-destined disunion!
In dusky gloom bizarre
She inhales to death, lucent radiance afar!
Professed silence
Battles in alliance
The smoke that intrudes her sober.
Only …
On nights that rain, that drool, that sprain
Flashing ablaze the eastern sky
She tells her pain. "We'll meet again
Once, of course, before I die.
My most fidel desire to lie
Unused! And you your wrath explain."

When we return to Anusua's living room, Stuart and Dr Bhowmik have started their political debate or should we term it war. Voices are rising as much as their temper, because none of them bother to listen and accommodate the logic of the opponent. They have much to say in favour of their own Leftist and anti-Leftist philosophies and both seem to be driven by the sole purpose of out-shouting each other. Zakir Hussain's tabla that plays in the background is aptly complementing their *jugalbandi*! Hussain gathers momentum with the magic of his hands; the gentlemen inside convert his efforts to black magic emitting smoke and heat all through! Anusua tries hard to control Stuart and support her HOD. Shayan is looking away, it's difficult to say whether he is awake or asleep. Dr Aniruddh is engrossed in some art book he has found on the book shelf. Sia and I conceal a laughter and sit quietly in a corner. Only dinner can put the quarrelling parties to rest. We proceed soon after to ensure that.

I am left alone with the sculptor while returning home. I know he is disturbed by the scene of me smoking. He is quiet. I start the conversation. 'Can you just put aside your conservative system for a while and look at more simple versions of things?'

'Don't use philosophy to explain away a bad habit, Sanghamitra.'

'I am not philosophising dude,' the casual *dude* slips out in the heat of the moment. 'If I have to smoke, I *will* do it; with or without approval. The point is I don't and that's a conscious choice. But what's the harm if I feel like trying it once in a while? Why are you so closed to life?'

He looks hurt. 'Maybe I am closed, but I am comfortable that way. There are certain things that are misfits. Nature has its own way of defining the beauty of things. It has made a man physically strong and he defines himself best when he protects. Similarly a woman cares and nurtures, and nothing portrays femininity better than her tenderness. I don't mean that women should not progress. But in the process of progression, it is not necessary that they give up the beauty and purpose of their being. If I have to put it rather simply, the cigarette doesn't look good in a woman's hand. It might make her look glamorous or sophisticated, but not pretty for sure. It takes the tenderness away and makes her look devilishly intimidating.'

I am a bit amused with this preachy lecture. Can't he just let go of everything and reside in the moment? Why is he bound to a format every time? 'You take yourself a bit too seriously, Sculptor. Let go, at times. Have you ever done something that you never thought you'll do? Have you broken rules for once to see what lies on the other side of the forbidden line? Liberate yourself from your restrictions, Dr Aniruddh, otherwise your prohibition is not honest enough.'

'To what extent are you willing to trade your line of forbiddance?' He sounds serious.

I can see that he's about to lose the argument. 'Just as long as I can justify my actions to myself. I won't commit a crime to find out what's in there. But I might take a smoke and say, I'm right I don't like it.'

He walks silently without an answer. I chuckle. 'Accepted defeat?'

He smiles too. 'Just exited the argument. If I were to be like you, probably I would lose my focus. I can't bathe without getting wet.'

I can't quite enjoy our silly fight with words because of the seriousness he has attached to it. 'You are absolutely fine as whatever you are, Sculptor. I was just trying to bully you, not convince you to behave like me. Formats disturb me in a strange way. I just can't fit into a routine. At regular intervals I need a change, a diversion, a variety. I don't even repeat my lectures. Every term I offer the same chapter from a fresh perspective. These help me to explore myself in multiple dimensions, understand my shortcomings and strengths, and I can work on improving them if I wish to. I understand you follow different ideals, which I appreciate and respect, but might not choose to follow.'

'I love my routine, Sanghamitra, and I am addicted to deadlines. I can't work with flexible time limits unless I tame them with a date of conclusion. I would like to believe that I know myself quite well to define what I am getting into, why and till when I would remain into it. Things are usually pre-planned and I don't accommodate diversions. It helps me to structure my existence.'

'Talking about deadlines, Sculptor,' I can't help giggling, 'try missing it once, for my sake! And once you miss it, no one can take anything from you; neither can you have anything to give!'

The serious face erupts into laughter, but sobers at my next statement.

'I spoke to Diya, your sister-in-law.'

He almost chokes and looks disbelievingly at me. 'How did you get to know her?'

I hand him a card I later discovered inside the *batua* bag that Dr Aniruddh had given me. It read, 'To Bhai sa and Mitra ... with love, Abhimanyu & Diya.' Their phone numbers were given below. 'I had sent her a text thanking her for the dolls. She called me back. Why did you tell her my name is Mitra?'

I thoroughly enjoy as the sculptor's face reddens in embarrassment. 'Your name is too complicated for our tongue. Please don't pick up an argument on this. Just accept that it actually is. What did she say?'

'General things. Why do you want to know?'

'Well, I don't want to know. I was just curious.'

I don't wish to tell him that my conversation with Diya was more than mere thanks. She insisted that I can treat the dolls as *shagun* from her and Abhimanyu! 'What *shagun*?' I had asked. She had said, 'In this family, men don't mention women so effortlessly unless they are bound by a special attachment!' My heart had skipped a beat at the mere anticipation of such a possibility. To her I had firmly pronounced that those words embarrass me to a great extent and that her 'Bhai-sa' was just reacting to my childish demand and certainly not to the demands of his heart. Diya responded with a monologue. 'Abhimanyu and I grew fond of each other since school. All our lives we had prepared ourselves to be with each other. Neither of us has ever been with anyone else, not even in fun or as a joke. Yet, it was I who had to take the initiative and reach out to Bhai-sa for help. Abhi never was the first one to speak out. The decision of living-in was mine and I proposed marriage. Men of this house are either too shy or too proud to declare their vulnerability to women! Bhai-sa would be no different.' I don't tell her that if such is the case, then I would prefer to withdraw. In my personal battle between love and pride, the latter wins hands down and I would never take any initiative. Moreover, I don't have an agenda, like Diya had. I do feel a strong attraction for the sculptor and something draws me hopelessly towards him. I do wait for his attention and can't deny that he reciprocates the interest by making himself available. But that is probably because he doesn't have a friend here. I'm not even sure though whether he considers me a friend. But he shares with me a lot of details, which I know for sure, are not for everyone. Equally true is the fact that I have not seen in his eyes the happiness that connects two souls. I have often felt that the sculptor comes to me for a purpose. I'm not sure what that is but the day that purpose fails or is important no more, I'll be out of his realm. My presence in his world is not so indispensable that it can't be substituted; not yet. And no, I will not make that extra effort to earn permanence within the scheme of his designs. I can just stop my journey for a while. If he cares to notice, fine. Otherwise he might as well pass by!

To Diya, I had just said that two people come together when they share a common interest. Unfortunately we don't have any! After greeting and congratulating them once again, I had hung up.

Few more minutes of silence. We walk through the rustic path to reach the main road.

'This year they are predicting rains early; it's going to be a moist summer. Would you be here during the holidays?' He finally asks.

'For the first fourteen days, yes. Then I am off to Manali. You?'

'I haven't yet decided. How long would you be there?'

'The entire vacation. An ex-student owns a furnished house there which I rent in during these months. One day I'll have a house in the Himalayas all for myself.'

'You mean you will live in Manali for a month and a half all by yourself?' Dr Aniruddh stops walking and looks at me.

'My mother would join me for some time in between. But why does it sound so strange? I do this every year.'

What he says next stumps me. 'Don't you ever feel the need of a companion?'

'No.'

'Why?'

'Some things don't have an answer. The way I live, is the life of my choice.'

'But how can you say that when you haven't crossed the forbidden line and experienced it?' He is smiling down at me.

'I did experience it Dr Aniruddh.'

He turns to look at me. I'm not sure whether he was thinking all this while that I have led a life of celibacy. 'You did?' he asks. 'What happened then?'

'No relation terminates in happiness, neither did mine. Can we call it a day?' We are standing in front of my house. I don't want to talk much on this. Dr Aniruddh takes a few steps ahead, then turns. 'Sure, but not before I say one last thing. That means this certainly is not the life of your choice. When something you wanted did not work out, you opted for the next available deal. Your life is but an alternate second-best!' He walks away without waiting for an answer.

Moist Summers

Dr Aniruddh Jain Solanki
Santiniketan

When I left Jaipur, Deivi-ma had taken me aside and asked me to find a bride. Or, she said, if I agree she would take on the responsibility of finding one. I had assured her that I'll let her know. Honestly, I don't know how it is to be with a woman. I have interacted with a lot of them at different levels and my subject of art usually centres around them. Rarely at times, I have flirted around without meaning anything. Yet, I have seldom been close to them. My exchanges with women usually follow a customised pattern, where conversations or meetings are neither too deep nor are they meaningful with anything beyond an agenda. Colleagues in the West have tried to explain my philosophy as 'practising celibacy' and have asked me several times whether I am associated with the Indian tantra yoga or other such faiths that they have half-knowledge of. There had been only two exceptions to my pattern.

I had a pen-friend. She was like a poisoned secret, yet holy, soaked in truth to the best of my existence. For months we had shared long notes on our lives and thoughts and passions and wishes. In all those months, we lived each other every moment of our existence. We loved sharing details about ourselves and our world with a strange connection that's beyond explanation. Those days I was battling multiple losses, a challenging work schedule and financial constraints. Life seemed difficult with every passing day and at times I wondered whether I did it right by choosing to follow my passion! But, it was a choice of no return. I had left too much behind to go back as a failure. As much as destiny subjected me to hardships, I reverted with a cold withdrawal, from everyone or everything around me. Evenings and nights, I earned to make a living. Mornings I worked on my course. Shivangi's letters were a pleasant break from this routine. The best thing about interacting with her was that she did not have a tangible existence in my world. I didn't know her face or body. She was only available in those neatly written words she used to express herself. I was primarily drawn to the beautiful, artistic handwriting that spread itself on plain white papers. Words were distinct and flawless, hardly any overwriting and definitely without even one word being struck out to correct a language or spelling error.

Since we had not seen each other, it was easy for us to write on things that we would ideally avoid mentioning otherwise, lest people judge us unfavourably. However, more than the frankness and absolute transparency of our lives, we did share an acute romantic instinct. None of us were loud on that; yet we experienced unexplained possessiveness and affection for each other. She portrayed the mixed emotions of a sister, friend and wife while attending to me and had made me feel emotionally secure when I needed it most.

Then one day she suddenly stopped writing. I never asked why! Reaching out to present my vulnerable self was not one of my core competencies, I was too proud for that. Going silent was her choice. I respected both her choice and the silence. Communication stopped, but I was still not done. I am not sure what pained me more … was it the sudden absence? Or was it an unwanted restriction to the flood of emotions that had started flowing out of me? Was it she who fascinated me more as a well known stranger, or was it I, who turned into a stranger while communicating with her? I depended a lot on her letters to make me feel that I have a place for myself that nurtures and cares for me. Hence, when she stopped writing, I felt violated and cheated. But I didn't pursue with her. My pride and ego came in between and the humiliation of rejection swept through my being.

Everything in life happens for a reason. I tried to find reason behind this brief pre-destined interaction. And eventually found one. Some force was urging me to carry on. It had got me started on talking about myself and in the process, revealing things that surprised me. With the pen in my hand and my senses exploring myself and nothing else, I realised that I had so much stored inside a mind, most of which I didn't know existed. An introvert in public or group interactions, I was not known to be an elaborate communicator. But often there remained an unspoken background and aftermath to the bare minimum that I spoke. My own stories started unwinding in my writing pad. Some force was telling me that I did not need a trigger anymore; I just needed to liberate myself from being coaxed to talk and feel free in the vast space that was left vacant for me. It's strange that time, which belongs to or waits for none, redefines priorities and cures bruises, pushing into irrelevance all pains that at some point of time had seemed irreparable. But I learnt to communicate and found language within myself to prepare my journey for a bigger world, where I needed to be known, heard and talked about to gain recognition. I had to create reasons and prompt clues for people to acknowledge my presence. Whatever I was writing about myself, helped me understand my sensibilities better, which in turn helped in articulating my vision, as I approached to conquer the world of art!

There's another name that disturbs my peace whenever I think of it. I was introduced to Crisanta Dwarf in a party we both attended in London. My participation in the occasion was strictly professional and I hardly had anything to do with her. When introduced, I exchanged pleasantries and moved on. When I was leaving, my car developed some trouble and I had to make alternate arrangements. Crisanta offered to drop me which I politely refused saying that the organisers would take care of it. The lady however insisted that I accept her invitation and managed to convince me. Since then, for the next few months, my life felt haunted. I had not watched much of her films and she was definitely not a budding actress. She was not one on the A-list either. Her presence in Page-3 was for all the wrong reasons. She saw my lack of interest as an insult and made my life miserable. While her inflated ego wanted to command my devotion, the Irish tabloids were feasting over headlines like, 'Crisanta Dwarf has a new man, a fresh Indian sculptor!' Those days I was recognised but not yet famous. As much as I wanted to get rid of Crisanta, she approached her task with a vengeance and let out spicy interviews regarding my involvement with her. The tabloids reached my door to verify and demanded quotes. When I could not persuade them or Crisanta to leave me alone, I decided to use this opportunity in a different way. I ended up saying that I am working on Crisanta as my subject and I have a project in mind. The tabloids started talking about the actor's body and face that would be captured in my work and their aesthetic value and to what extent would I exploit my 'personal relation' with her for professional gains! I answered them all with patience and strategic non-commitment towards pronouncing my plans in advance. Three things emerged out of this. One, while giving the tabloids their share of spice from my end, I made some friends who understood the truth about my peace being ruined by the actor; they offered to help. Two, I was suddenly a Page-3 celebrity. Three, slowly, owing to the sudden popularity, my industry had started taking note of my work more seriously because popularity sells better than talent and hard work. Crisanta's madness thus became a blessing in disguise. In two months time, an extremely ambitious solo exhibition was held in Athens and it registered 100 per cent success. All my work was sold off at unbelievable prices! People came to visit the gallery out of curiosity to investigate and gossip on the work of

'Crisanta Dwarf's boyfriend,' but went back impressed. Critics shared extremely positive reviews and word-of-mouth spread. Soon, a large number of art lovers were visiting my work and sharing impressive feedback. Some renowned galleries from other cities wanted to sign me on for my own merits and not because of a false relationship status. By the time Crisanta realised what had happened, it was too late. She tried to give out enraged statements on how I had been 'using' her to promote and elevate my career. I called a press conference and declared that I have always resisted from being called 'her boyfriend' because I was not; I had said that she was just the subject of my upcoming sculpture and she was nothing more than that; I validated all these with proofs from my statements in old news reports. The friends that I had made in the media kept their promise; they jumped to action with fiery articles revealing and justifying the truth behind my words. One of these articles even dared Crisanta to file a defamation case against me if she believed her claims to carry even an ounce of truth in them. Silently, Crisanta stepped back.

Howmuchsoever weird it might sound, I have actually never got involved in a romantic relationship. Having been abandoned by my family, I was too scared of relationships as a rule. Moreover, I don't have the temperament or energy to invest time and mind into it. If something has to happen, it will without my effort or intervention. Usually all through the day, my body and mind are brutally active in work, leaving no space for idle thoughts on what lacks in my life. On tired nights, at times, I do wish to feel nursed, sheltered and loved. Male longings do come to me complaining undeserved deprivation. I have explained to myself that this deprivation might also be a part of the package that I had wilfully disowned to achieve whatever I have achieved in the last decade. Though my body reacts to this non-availability, I haven't ever felt any self-destructive desperation. Rather, I am quite controlled in my behaviour towards women and never looked at their body driven by carnal desires. In my heart I know that if my body ever touches another then it will be only because the minds have already met. Unless there is a soulful union, my urges would never be satisfied with an incomplete physical intimacy. At thirty-seven, I feel young and vital, but I don't expect romantic miracles. Deivi-ma had warned me that when I grow older and work pressure slows down with diminishing physical firmness, I would realise that staying alone had not been a good idea. I had listened to her silently, but I am not ready to trade my body and mind in isolation. She wouldn't understand my logic. When the body and mind are not together, there are chances of them going in different directions. If my body is married off and mind stays disconnected, it will try to find its match somewhere outside the marriage. Hence, either both go together to the same person, or neither does.

It is almost 1:00 am and I get out of bed. These thoughts had not allowed me to sleep. I open the door and come to the staircase to breathe in fresh air. May is hot and humid here. Everyone around is praying for the rains to come soon and quell the heat. Few steps away, lights are on from inside closed curtains. She usually doesn't stay awake till this late! I pick up my phone to text her whether everything is fine; but decide against it the next moment. My diagrams are still incomplete and it frustrates me to death. I just don't get it right. There is massive work to be done on this and I have already informed some media people on my upcoming project. They are waiting for its completion to cover the story and declare exhibition dates. Limestone has already been ordered; it'll reach me any day now. The vendor is an old acquaintance and has been supplying it for years. Yet, I personally check on the texture of the stone every time it is delivered. I sit on my table once again trying to visualise a shape and form for my Kalindi.

Next morning I arrive at the department around 9:00 am. It is vacant and there is no one except the HOD. I exchange pleasantries and get along with my work. Considerable time needs to be spent in the library and some Internet job. Signals through my data card were bad this morning;

so I have to considerably rely on institute resources. I am deep in my research when Sagnik comes to say 'Bye.' He's going home to Kolkata for his vacations. I come out with him for a chat and discuss general work. Just before leaving he informs me, 'Today is Prof. Sanghamitra's birthday, maybe you should wish her!' For a moment I am taken aback. She never told me! But then I calm myself. Sanghamitra won't say unless asked. I ask Sagnik the source of his information. He says, last year he bribed the authorities and secretly dug out the professor's information register! This boy has got some guts! I just ask, 'Have you wished her?' 'No,' he says, 'she won't appreciate it. I just left an anonymous gift on her doorstep. Some Jasmine flowers I had collected early this morning. Those are her favourites but I know she won't accept them. They'll lie at her door till the wind blows them apart.' He smiles and departs.

I put in a few more hours of work. At 3:00 when I am almost done, it's dark. Even a while ago the atmosphere was calm and composed. Not a single leaf stirred. Not even a bird chirped. Nature was gloomy suffering the horrible summer sun at its peak. Sudden resounding clap of thunder and a violent gust of wind interrupt my concentration. A flash of lightning dazzles through my eyes. The sky is overcast accompanied by strong winds forecasting a storm. Soon a dusty squall followed by spells of thunderstorm and heavy rains lash around, bringing huge relief from the humid heat. The balcony door bangs open and my room is filled with a cloud of dust. Beautiful smell of the rains emerging from rain-bathed moist soil takes over. Trees sway violently against each other, welcoming pleasantly the change of temperature. There are sounds of undisciplined windows and doors opening and shutting in glee. Some cycles parked afar have fallen down and papers inside the room are flying helter-skelter. The paper weight falls from my table and the room is instantly messed up. But I don't wish to give up the pleasure of experiencing this moment in rearranging the room and making amends. I recall, this is the *kalboishakhi* I have heard so much about from the locals. I wait by the window expecting the natural elements to make peace. The storm ends in a while, but not the rains. They erupt every now and then. Quickly at an opportune moment I start my bike and whiz through to park it at Mridangam. I run upstairs to drop my stuff and come out once again to take a walk down the backside country road, developed naturally by people frequently walking over the soft grass. A few steps through this barren, undeveloped path leads to a vast Sal forest. This area is usually less visited, unless love-struck and physically starved couples find no other place to go. At this hour though, it is empty. Heavens has let loose its blessings and the earth seems to be more thirsty than what the downpour has to offer. Visibility is less because of the showers and also because I have left my glasses at home. My clothes, heavy and wet, are hugging my body as the rain washes my insides as much as it affects my exteriors. There's a refreshing joy in my spirits as I take slow steps forward, allowing the showers to pour on me their best benevolence. In between such ecstasy I am shocked numb by what I see a small distance away. With less control over my actions and emotions, I hastily move behind a sal and watch her. Sanghamitra it is, walking away in the rains a few steps ahead. Her yellow dress clung on to her, made transparent by water, suggesting explicitly the curves of her body. It is difficult for a man to look away from this woman, beautifully and enigmatically mysterious in the way she carries herself. Wet hair is scattered all over her and a loose *dupatta* touches the ground as much as it touches her. She is walking ahead unaware of my presence or any presence around. I walk a few steps behind her, fully conscious that I am caught in an undignified act. But she has taken my resistance with her. She is feeling cold perhaps, because she clutches on to her body with both hands and rubs her palms on her elbows. The head is held upwards, as she stops for a while, allowing the downpour to wash away whatever she is offering to the rain gods. Should I make my presence felt? Yes, my moral brain says, and lead her back to her house; it might not be too safe for her to continue being here like this. What

I see would be seen by many others and not all would be sophisticated enough to maintain the distance. But I can't gather the force to reach out to her. I remember Sagnik's words; can't blame him for being mesmerised by this woman. Sanghamitra looks elegance personified even in this state of detachment. I survey the area around. There is no one visible and she is standing still now; not moving any further. After a while she turns. I assume that she is returning back. Stealthily I escape in hiding so that she doesn't know that I had been watching her. I run though the slippery roads and stop right in front of her house, gasping. I decide to wait for her at her doorstep. As I approach her veranda, I am in for a shock again. Her door is open, the curtain flings in and out with the breeze. A few white and beautifully fragranced jasmines lie scattered near the door. Are these the flowers that Sagnik had been talking about? I look inside hesitantly and find on the floor an open envelope with lots of folded papers, torn and yellow with time. One of the papers that is stuck on the inside of the door reads, 'I am the melody that rises from a thousand songs. I am the unacquainted breeze that walks through your hair. I am the Nature who smiles at you in passing leaving you happier than you were a while ago. I am the sun who touches you first, every morning. I am the strings of veena that wakes alive to your attention. I live in your being; I travel in real and in fantasies, guarding you, holding you, possessing you ...' The handwriting is definitely not hers!

I have probably crossed all limits of decency to the extent of criminal imprudence. I come out of the door and lock it from outside; without waiting for Sanghamitra I leave for my room. I am restless with too much information, none of which are compartmentalised and they are all approaching me simultaneously making it difficult to prioritise and comprehend. As much as I detest my action, the immediate thought that comes to my mind is that this woman has had an impactful past from which she hasn't broken free yet. Last night, I presume, she was up till late reading those papers that peeked out of the envelope. In all probability, they were letters from some romantic interest of her past. I brush off the thought and pull myself together to go in for a shower. As I come back to my room, the rains have stopped. I look across the lane and find the lights on. She has returned home. Today I no longer possess the strength to walk up to her and wish her a happy birthday.

I walk towards my table and open my sketch book. I remember a particular length of conversation we had some time back. In my quest to understand the woman better, I had asked, 'What are you like, Sanghamitra?' She had shrugged and smiled. 'I don't know … not bad I guess!' Not ready to give up, I had probed further. 'What are those things that you are especially fond of in your life?' Looking away she had mentioned, 'Everything beautiful and natural. I find myself in them. Beautiful places, beautiful music, beautiful art, beautiful books, beautiful people, beautiful faces, beautiful habits, conversations, language, expressions, even clothes, jewellery, bags, shoes…! I have a sophisticated and a cheap list of all beautiful things I adore. Which one do you wish to hear?' She chuckled and continued in soft melancholy, 'And everything ugly distresses me. Narrow-mindedness, rude behaviour, loudness, noise, nastiness, jealousy, foul language, all these threaten me as much as they threaten the beauty I so much appreciate.' Eyes closed, a visual appears to me. Raindrops trickling down Sanghamitra's face, neck and body; her face is bent backwards to give space for the water to spread. And the faint knowledge of a past that enslaves her, haunts me! No other image of any earthly being has ever perched on my memory as this woman's, wet in all her sensibilities. The image leads my imagination to the one I wish to sculpt on limestone. With fast, steady hands I prepare the diagram and put approximate measurements at relevant places. My Kalindi, a form of water herself, will appear as the legitimate companion, complementing the rain gods; aggressive torrential downpour makes her boundaries overflow and she dances in fury awaiting the attention of her beloved, Krishna. She will eventually have to return to her calmness just as Sanghamitra still returns to the curse of her past!

Manali

Sanghamitra Banerjee
Katrain

From Santiniketan I had travelled to Howrah, and boarded the Rajdhani Express around 5:00 in the evening. There is a spectacular charm about travelling by trains. I love the sound and rhythm of the journey, and those unhealthily prepared beverages and snacks that are available in important stations. I don't have to bother about food and drinks though; they're being served from time to time by the Rajdhani personnel. Approximately seventeen hours, and I am welcomed by the dry heat and hustle of New Delhi. For two days I am stationed here in Kalkaji with a school friend. We sleep to beat the heat during the afternoons and hop around Sarojini Nagar, Karol Bagh and Dilli Haat in the evenings, shopping for things that we don't require. The day next, I take a bus to Manali.

Since I come here every year, I know quite a bit of this place. My accommodation is in a two room house in Katrain. Caretaker Dhonai and an old cook whom I call Thapi Aunty because of her Nepali origin welcome me with a big, happy smile. They share their social and family issues with me and know that I have carried for them and their families, gifts from the 'town downhill.' Tea, as per my taste, is waiting in a flask on the table. I rush to wash and come back in loose, casual clothes to sit in comfort. This time of the year is not too cold at noon; I discard the shawl and sit outside with my tea and a few cookies. Driver Narayan Singh pays a customary visit to let me know that he with his ambassador is there at my service. This area is located few miles away from the main town, though all facilities are just a kilometre away. Outside the main gate, the road goes down to meet plush apple and pomegranate orchards. On the terrace, there's a music room to die for. It has tabla, violin, tanpura, sitar, drums and a sarod. Owners of this property worship these instruments as their ancestral magnificence. Regularly they are cleaned and tuned up. I am free to use this room as long as I am here. Since it is located on the terrace, it is practically disconnected from the rest of the house and I can exercise my vocal chords for as long as I wish to. Considerable hours of my days are spent here. These are lazy days for me when I read in the early mornings and evenings and go for long walks or sit by the Beas till there is daylight; otherwise I practically have nothing to do. My mother will come to join me sometime soon.

Almost ten days after I have reached here, I get a mail from Dr Aniruddh. After the first few sentences enquiring about my health and safety, he writes he has a confession to make! And he adds,

> ''Twas mist and rain, and storm and rain:
> No screen, no fence could I discover;
> And then the wind! In sooth, it was
> A wind full ten times over.
> I looked around, I thought I saw
> A jutting crag,—and off I ran,
> Head-foremost, through the driving rain,
> The shelter of the crag to gain;
> And, as I am a man,
> Instead of jutting crag, I found
> A Woman seated on the ground.'

This morning I have come to the Naggar castle with a book in hand. Built by the Sikh rajas of Kullu in the fifteenth century, this beautiful fort has been built alternating stone and timber style of Himachali architecture. It is a heritage hotel now with a one-room museum downstairs, and the Jagtipath Temple in the courtyard that houses a slab of stone which is said to have been carried here by wild bees. The manager, Mr Goel, comes to greet me and enquires about my well-being. He also asks about my mother. His family, especially his wife, is extremely fond of the Bengali food the old lady prepares. Ma has the urge to visit all the temples every time she comes here. There are a lot of hot water springs around this region. Last year his family had joined us on the way to Manikaran. The Manikaran Temple and Gurdwara is a pilgrimage centre for Hindus and Sikhs. The Hindus believe that Manu recreated human life in Manikaran after the deluge, making it a sacred area. Shiva, Rama, Krishna and Vishnu are worshipped here. Legend goes that when lord Shiva and his consort, Parvati were walking in the valley, Parvati dropped one of her earrings. The jewel was seized by Shesha, the serpent deity, who then disappeared into the earth with it. Shesha only surrendered the jewel when Shiva performed his cosmic dance, the Tandava, and shot the jewel up through the water. Apparently, jewels continued to be thrown up in the waters at Manikaran until the earthquake of 1905. The area is well known for its hot springs that can cook rice and potatoes. Vegetables boiled thus are used in langars of the Gurudwara. They say, to pacify Lord Shiva Sheshnag hissed thereby giving rise to a flow of boiling water. Science attributes the emergence of geo-thermally heated groundwater to natural presence of sulphur in the earth's crust. The Manikaran temple has a huge statue of Shiva in wrath, carved on black rock. Mr Goel suggests that this year we can repeat the visit. Also, a fair is supposed to be held in the monastery and his family could help us avail things at cheaper prices. He orders tea to be served, the first cup is complimentary. I move upstairs of the Naggar castle and sit at an isolated corner of the balcony.

Vaguely I turn the pages of Chitra Divakaruni's *Palace of Illusions*, but can't concentrate.

The sculptor's reference to Wordsworth, I am afraid, doesn't quite clearly disclose what he wants to confess. But it does send a shiver down my spine. Does it allude to my rendezvous with the first rains of the season? The evening before, Stuart and Anusua had come home to celebrate my birthday. Both of them were to leave Santiniketan early next morning. Anusua had prepared *payesh*, a traditional Bengali sweet dish which is being increasingly replaced by lavish cakes on birth anniversaries. Stuart offered to prepare chicken-rice and that was all about our small celebration. No extravagant gifts, no additional nonsense. After they left, the rooms smelt of cooking and chaos. I decided to start my cleaning operation at 11:00 in the night. After the floor, bed and sofa were done up, I was still not tired. I pulled open the drawers and storage spaces to trash out all unnecessary papers and stuff that I would not require any longer.

From one of the chests, unwittingly I pulled out that large envelope which carried Shekhar's paintings, letters, notes and a few photographs that I still have with me. Instantly overtaken by memories, I travelled back in time. I wished I hadn't gone home that summer. I wished he hadn't left for Delhi. Sleep eluded me for the rest of the night and I sat on the ground taking myself through all those neatly folded pages that have started turning yellow with edges tearing out. Even as I navigated through them, I realised I still remember every word that followed along with the punctuation; I could sleep-talk the content of his paintings. Caught up in a numb wistfulness, I sat on the ground motionless and speechless, a heavy head rested on the bed at the back; did not feel like getting up even when the eastern sky had started changing colours. My mouth felt dry as sand and I didn't get up to prepare tea. The tanpura remained unused that morning. I could sense those stealthy footsteps walk up my stairs, wait for a while and leave subsequently. Sagnik! Since last year we're playing this unspoken game. He leaves those beautifully fragranced jasmines at my doorstep with full knowledge that I won't acknowledge or accept them. After he left, I switched off the light and pulled myself up on the bed along with the envelope. Lazily I buried myself in the pillow, unwilling to welcome the morning. Time passed in its own pace, disregarding the fact that I was not bound by a schedule. I stared at a bit of the sky visible from half drawn curtains of the window. Once again I stood facing the fierce truth that I choose to ignore every time it raised its head. Shekhar sadly, hasn't remained the positive force with which he commanded my life once! His non-existence pulls me down and I face death in repeated succession every time I come across those evidences of his absence.

Around 3:00 pm, the grim of the weather made way for a pleasant breeze and the sun was guarded by black clouds. I got up from my bed and stepped out. I was aware of those symptoms; a storm was on its way. I sat leaning on the pillar of my veranda. Winds were stronger; curtains fluttered and doors and windows opened and shut vigorously. I heard utensils falling in the kitchen but didn't take precautionary measures. I felt a bit weak as I stared outside. The storm came bringing dust balls with it. Didn't matter to me that I had cleaned just the evening before. Let the fury take over and spoil whatever it can; I would rather start afresh with the leftovers. Soon the whirlwind started followed by torrential rains. Thunderous clouds declared war as houses in the neighbourhood played conch shells to please the gods. It was as dark as twilight and lights went off immediately. I didn't realise when I had started walking down the muddy, slippery path, towards the Sal forest. Heavy drops of water fell on me hurting the skin with their speed and rage. If only they could cast the cooling effect to soothe more than the moisture-starved soil and plantations that begged for relief. I could feel the cold of rains reaching my insides, unable to comfort what burnt there in permanence!

After I return from the Beas on a particularly cold evening, I write a note to my mother claiming to know her exact arrival plans and I write back to the sculptor nonchalantly that he can offer for my reading anything that he wishes to share, without formally naming it a 'confession!' My heart beats loud thinking what is waiting for me in his upcoming mail! Next morning, around 11:00, I am off to the Hidamba Temple. The temple is surrounded by a cedar forest at the foot of the Himalayas. The sanctuary is built over a huge rock jutting out of the ground, which was worshipped as an image of the deity. The structure was built in the sixteenth century. The most surprising feature of the temple is that inside the temple the imprint of the feet of the goddess is carved on a block of stone for worshippers. This area where the temple is located also represents the imprint of a giant foot spanning across the valley in the area near the temple. I love walking through the cedar trees and relishing the soft sun rays. Off and on, I open a book and read a few pages.

His response comes late in the night, 'I am guilty of encroaching a bit too much into your private space,' he writes. 'That afternoon you were not alone in the Sal forest. Three sublime beauties of Nature–the rains, the forest and a woman–had come together before me to experience and I just could not gather myself to disconnect away. I didn't mean to follow you; neither did I wish to put you to embarrassment by making my presence felt. But you were treading too daringly in an isolated area. As much as I was mesmerised by the majestic view, equally was I worried about your safety! Though it would be inappropriate for me to ask what celebration brought you so dangerously close to the divine, I couldn't help wonder about the adventure! When you finally turned, I moved away from there quietly. I thought I would wait on your veranda. I was surprised to see that the doors were open and things scattered. I had thus, more reason to believe that something was amiss and your eccentricity that afternoon was not impromptu. I peeped inside and found a paper stuck at the door, which disclosed lots more than what I aimed to know!'

I stop reading and close my eyes, as if to hide my face from the author of this mail. He has seen nevertheless, a little too much for any corrective measure that I can now undertake to undo it. I curse the foolish, whimsical actions that led to this mess. His last few words read, 'Even though these words might mean nothing to you, I extend my sincere apologies. Please trust that I am guilty of circumstantial forces more than imprudence by choice. My confession might embarrass or enrage you, but I was not at peace till I didn't mention that I sinfully bear the knowledge of something that was not meant to be mine. Whatever your reaction, Sanghamitra, please pour it back. Don't return silence in response to this mail.'

I take myself away from the laptop for a while. Not every expression can return in language, Sculptor! Few lines from Shelley that I had read during adolescence reappear in my thoughts.

'As in that trance of wondrous thought I lay
This was the tenure of my waking dream.
Methought I sat beside a public way
Thick strewn with summer dust, and a great stream
Of people there was hurrying to and fro
Numerous as gnats upon the evening gleam,
All hastening onward, yet none seemed to know
Whither he went, or whence he came, or why
He made one of the multitude, yet so
Was borne amid the crowd as through the sky
One of the million leaves of summer's bier.—
Old age and youth, manhood and infancy,
Mixed in one mighty torrent did appear,
Some flying from the thing they feared and some
Seeking the object of another's fear,
And others as with steps towards the tomb
Pored on the trodden worms that crawled beneath,

And others mournfully within the gloom
Of their own shadow walked, and called it death …
And some fled from it as it were a ghost,
Half fainting in the affliction of vain breath …'

Why did you have to witness this, Dr Aniruddh? But this is not the question I will put across to him in person. Rather, I pull the laptop and write back, 'What exactly draws your attention towards me, Sculptor? Why do you bother to know about me and let me know these details?' Response comes almost immediately. He's online.

'I am an orthodox Rajput who had returned after years abroad and met an open-minded professor living her life in liberation. Our isolated souls connected and collided in the land of art, music and poetry. You exposed me to a different perspective of living, loving, sharing and understanding, beyond what I have believed and followed over years. The dissimilar worlds threatened a budding friendship; yet nature conspired to bring us together. At a crossroad, I have an intense realisation–I love myself and completely approve of my personal practices; yet I can as well sense the beauty of being something that's not me! In you I have experienced philosophical and functional opposition that does not challenge, but co-exists to make the distinctions clear and visible. I am aware of my choices with deep knowledge of the alternatives I have discarded. I own myself and my life much more than what I did few days ago; and I owe this ownership to you!

'It would however be morally improper to not mention here, that you have been one of the subjects of my upcoming project. Before you spring to conclusions, let me assure you that I am not going to replicate your face or identity. I have just borrowed and interpreted from your existence, the image of a woman who hides her sensuousness with indifference!'

Note to My Mother

Dr Aniruddh Jain Solanki
Kolkata

Dear *Bhabhu*,

One of the early assignments that hired me as a creative consultant was for an ambitious architecture in Venice, being built by the family of an erstwhile Doge (a Venetian word for Duke) in memory of his half-Indian mother. The project was supposed to develop into a holy place for rich, cultural exchange, a Piccadilly of sorts, meant for enthusiasts to come together for art, literature, drama, music, dance and cinema. I, along with three other architects, was instructed to visualise this as an attraction for international performers and audience; simultaneously it was to refer to a strong Indo-Italian context in its design. The late lady inherited her tastes from a Hindu, Sanskrit-educated mother and an Italian father. Matrimony of the parents was not well accepted and was vehemently opposed by the family, who believed in keeping their pride and procreations within the royal community. After much turbulence, the marriage had taken place only after the father had declared, he will not marry anyone but her! The new wife was christened to Italian culture under strict vigilance so that she didn't mess up with the sophistication of royal decorum. Soon after, a daughter was born to the couple. Captivated by her prejudiced in-laws, the mother created for her daughter a world of Indian finesse inside the ancestral palace, without anyone's knowledge. She would tell stories and recite poems to arouse her interest. While the girl was never permitted to travel to India and explore her mother's cultural wealth, nothing could stop her from taking deep interest in the foreign land that bore testimony to half of her roots. By twenty-two, as she grew up to be a beautiful young woman ready to be married off, hardly anyone knew that she could read, write and speak fluent Sanskrit and had already read our epics. She was married off in a family of equal riches, bound by tradition and orthodox rituals. Her marriage, however, gave her the liberty of practising her interest without being judged under the elaborate, magnified vigilance. She sourced, read and indulged in Indian Literature and explored further with the help of a hired tutor, while her husband discarded the depth of her pursuit as just another expensive hobby of his royal wife. Before her death, she ordered her collections to be kept in a house built afresh to promote art and culture. It was also her last wish that the architecture carries strong Indian influence as it stands in the heart of Venice.

When I was hired as the Creative Consultant for this project, my task was not easy. My employer was an important Italian citizen with ego richer than his tastes, basking in the glory of an office-bearing Italian heritage but bound by a promise made to his mother on her death-bed, to welcome and appreciate Indian expertise. He ordered for Indian exteriors and Italian interiors. After a month-long deliberation, I submitted a plan that came more from the heart and less from the brain. I had visualised a three-walled tent structure in dark mahogany wood and white stone. The three-dimensional structure would accommodate three doors for entry and exit, from three distinct directions. On the upper tip of the triangle would rest a huge conch shell that doubles up as a lamp filling its belly with fuel so that the tail burns. I could foresee this building as a torch-bearer of art and craft, and the fire that burnt on top would pledge for its purity and sanctity. From each corner of the building where the two walls meet, an arm would extend itself in three specific directions. These three arms would be the boundary walls for three open-air auditoriums for displaying dramatics, theatre, dance and music performances, book launches and inaugural discussions, poetry recitals, etc. Each auditorium would have its own gallery for the audience. The arm pointing north-west would have a huge Buddha seated on a lotus; this arm would have inscribed on it, *asatoh ma sadgamayah* meaning 'from the unreal, transitory existence lead us towards truth!' The arm pointing north-east would have engraved on it the traditional picture of Krishna-Arjun as depicted in the Bhagvad Gita; below this it would be inscribed, *tamasoh ma jyotirgamayah* meaning 'lead us from the darkness of ignorance towards the light of divine spiritual wisdom.' The third arm that points southwards would convey the story of Vasavdatta, a classical romantic literature in Sanskrit composed by Subandhu, a courtier of king Kumaragupta. Vasavdatta is said to have faced many hurdles before she could unite with the prince, who was her companion in many lives. The wall on the southern arm would have a rock statue of the princess, being brought back to life by the touch of prince Kandarpaketu. Along with the tale of this companionship, transcending lives, it would convey the message of immortality, *mrityur ma amritamgamayah* meaning 'lead us away from the fear of death to the knowledge of endless life.' The interiors on the building would have green rooms, attached to each auditorium. There would also be a huge exhibition hall for art scholars and stalwarts to share their work. At one corner, there would be a small museum that houses acquired possessions and remains of the late woman who visualised this project and named it as her last wish. The insides would have rich Italian designs, which were being planned by an Italian designer.

My plan was accepted without much alteration. Only the lamp I planned on top was decided to be electrically lit instead of feeding on fuel.

As I write my first ever letter to you, *Bhabhu*, I could not help remember this building which carried my most sincere blood and vision. All the while when they narrated the story of a woman who pursued her interest in hiding, I felt I was hearing a story I have known before. Just as the country had changed so had the accessorising pillars of the story to bring region and time specific relevance to it. No one in the family knows that you have been a gold medallist in Sanskrit and English literature in your college. You never told anyone because it would cause distinctions among the females of your generation which would have been undesirable. I knew about it only when I was busy studying the elaborate designs of your jewellery in gold and precious stones. You had laughed thinking that I am weighing those for a future wife, and then, unmindfully two different boxes dropped from your locker displaying the medals. I had picked them before you realised what happened! I had agreed to remain silent about them only if you taught me the language. You did, in all elaboration, with the best that you had.

In our family, women never got into teaching the children. Not everyone had the expertise or education to support this activity. Education had never been a deciding factor for matrimonial alliances. *Baa* always attached more importance to family history, status, business achievements and political contacts while judging their worth before exchanging her sons and daughters through marriage. Those Sanskrit sessions between you and me were something exclusive!

My earliest memory with you goes back to my schooldays. Having left your hand and going inside the huge building with an unknown escort, crowded by many others like me had made my heart beat faster. Before the big gate closed, I turned to look at you finally. You had smiled from there and it told me, there is something happy about being in school. I looked forward to explore the happiness. Almost a year later, the results of my first examination were out. They had given me a report card and lots of toffees. When I met you, I tried to give you the toffees because I considered them more important. You ignored those and took the card from my left hand. A smile flashed across your face and you hugged me. I had come first in class. Sweets were distributed to everyone at home and loving voices blessed my efforts. I probably did not know then what exactly was it all about to come first in an examination, but I learnt that I have to stay ahead if I were to keep that smile on your face. For once *Bhabhu*, it also crossed my mind that had I not come first that morning, would anything have changed? Would you still have smiled at me with equal charm?

Since I was a child, I never quite appreciated your attention towards others. When someone in the family loved your sari, it was hers immediately. A cousin appreciates your food and it is heaped on his plate, ignoring the fact that I too loved whatever you cooked, every day. Whatever was mine, clothes, books, toys, I was encouraged to share even if reciprocation did not happen. Anyone could come to you any time and claim to be with you, discussing their problems; I stood there awaiting my turn! I actually never got a chance to spell my interest to you. I wanted to tell you that I love carving and sculpting, to find life in a rock. I love replicating life in a miniature way compared to the life that runs this world. When I create an emotion, I feel like God. Each of my creations talks to me; they tell me things that the inspirations had not. But while working on them, I can see a person inside-out whom I consider my subject and it helps me understand them better. Nothing remains hidden and I can relate to their depths; I forgive and seek forgiveness. It heals my mind of everything negative I ever bear against them. And I heal, not by deleting them out of my memory, but by an acquired indifference.

All my childhood I had aspired to own that one moment of exclusivity with you. Something that comes from you exclusively for me and no one else. Your charm, your love, your food, your bed-time stories, everything was otherwise shared! I finally got that exclusive treatment when you gave me those Sanskrit lessons. Late in the night when the rest of the house slept, we stayed up for that forbidden secret which belonged to no one else, but just the two of us. Those nights are what I treasure in my memory. Even when you scolded me for my mistakes in a hush tone, which was unusual compared to your standard of decibels, I never felt bad. Nothing claimed our unconditional attention from each other in those hours; so what if we felt sleepy the next morning and would pass a secret smile at each other every time we yawned!

And the resentment, the hatred you shower on me today. This too is probably equally pure and exclusive. Last time I visited the haveli, I had learnt that the family doesn't feel as violated as it did few years ago. They have accepted my decision. There might be sadness, but not resentment for sure. Not any longer. I can sense only in you, a vast dissatisfaction concerning me, exclusive with its depths.

I am not as strong and generous as you, *Bhabhu*. I didn't have the capacity to hold back and hide my talent like you did. At times I wonder, what exactly depresses you more about me? The fact that I fled from home to pursue an interest which I couldn't have sustained, had I not taken the drastic step? Or is it that you felt violated as I refused to replicate your model of sacrifice and collective living in my life? How much ever you and I disagree with each other on our approaches, there's no denying that your tutorials were with me, philosophically, all through my years of struggle. You taught me the healing effect of meditation. I owe to you my knowledge on Hindu scriptures, epics and other ancient books and stories emerging from our cultural roots. While I worked extensively in the West, juggling with accolades and criticism simultaneously, I would often close my eyes and think of you. I remember learning several *slokas* from you along with their elaborate meanings and relevance. I learnt such difficult words easily and never forgot them in life. The mantra I referred to earlier,

Asatoh ma sadgamaya
Tamaso ma jyotirgamaya
Mrityur ma amritamgamaya
Om Shanti! Shanti! Shanti!

was one of the most beautiful mantras you taught me with great care. You even encouraged me to recite it every morning after leaving bed, and I still do that. When this assignment in Venice came to me, I approached it as if I am giving something back to you. I used from my memory the stories and knowledge I acquired from you, and refined the presentation format through whatever I had learnt from art college. You never gave me a chance to say, that this building, named Tappa Sul Fuoco, meaning 'stage on fire,' was my *gurudakshina* to you.

Bhabhu, do you ever realise that I am nothing but an extended existence of your prejudiced presence in this world? You had laid your own rules while operating within the boundaries dictated by the family and so did I. You may or may not believe that I have never for once violated the practices that the family had brought me up with, only difference being I did not stay with you to prove that. You are domestically ambitious and so am I professionally. During Abhimanyu's marriage I had seen you preparing the gifts. All those colourful sweets soaked in ghee and dry fruits, which you had prepared experimenting with various ingredients to bring up a fresh offer, way different from what was available in the market. Those sweets declared our sophistication in their design, our riches in their expensive ingredients and our kitchen-crafts in their taste, to the new relations developed through marriage. And then you ideated and supervised the package and presentation of the gifts, the *shagun*, be it food items, clothes, jewellery, accessories or others. The beautiful trays that you had sourced with special orders, the silk that covered them–a distinctly different colour for each relation for whom the gift was meant, the ribbons, beads and glitters as fillers to adorn them, all neatly packed with a bright coloured jute-net cloth hemmed at the borders with matching lace to cover the trays from above. And not to forget the return gifts passed on to all those who attended the marriage–a little pink box with a pearl and a peacock feather on top. No one else could have planned such a magnificent *shagun* with accurate elaboration. Had you been holding the Public Relations office in a multi-national or planned a career in event management, you would have probably been a bigger person than I am! What I am appreciating in you is a creative vision, an innate instinct to capture and translate beauty, the capacity to make a statement about yourself and your inheritance. You don't realise that creatively, I am in the same profession!

Bhabhu, this letter reaches out to you from the deepest corner of my heart. Please understand, there is only one medium through which I can ever communicate my love, loyalty, sincerity and obedience; that medium is my art! For once, I wish you come and touch my achievements and bless me for being your child, having taken your creative presence forward. I plan to launch my most ambitious exhibition till date, in May next year, at London. This time, I want my family to be with me while the sculptures unveil themselves. I am working on the last statue and it is nearing completion. I have come to Kolkata to move certain things from my end. Last night I have activated my PR and organisers have been informed. I have never given myself so much as I have given to this project and its detailing. I wish to dedicate this series to *Baa*, Gayatri Devi. However, as much as I may have worked to strain my muscles and brain to develop these sculptures, I would not let the exhibition happen if you and Jisa are not with me for this. I don't wish to bring myself yet another imperfect dawn when I wake up to praises, ravishing reviews and congratulatory notes, while my close family remains oblivious to my achievements. I know I have never sought forgiveness from you in person because for a long time I didn't believe that I had done anything wrong. I had held it against you that my family did not support my dreams; but equally do I realise now that I did not support yours' either. *Bhabhu*, all these years of indifference and ignorance may have created a huge barrier between us, but I don't wish to lose you to this vain pride. I beg your forgiveness; I crave for your companionship. Please come and own me, own all the dedication I have invested to be what I am today, and bless my determination of not breaking away from the family values in principle. I would work ahead to send out the press release only after I hear from you an affirmation.

Love and regards.
Yours,
Aniruddh.

The Imperfect Dawn

Sanghamitra Banerjee
Santiniketan

My vacation ended sooner than expected. No, I didn't have to prepone my journey back; I just wanted to stay on. I feel like this every year. Thapi Aunty and Dhonai would bid me farewell with misty eyes and I would actually contemplate tearing off my tickets in the last moment! And then I would return. After my return to Kolkata I spend a day with Ma at home. Post that I reach Howrah station to catch the train to Santiniketan. Ma will spend a couple of days here to pay customary visits to relatives before she returns to Bangalore. I get down from the taxi that brought me to the over-crowded Howrah and pay off his due. Suddenly I realise that someone has taken away my bag while I was unmindfully counting money. I almost shout, 'Catch the thief,' but thankfully care to look up before that and spot the sculptor smiling down at me. I am pleasantly surprised at his abrupt entry. I conceal my happiness though, and scornfully ask, 'What are you doing here?'

'Trying to disturb young, pretty women!' He grins shamelessly, hands inside the pockets of his cargoes, a blue cotton T-shirt hanging loosely and my bag on his shoulder!

'Really! Do you know you have no sense of complimenting women?'

'Hey I was not talking about you,' he smiles through his eyes.

'Oh I see.' I snatch my bag and start walking away swiftly. He is bewildered for a while and runs to catch up with me, blocking my way.

'What?' I demand, and break into a smile.

'I came to receive you, your highness. And I seek permission to travel with you to our common destination.'

'Wait here till I get the tickets. Please move so that I can go ahead.' I try to walk past him. He doesn't care to shift an inch. For a while he looks at my face in silence and says, 'This time we are travelling by car.' I start raising an objection which he refuses to accept. 'Please don't say no. You are coming with me in my car.' He lifts my bag again and gestures me to follow him. Hardly do I have a choice. As he puts my baggage in his BMW, I remark, 'What an expensive thing you possess. I don't quite match this. Feels like a prince and pauper! Can't you afford a lesser car?' He breaks into laughter and so do I. After a while he responds with a smile in his eyes and an odd seriousness in his voice. 'I'm afraid, I don't have anything that matches you, Sanghamitra. A swan spreads elegance and moves in its own rhythm; who cares for the water that carries it!'

Dumbstruck, I look at him. People don't talk to me like this; I mean not any longer. Is he trying to flirt? Gone are the days when I used to be in college inviting a pass or two on certain days. Did he seriously say that? Or is he in a state of trance again, unsure of what can help him recover? I may have stared a bit too long in astonishment. Dr Aniruddh starts the car and throws a glance at me. He smiles while I force myself back to composure. The car races through the outskirts breaking away from the noise and crowd. I end up saying, 'Can we do something about this weird smell inside the car? Open the windows for a while maybe?' His voice in response sounds amused and scornful, both at the same time. 'It's imported.'

'It's fantastically suffocating,' I remark, but can't stop smiling. He smiles as well, nodding his head at my taste! Then stretches his hand to remove the car perfume resting in between.

'So how was your stay at Manali?'

'Beautiful as usual. How was yours? What did you do?'

'I drowned myself in work. And at times, when my brain revolted, I went for long walks. During one of my walks I discovered this new place you have never taken me to. I had started walking to reach Kopai river that evening. I stood on the bridge watching the tough, dry landscape with water levels reduced to a bare minimum, struggling hard to maintain the "river" status. After a while I ventured further inside, to explore what lay beyond. A few miles ahead I came across this deserted land with a beautiful lake, surrounded by coconut and banyan trees. No sign of habitation was visible till far, neither was there any human presence around. On one corner of the lake stood a coconut tree bent in shape by the weight of a younger banyan tree growing concentrically around it like a huge, possessive, captivating snake claiming rights on its life! Remember you once showed me a *pankouri* bird? There were many of them on the water body. The sun had already reached the western horizon and all of them suddenly flew away together, throwing beautiful reflections on the water below. I wished you were with me then, to witness the view. You had told me your date of return over mail, but every day while coming back home after my walk I looked at Mrigaya expecting to be surprised. That didn't quite happen!'

Once again I am quiet. Something has changed, in him or about us. He is trying to say or mean something, planned or unplanned; I am not sure whether I am prepared to grasp and comprehend. Maybe, his loneliness in Santiniketan for so many days at a stretch is making him talk more than he had decided to disclose.

'What were you working on?' I ask finally.

'You!'

A sensation runs down my spine. This is not the first time I am hearing something like this. But how do I react to it? Should I feel happy or embarrassed? Should I ask more, or stop all conversations on this right here? What if I don't appreciate whatever he has actually worked on? The thought that plagues me further is that Dr Aniruddh had seen me unrestrained in the rains and God knows to what extent that would translate into his work, if his subject is really me, as he mentions! Next moment, however, I convince my wandering self otherwise. I must trust his aesthetics; he has never given me a reason not to! But why is the sculptor doing this? I wonder! He is practically nudging that soft area which I chose to discard without exploring. I look out of the window and hear him saying, 'Won't you ask further?'

I don't turn to look at him. Just respond, 'I am scared of what exactly you have to say if I ask, Dr Aniruddh!'

The car stops and I unknowingly turn to face him, to find out why the vehicle came to rest. He removes his glares and looks me in the eye. 'You must call me Aniruddh!'

'This is not the context. We were discussing ...'

'We are not discussing anything further till you drop this formality.' He interrupts with a firm voice.

I am truly uneasy and sit quietly looking away. I can sense my heart beating too fast and I struggle to transport myself away from this situation. I know he is watching me and it feels his vision is touching my insides. I am getting caught on something I chose not to ever disclose. Finally he speaks.

'Do you have any idea what exactly I specialise upon? I am talking about my work, not the abruptness I often inconvenience you with. Do you even know who I am? My credentials, my excellence or my professional pursuits?'

I sit motionless like stone. God knows what he is trying to get at. 'Anusua did explain a bit.'

'And you never bothered to find more! Never wanted to invest in details even though we had been spending so much time into chit-chats. Are you naturally indifferent or am I specially blessed?' His voice sounds grim!

Softly I try to reason myself in response to his sudden rudeness. 'Professional interests and achievements at times create boundaries and barriers. If I have to understand the details of your expertise, I might feel too intimidated by your experience and exposure. Right now, we are just two individuals with similar and dissimilar interests, complementing and contradicting each other. That's much simple. Nothing exists before, nothing happens after. I and you, and this moment–that is more fascinating than a bygone past or a pre-scheduled future. This however, is just a thought. That is not the reason why I never asked about your specialisations. I am saying all this in response to the pointed question you ruthlessly threw at me. The truth is, it never occurred to me that I need to know more about your work.'

'Profound,' he says and restarts the car. I can see the sides of his face as he drives, but his expressions convey nothing.

'Why is my knowledge about your work so important suddenly,' slowly I ask.

'You have your own way of telling people that they don't make much sense in your life and you are not interested beyond a point! You don't care to know about others as much as you don't share yourself.' Seems the words come from somewhere else as his sole concentration rests on his driving.

I am disturbed by his words. Yes, I am not comfortable getting too personal with anyone. And I practise greater precautions with the sculptor because my system responds dangerously to his moves. From whatever I have known about him, his background achievements and thoughts are a few light-years away from mine. What would I achieve by knowing further about him? It would take me emotionally closer to him, only to come back with injured sentiments. What would I gain? He lives in a world dominated by his work and his expertise takes him places. I am certainly not the first or last woman with whom he shares a basic comfort. Beyond a level, I don't even understand his world. Without getting into much details, I just sadly pronounce, 'That's not true.'

We drive in silence through plush meadows awaiting rains. Rains are expected sometime soon. Dark clouds are already visible in the horizon. They predicted an early monsoon this year. And this year, I have to be extra careful about my conduct during rains. The climate inside the vehicle is heavy. God knows what thunder is brewing inside the sculptor. I try to make it lighter. 'It might rain today.' I add a smile.

'Why are you so fond of rains?' He smiles back.

'I just love them. Everything changes so much around. The chill of the breeze, the thunderous clouds, the uncompromising downpour, the glee of the plants, the darkness, and then the wet sun that reappears. I especially love it when it rains all night and you wake up to its droning sound.'

'Do you even remotely understand that rains are a threat to my work, especially when I am teaching clay? Everything needs to rush inside and it's a complete mess! The other day I was walking back with some diagrams through the huge mango orchard and unseasoned rains spoilt quite a bit.'

'Who works during rains?' I retort with a frown, inviting laughter. He takes a while to regain himself.

Abruptly then, he remarks, 'What is your real interest in Kala Bhavan, if I may ask?' I am caught off-guard but I knew I had to face this question. 'I was close to a painter once.' He remains quiet, waiting for me to share further or just allowing silence to breathe in between. I hesitate for a while and continue. 'I don't consciously maintain a distance; I mean not always. If I get to know too much about you, I might get judgemental. So, I just take it as it comes. As much as you pour on me, in the time we have spent in exclusivity, is something that's not biased with unconcerned details about the time you might have spent otherwise. If I were to take a deeper interest in your work, I would have got intimidated. Or I might have expected favours, given your worldwide contacts. Without such indulgence, I just know that it is nice being with you. The train journey we had together, the evening at Dakshineshwar, the moon-lit night on the boat, those Rajasthani dolls, this journey sitting in your car, all are exotically beautiful! And as for me, I live separate lives with myself. I hide considerably about myself but that is not because I want to insult my relation with the world with non-disclosure. It's just that it allows me to be two different persons at the same time–one who is open and known, and one who is hidden and subtle. This is the fun of my life. I am isolated, but not lonely. It actually happens with everyone. You find this particularly visible in me because I consciously don't waste words or energy in self-explanation.'

'What if I claim an access to everything concerning you?' I am no longer taken aback by the sculptor's unrestricted boldness. Today, he has decided, he'll not hold back anything that approaches his brain! Playfully I respond, 'You will have to earn it yourself. I won't give it to you for free.'

'I am ready to compensate.'

'Compensate with what, Mr Sculptor? How rich do you think you are?'

'Not all that rich, Sanghamitra. But would you take if I were to give myself to your secret world!'

I think I didn't hear him correctly. A flash of thunder had roared while he spoke; I pretend disabled audience to his last few words and continue with my non-responsive reserve. The small dark cloud on the horizon has spread all across like an epidemic, engulfing the sun and flashing huge cracks of lightning tearing through the sky. Trees are swaying violently, welcoming the obvious. Droplets start appearing on the glass of the car and on the windscreen. The sculptor has parked the car and in silence we both sit watching the exotic, uninterrupted view in front. There's nothing more beautiful than this engrossing submission to nature. In a while, downpours come in ferocious vigour, blurring all visibility. Raindrops hit the top of the car producing a typical sound and water flows down the glass like a never ending stream. I feel like running out, but equally am I conscious that there's another soul watching me intensely. He pushes the car seat back and relaxes himself. And then, he shocks me to the extent of paralysing my brain. His left hand touches my right palm, and takes it inside his. For a moment I don't believe he did this. I try to slide it back hoping that it must be a mistake, an unmindful gesture that means nothing. But his grip is stronger than my attempts. I look disbelievingly at my bare, dusky fingers entangled between his fair ones, adorned by multiple rings. The throat is too dry to speak. For a while he keeps looking at my hand within his, touches it with the other. His forefinger walks softly through the soft of my palm. It sends a shiver down my body. The other hand caresses the back of my palm for a while, and the fore-finger lingers through the tips of my nails. His thumb softly moves around my pulse till both sets of fingers find themselves and interlock. He turns and bends towards me. I sit there motionless, unable to look at him; all thoughts are jumbled up, the heart thumps aloud, the mind goes blank! The deep voice says, 'I am leaving Santiniketan in a few months, Sanghamitra. Come along with me.'

Krishna's Sixth Woman

Dr Aniruddh Jain Solanki
Jaipur

As much as I had shocked Sanghamitra with whatever I told her, I was no less astounded at my own audacity. I have never offered myself so blatantly to a woman. Her absence in the last few months brought me to face some facts that I hadn't delved into earlier. Not for once could I forget that image of hers, soaked in the rain, walking away direction-less towards nothing! Twice after that it had rained in Santiniketan; and my soul reached out to her in those moments. It felt as if the showers were incomplete till they had touched her, calmed her, healed her and refreshed her. It also disturbed me that the woman, who elaborated herself so beautifully in the rains, was actually expressing her pain! I was driven by a strange pursuit to unbind her from an inopportune past and set her spirits free. First step to this was letting her know that she doesn't singularly hold that deep, dark secret within her heart; not any longer. Today it stands to be a shared property. With sharing, ownership of a deep rooted sorrow would be automatically divided; she would be forced to take precautionary steps to protect the story from divulging further and would single-mindedly shift her focus on me. And once the disowning process starts, it would fade into irrelevance if I can fill in that vacuum with time. I had promised myself that rains would speak differently to her very soon; I would be the difference.

On our way back to Santiniketan that morning, she seemed to be singing with the rains. Water poured down the windscreen and window; she leaned against the window so that the skin of her face touched the glass, watching the drops trickle down with great satisfaction. Her eyes reached the ceiling from where the stream of water started its journey downwards and followed the movement as the droplets dispersed at the base. From inside she tried to touch them; her palm reached the top and came down as if chasing the downpour through the closed glass. At some point it felt as if she wanted to open the door and go out in the rains; but she stopped herself; maybe because she did not want to give me the same pleasure once again. Words flew impromptu, beyond my control. Before I knew, the rains had marked a new beginning for her. For us!

For the last forty-five days I had been working day and night on my Kalindi. At times I would sleep for a few hours or go for walks to declutter my brain. Most of the times though, I would be possessed and engrossed in the black sculpture, as it took shape from a tough rock to a lively sensuous woman. When all Santiniketan was practically disabled under vacation mode, my first floor constantly registered the sound of my tools hitting against the stone, experimenting and finding aesthetic curves adding features to a womanly being. It stood up to be a four feet tall structure, maintaining uniformity in measurements with the other statues of this series. My diagrams underwent fundamental changes in design. Many improvisations later, I had agreed with myself on certain alterations to the plan and structure, from what I had thought of earlier. The woman here stands with a long nose, half-closed Buddhist eyes and full lips, head tilted sideways delightfully receiving the rain gods. She has a full body, voluptuous in design, well developed with rich, hedonistic features. The statue stands on its right leg. The left leg is bent from the knee and lifted up backwards, parallel to the ground. The woman is romancing the showers with the calm of her half-closed eyes, oblivious of a serpent, symbolising Vasuki, which winds itself at the base of her leg and goes all the way from her back raising the hood to cover her from top. The figure is supported at the ground by the body of the serpent on one side and her right leg on the other. Bereft of any jewellery, she stands oozing feminine passion that adorns and defines her. Her hair is messy and scattered all over suggesting strong winds. A loose cloth entwines her waist and comes up to cover her top. Wet with the rains it clings on to her body in folds and curls, giving the figure its ultimate sensuousness. Touching her shoulders, the loose end falls behind and spreads itself to offer greater support to the structure. From the waist, the same cloth covers her bottom as it ends in curls a little below her knees. The statue has a bare back with a prominent line that defines her erect spine. Her left hand softly touches the edge of her cheek and forehead, attempting to tame the hair and keep it away from her face. The other hand hangs down loose from the side. The serpent has a criss-cross design with a dot in between, signifying the richness of King of Nagas. A beaded necklace falls from his neck, just below the hood.

With all the other sculptures that I worked upon, I always hired an intern who would do the initial polishing and drawing the lines. Refining and polishing is required even at the end of sculpting to round off the sharp edges and process the finishing. With this one, I did everything myself. With a strange possessiveness, I didn't want anyone to touch my Kalindi. After doing the basic rock-work when I started carving, I came across a strange passion, none of which I had ever experienced before. This was not the first time I had been working on a feminine figure. That in fact is my forte, my expertise, my experience over all these years. Not for once had I ever broken the unspoken code of conduct; I have always handled my subjects with ruthless professionalism. Not even in the darkest corner of my mind did I ever fantasise the inspirations of my sculptures. As I invested my concentration doing up her hands, hair, spine, waist, the belly button, her entangling cloth and feet, I felt I was touching a woman. Sanghamitra! Each and every moment that I spent on this statue was my forbidden moment with Sanghamitra! I was giving her a new life. Or maybe, I was inviting her to my life. In the dark of the night and in midday heat, my senses rested around her rocky presence. It felt that I was destined to touch her, feel her and explore her to the depths. My soul worked in unison with this block of limestone, constructing a Kalindi who was coming out to be the first ever escapade of my life.

I could not stop working on her! Neither did I ever feel tired. I just knew that I had to make this happen, and it had to happen as early as possible. I was mysteriously addicted and obsessed with the structure; liberation lay in its completion. My hands worked faster than usual and my brain spoke to her constantly discussing everything under the earth. All night and all day I would spend with her, working out the curves of her cheeks, lift of her nose, the hair as it flew haywire, the hands bent in feminine softness, legs with their rhythm, bosom with a fullness and spirit that was mysterious. I had captured her inside out! The day I finally completed the basic work, I watched her from different angles, from near and far, experiencing the joy of re-creation like never before. She had evolved from my deepest sensibilities, combining absorption with desire. I looked out of my window and stared at Mrigaya, standing equally abandoned as I was, without her. I couldn't help wondering what the lady might be doing at Manali. I smiled at myself, as I remembered her interactions with me during the last few months. Her smiles, her mischief, the rebellious ideas, the beauty that is close to Nature and her detachment! This was probably the most wonderful work I had produced so far. It involved me intensely as much as it projected her. I turned to look at the face of the sculpture, and my eyes travelled down to its base exploring each part of the rocky design. I decided that this statue in the series would not be for sale. I'd place it along with the others to complete the thought and vision I started with; but I would certainly not give this one away. If anyone deserves to own this Kalindi, other than me, then it would be Sanghamitra!

That morning I had been to Kolkata only to drive her back to Santiniketan. Amidst rains when I had held her hand, she quivered but did not resist. The trembling fingers, the heat of her palm, a higher than usual pulse rate had got my system speeding through. Masculine desires urged me to proceed, further exploring her physicality; but I forced myself to stop. For a while I did not speak to control myself and submit in clarity whatever I wanted to say. I used very less words to define my state of mind as our hands held each other, fingers interlocked in between. I need to hear her out in affirmation, before I can take any further liberty.

I was to travel to Jaipur the next morning. Before leaving for Kolkata, I have left a note at her door. My week-long stay would give her enough space and time to think about it.

Bhabhu has invited me back to the haveli after I had written an elaborate letter expressing myself unambiguously and seeking her forgiveness. When I reached the doorstep this time, she was present there to greet me in along with Deivi-ma. The house is always ablaze with activities; a celebration continues in permanence. I go around and meet everyone after I have bowed down to the family deity at the *puja-ghar*. A bath and refreshments later, everyone has gathered in the living room hall. This, however, is a rare occasion and happens only during marriages or other social functions when the family has to take joint decisions. It raises my spirits to understand that today, I am the occasion.

Some time in between, Diya, my newly-wed sister-in-law, secretly hands me over a pair of earrings made up with gold and diamonds. The day I had bared my heart to Sanghamitra, I had called Diya and told her about the developments. It was late in the night when Diya had picked the phone, and almost for the rest of the night she didn't allow me to hang up. Her countless questions on Sanghamitra, her habits and looks and choices kept us occupied. When Diya placed the small red box on my palm, Abhimanyu stood around the corner. His mischievous wink does not miss my attention. They must have already shared all information with each other and the knowledge of Abhi knowing it all makes me feel uncomfortable. Without a word I just smile, thank and try to move away. My shameless cousin calls me from behind and asks, 'Bhai-sa, who proposed to whom!' I exude a frustrated shrug and hurriedly walk off.

There is a free spirit about the house today. Having received a final approval from one of the most dominating characters of the family, the younger generation is approaching me with more than warmth. They ask me about my days abroad, my struggles, how I made it to the top, the creative visions that work with me and the inspirations. I answer them in all elaboration consciously taking care that I don't touch upon anything sensitive. Like we did in our childhood, the elders are sitting on the sofas and divans; my generation has made themselves comfortable on the floor. Jisa is seated just behind me; I am leaning my back on his knees and legs. In our family parents and offspring do not publicly display their love for each other; Jisa's fingers unmindfully run through my hair and abruptly withdraw. I bend my head backwards and smile at him to acknowledge the affection. There is a beautifully crafted chair with a low seat and longer stand at the back, built in ivory with explicit and delicate designs. It is seated in between the gathering but no one occupies it. It belonged to *Baa*, Gayatri Devi. Ideally Deivi-ma deserves to be in that seat with her rightful inheritance, but she has never touched it. Instead, after her morning and evening pujas every day, she bows before this chair before starting on her regular duties and activities. This decision is part of her leadership extraordinaire; she rules without calling herself the ruler. It helps her maintain healthy exchanges with ladies of her generation as she proposes to continue being one of them instead of being their dictatorial guardian. Every one reports to her; she applies her keen restraint on what she chooses to comment on and what she just quietly absorbs like a passive listener. The clan takes a huge interest in my upcoming project. My generation asks vivid questions about my life, career and work; I ask about theirs. They ask me how I happened to choose Krishna's women while I had always been smitten by Shiva, the Nataraj, particularly. I tell them that this series is dedicated to my family deity and to *Baa*. I don't nurture any belief that separates me from them; it is just that Shiva questions and raises my imagination to stimulate creative instincts far more than Krishna! Elders sit back and listen and intervene occasionally attempting to know more. Young ones, my nieces and nephews play around. They had maintained a distance last time, unsure of who this sudden entrant was. Today they feel no threat having realised that I have been seated with the family in a core, private exchange of conversation. They have been told that I am the uncle who created the glass room beside the pool, locked doors of which attract their attention like nothing else. I promise them that I will get the room unlocked and they can be with me inside as long as they wish to. *Bhabhu* is watching me intently from a corner. Her questions are less, in fact none, but I know she is absorbing the most. Her expression, after a very long time, is reasonably affectionate. As I scroll through the rest of the family, playing with the young ones and talking to the elders, amidst dry fruits and home-made sweets, we exchange an affirming look with each other. Tonight would be a sleepless night when mother and son would heartily catch up. When everyone is engaged in delighted conversation, Diya drops a bomb that silences everyone. 'Bhai-sa, how is Mitra?' Everything comes to a standstill suddenly and the entire house is looking at me, waiting for my response. I for the first time experience my face going red and I have no control on this situation. Before I gather my wits to respond, she opens her mouth again. 'She told me over the phone that her actual name is Sanghamitra. So you call her Mitra?' Abhi laughs out loud and runs away from there. God save this girl from me now. I throw a ferocious look at her, but she is undeterred. Instead she chuckles at my discomfort. I just manage to say, 'She is fine.' Rest of the clan pounces on me throwing all sophistication to the winds. Questions are bombarded at me as I struggle to get out of this mess. What do I have to say? I can't shrug off by naming her as just another colleague or professional acquaintance. I can't call her a friend because my family still doesn't understand the concept of no-strings-attached friendship between males and females unless they are together as kids at school. And I definitely can't declare the details till I hear what Sanghamitra has to say. I somehow convince everyone that it's too early to talk about this. But the clan has already started discussing about another upcoming marriage in the family! As the gathering breaks for dinner, I am pierced inside out by two pairs of eyes. *Bhabhu* and Deivi-ma. I am answerable to both of them.

After dinner when I enter my room, *Bhabhu* is already waiting for me there. As I enter, she says, 'A mother parts with her son considerably when she gives him in marriage. You have come back to me only to part ways again.' I remain quiet for a while. Then repeat what I had to say regarding this. 'It's too early *Bhabhu*. I have no clue how and what she feels about me.'

'Which mad woman would say no to my son?' A typical mother remarks, forcing a smile out of me. But I hammer back, 'The same son had heard a no from his mother for so many years; how would you blame the woman if she does the same?' Her jaw immediately clenches; she is ready for a fight. Before she hits back, I utter, 'I missed you, *Bhabhu*. Terribly. Every time I created a masterpiece, I wanted to come and show it to you so that you would forgive me.' Her expression softens as I allow myself to fall on her lap. Tenderly, she keeps her hand on my forehead. In tears and laughter we share the rest of the night, telling each other the tales of our lives through which we grew in separate lands. She asks me about Sanghamitra and I tell her everything in detail. 'Doesn't she love you?' She asks finally. I let out a sigh. 'Only thing I know for sure is that she tolerates my presence with a smile and allows me to be with her as and when I wish to be. She never calls me herself; neither does she ever express her inner self with spontaneity. She shares some level of comfort with me. That might be because we are polar opposites in nature and every time we meet, we learn something new from each other; we experience through each other something that doesn't exist in our lives.' *Bhabhu* is not pleased at this uncertainty. In her usual dominating way she remarks, 'Don't complicate things. Talk to her straight and sort this out. Philosophy might be romantic, but it doesn't take life forward!' I smile and bury my face in her lap, hugging her waist as she sits.

Bhabhu sleeps off around 3.00 am. In a while I get up, take a shower and at 4:15 am I am at the *puja-ghar* waiting for Deivi ma. I owe her an explanation. She was horribly quiet at dinner last evening. Deivi ma arrives at 4:30 am and frowns at me. 'What are you doing here so early in the morning? I see you have taken your bath as well.'

'Last time when I said I don't have a girl in my life, I really didn't have one, Deivi ma!'

'You told Diya, the daughter-in-law to the family, but you kept me in the dark! That hurt.' She remarked looking away, working her practised hands through the preparations for the morning puja.

'I didn't tell her anything when I visited the haveli during their marriage. Last time Sanghamitra had asked for a pair of Rajasthani dolls and I sourced them through Diya since she is an expert on those. She created a story out of it which was not true then, but has some relevance now! I earnestly put my words across.

'A Buddhist?'

'Bengali Hindu.' I look down, and tell her more. She listens quietly, smiles at times to herself.

'This woman has a mind of her own, Deivi ma. I won't be surprised if she doesn't agree to a marriage thinking that it would limit her movements. She is not the one to follow rules. I don't even know whether she will understand my family. Just that, I am brutally attracted to her without any assurance of reciprocation!'

'She will reciprocate,' Deivi ma says finally, 'Every woman loves a home. She might choose to play it differently though. As much as I hear from you, I'm sure this girl will first ascertain that you are bound to her as much as she is bound to this family. The day you break the deal, she'll break hers. She'll make sure you give her her due. You might feel insecure about her at times because of her whims, but she'll never betray if she chooses to be with you. When can we meet her?'

'Come to Santiniketan, Deivi ma. You might be inconvenienced to stay in my small room without an air-conditioner, but you will love the place nevertheless.' Deivi ma looks blank; then turns and smiles. 'Don't worry, if you are comfortable there, I will not be inconvenienced either.' It's 5:50 in the morning already. Rest of the family are approaching for the morning puja. I throw a venomous look at Diya; she ignores and grins triumphantly.

The Escapade

Sanghamitra Banerjee
Santiniketan

Monsoons this year had been scanty initially. They would just come and go away unpredictably. The constant downpour that continues through days without a glimpse of sunlight hadn't happened. It was only in late September, that the nature did unwind itself in vigour. The downpour lasted for about seventeen tiring days making it difficult to step out of the house. Furious winds made scary, ghostly sounds as they explored the open terrain and knocked on doors and windows with fierce velocity. Anusua at times would come down to stay with me, or urged me to move in with her. She gets scared during such times. 'For days when the sun isn't visible, it dampens more than the earth. The very spirit of life goes down and it feels irritated.' I don't understand this, of course. I can spend countless hours looking at the downpour–the way the leafs dance, trees sway, thunderclouds roar, the crackling lightning across the sky, soft sound of water running in streams to find escape, smell of the soil, wet corridors, daylight submitting to the sudden darkness and darkness slowly sliding back to light–I love every bit of it. Anusua utters curses at me.

Late September it came. The floods. As much as I love romancing the rains, it hurts and aches to absorb the destructive effects of Nature.

It feels, I am privileged to enjoy what others mourn because of their lack of resources. I with my team of students ride on to the villages in the interior where flood has drowned many huts made of clay and mud; people are devastated without food and shelter! We offer them a safe haven temporarily helping them to accommodate in a local school made of cement; we carry food and clothes for them. Once they have survived the water, they lament over what is lost. Their tears pierce through the heart. Often kids and old people fall ill and need to be treated immediately. We have in our team a doctor from the Viswa Bharati Hospital, who volunteers every year. Throughout the year our team is active enough to collect money from contributors, preparing funds for flood reliefs. We all put in a percentage from our monthly income and keep a count of the amount accumulated. We cannot help everyone, just pick out a village and offer help with our meagre capacities. Whatever we give, we can't ever claim to replace what is lost. It had investments of time, money that is scarce and emotions to build a home and gather up those little belongings these poor people owned. Losing them meant losing a part of their existence. I and my team of thirteen students and three professors work day and night helping them to build up again emotionally and go back to life; the money that we have to offer is much less compared to what has been drained out.

Dr Aniruddh vanished after that morning. He left me a note which said that his mother had called him to Jaipur and he had to leave! I have no idea why he said whatever he did during that eventful journey together. Knowing the kind of person he is, I can say that he was, under no stretch of imagination, playing a prank. Yet the disappearing act left me confused. True that I am attracted, but I am not desperate. There are certain answers I need to have before I think further. I am not sure though, whether I'll be able to ask them when he is around. I am not even sure about what I wish to specifically ask! I am worried about losing my independent lifestyle as much as I want him to continue being around. I love the way he looks at me at times; I wish to feel him around me; I want to touch him, that clean shaven face and soft hair unruly in front; yet, on certain moments I need to be left alone. I don't know whether he is ready to understand my whims. He is conservative, not only in actions but also in thoughts. His practices do not match mine. We are two distinctly different people with very well designed choices that emerge from our faith! To what extent is he ready to travel with these? And to what extent am I ready to welcome him as a permanent contradiction in my life? Is he at all interested in something permanent? He must be; his kind of people don't try temporary fitments. But what if we fall apart? What did he tell his family about me? Was that 'Mitra' a significant hint I misunderstood? Why did Diya know what I could not decipher? Questions, that I might never ask, endlessly hover around my idle brain whenever I try to relax.

There is something common between us. We both appreciate beauty. Cosmic beauty, beauty of external appearances and internal devotions, beauty of language and art, beauty of articulation and expression, of each enlightened day fading into the dark, and the beauty of life–where people come close and drift apart by shrewd interplay of destiny and yet, nothing stops because almost everything or everyone has a time-relevant substitute. Perhaps the only difference between the sculptor and the professor is that the sculptor wants to capture the object of beauty, the professor can let go.

Quietly I have been dealing with his absence after all the drama that morning! A pang of anger erupts inside. He should have been here to answer me. On the exterior, I am a goddess of patience. I would however be fooling myself if I try to pretend that his actions that morning did not rekindle a sinful desire all across my body. His hold was tender, but strong. I haven't ever seen him bare on the top but I can say he has an athletic build. His back shapes into a beautiful V and I am tempted to know how it feels when those biceps bend to hold a woman across her neck and shoulders from behind! What magic is inspired when a woman's bare back touches his chest? Did his face and nose ever dig into a woman's hair? When did he last have a girlfriend?

During floods all train lines and roadways to and from Santiniketan are blocked. Water logging is rampant everywhere and even telephone lines are jammed. This area becomes a true recluse, cut off from every mode of communication. After seven days of camping around Satkahonia, a village near Ilambazar, we return exhausted. It rains heavily when we reach Santiniketan and we, the professors, allow the vehicle we had hired, to take the students safely to their hostels. I get down a little ahead of Ratan Pally market and start walking towards Simanta Pally. Half way across the rain comes down again in huge torrential showers. There is not a single rickshaw; neither a tree under which I can take shelter. Such moments though, don't embarrass me. Without waiting for the rains to stop, I choose to walk ahead so that the path comes to an end. Not that I am unhappy with the downpour. It washes me from top to bottom, inside out and it feels very cold with the strong breeze. There is not a single being to watch my pleasure, or share the fun, as I kick the water that stores in potholes and wipe my arms with my palm only to be washed away immediately. I am also singing something, not sure what.

The glory that's yours
A light that's mine
A pride that shadows a tale sublime!
Monsoon glitters, the Heavens lit, drizzling mists unrestrained,
Unguarded, robust falls hails the earth as it rained
The dark of night, its serene split in merry and bliss, leaflets cheer.
An orphan bird shivers in cold, her secured nest broken afar!
Few leafs above in beauty and grace, melodious and serene after long,

Feathers in white, in royal might humming soft a rain song,
Princely wings leisure in peace,
spreads his arms in bounteous charm.
The orphan bird smiles unaware the downpour does no further harm!
In strange delight their being was roped!
Together they lived, and smiled and hoped,
Can the bird of glory, the bird of light,
Come together once tonight?

I take the turn towards Mrigaya and abruptly halt!

My vision is blurred because of the heavy rains, but not so blurred that I can't recognise the figure sitting on the wet floor of my veranda. He stands up as I slowly approach; few steps away from him I stop, as we stare at each other. A strange moment when all my questions, all that I wanted to tell him and hear, are all silenced by abrupt lack of language. We stand apart watching each other. The rain is pouring down my hair, my kurta clings on to my skin. A soft dupatta wraps my body and the bag hangs weightily down my right shoulder. He stands there protected under my ceiling, in his blue check shirt tucked inside khaki trousers. He breaks the spell first. Quickly opens an umbrella lying beside and comes forward to drag me inside. Not taking my gaze away from him, I drop my bag and cover myself with both hands fiercely fighting the cold winds. The already wet floor redefines its wetness! 'Are you mad?' he asks, 'How often are you seen like this in public?'

'Like what?' I demand to know. He takes two steps behind and his eyes rove over me from top to bottom. 'Like this … the ultimate seductress!' I throw him a violent look. 'I am coming from Ilambazar after helping out the flood prone!' He leans on to the wall, stands with one leg crossed over the other, watches me for a while, and says something with an amused expression, which makes me uneasy. 'Your body is covered, Sanghamitra, but the curves are explicit! There could have been more eyes feasting themselves on you. Understand what I mean?' He smiles down at me and gestures to open the door. My Saraswati has been washed by the rains while I was not there. Quietly I open the door and enter; he has picked my water-proof bag already. I arrange to go for a shower, first thing, and Dr Aniruddh offers to prepare tea. Black tea.

I come back to the room feeling warm after the shower and getting rid of the wet clothes. A piece of cloth is tied through my hair in a bun. I wear a sari expecting that I will have to go out again to shop for vegetables and other essentials. Discussing routine purchases in mind, I enter the kitchen and stand astonished. The sculptor has shopped for groceries and milk! I didn't see these before. They are waiting beside the fridge while he has filled water in my bottles from the water purifier. All bottles are washed properly. Instead of tea, he is brewing coffee.

'What are you up to? What's all this?' I ask.

'You don't need to go out again today. Take rest.' He smiles, keeping his eyes on the milk that's boiling. 'I didn't do much to your kitchen. Don't know how you do things. If you agree, I can help you activate the house!'

I lean against the door of the kitchen. This man doesn't seem to be romantically inclined towards me. But he cares, for sure. Maybe he'd be equally traditional in his way of expressing fondness. I can't yet convince myself to accept that his feelings towards me have got anything to do with love. It's not my kind of love, doubtlessly. I have known love to break barriers and take two people by storm. There is a hopeless madness of knowing and exploring each other and uniting into an irreversible *one*. Tastes, actions and priorities match more often than not and achievements are defined by a heart-warming togetherness. Here, we haven't known each other for half our lives and most of our habits are strangers to each other! Dr Aniruddh's voice snaps me awake from my day-dreaming. We move to the living room with the coffee and I narrate my experiences of the last few days. He had tried to call me all through, but the phone lines did not connect. He came to know from my department that I would return today morning and had been there, waiting.

The coffee makes me feel good. I hold it with both hands, fingers drawing warmth from the cup. I look around, preparing to start cleaning the house. He offers to clean the refrigerator meanwhile; that puts me in splits. 'Are you serious? Does your diamond merchants' family know that you want to clean the refrigerator of a woman who lives in a modest two room house?' He stands resting his back on the wall behind. 'No. But they are aware of a woman who refuses to define how much I am allowed to enter her life!' I look away from him, at the cupboard and the cup in my hand. 'Have you thought about it enough, Sculptor?' He bends forward. 'I haven't thought. I am just speaking my mind. I have no clue what lies ahead, neither do I know whether you are prepared for my proposition. Just that, I don't want anyone else to watch you the way I have, speak to you at weird hours the way I did, or confront you the way I dared.' He pauses, then speaks again. 'I have never said these words to anyone before; so I'm not sure of a better way to convey this. I also understand that your choices might differ and I won't dig in further if you don't want to take this anywhere.' I look up at him. Is it really that easy for him to say these things? And he claims to experience this for the first time in his life? I know the turbulence he must be feeling inside. A strong adrenaline rush, a restlessness, some helpless fantasies that refuse to leave alone. Yet he restrains because he doesn't know what I think! I can't remember anything of what I wished to ask him. It feels feverish sitting in front of him, being fully aware that I am being watched. 'Don't you feel scared of my whims that can tear us apart? We are so different as individuals.' Slowly I manage to say. He walks suddenly and comes in front facing me. As if in trance, unsure of what he is up to, I stand up as well, looking into his eyes. 'There is something inside you that's mine, Sanghamitra. And that has always been mine. I don't claim to own anything more than that. But yes, I need to know more about it. And I am capable of expanding it to the extent that everything else falls apart!' He waits for a while watching my reactions. There's none visible, but I can sense a storm inside. It is dark again outside and we need to switch on the lights. But none of us move. 'Think over it, and come to me if you please.' The sculptor turns to walk out. His ego is bruised by my apparently indifferent silence. Involuntarily my palm touches his shoulder from behind; he stops and turns. He waits for a while trying to judge me and the moment, then touches the right of my neck. I shiver at the warmth. Slowly he takes me in and I rest my head against his chest, placing my hands on his waist and back. Strong hands pull me further towards him, eradicating every bit of space that could cause a separation, and his chin rests atop my wet hair. Unskilled fingers split open the bun to throw the cloth aside and let loose the untamed growth, exploring through entangled hair and then the bare of my back that the blouse had left uncovered. They scroll downwards to touch the skin on my waist and halt as they rest on the sides. Incredible desire flashes through my body and soul, amidst thunderous roars outside. Dr Aniruddh seems to be on a similar journey. His head bends down touching my hairline and softly his mouth feels my ear, neck and bare shoulder. Softly I pull away a bit and rest my hands on his chest, looking up at him in anticipation. He pulls me closer again, so tight in his arms that it hurts, and his lips lower to reach mine.

There is something about the way he holds. As if he is afraid to lose and hence reluctant to set free! It hurts but it feels nice and secure too. Even after I release myself, my body aches. The evidence of his touch lingers on as we try to concentrate away from each other, contributing to other chores of the house that need to be settled. But before the soft pain in my elbow and back disappears, he replaces and restores it holding me from behind and digging his mouth into the shoulders. He pushes me towards the wall to block all movement and leaves a mark at the corner of my left shoulder. I push him away but he falls back on me. There's flood inside this man as well; overwhelmingly he spills raw desire to engulf my being, my world. A secluded life, that I called my choice, seems to be drowning in the vigour of his wild, outrageous invitation!

Santiniketan is not aware of this development and we choose to keep it under wraps for the time being. We talk about work, the forthcoming project and his plans in the days to come. He elaborates in detail the concept behind Krishna's Women and the story behind each sculpture. Specifically the one on me; the way he visualised it and brought the figure into being, felt amazing. These art enthusiasts source their inspirations from weird corners. He took me to his place, the first floor of Mridangam, to show it to me. For the first time in all these months I knew how his room looked like. Exceptionally well maintained for a bachelor! 'I have stayed alone for a long time in places where discipline is valued and worshipped. I had no choice but to learn,' he reasons. Having him in life would mean bidding goodbye to this cosy little home of mine in Santiniketan. But I guess, everything comes for a price, with a challenge. The biggest challenge would be to mingle and understand the huge family in Jaipur. I am a bit too much habituated to my space, not being answerable to anyone. A lot will change about my living and with Aniruddh, I am about to embrace orthodox practices which are specifically contradictory to my system. I am not sure how I'll play that. Only thing, probably I'll not have to spend my entire life with them. He keeps travelling. Whenever we meet, he discusses the progress of his work. His world revolves around the life he creates on stone and he is never tired discussing it. I keep watching his expressions of joy and innocent excitement and he narrates his achievements and creative discoveries to me. Very soon he plans to move out of here and take me along, once he has arranged for work and accommodation abroad. Sometimes he rests his head on my shoulder discussing 'us' the beautiful togetherness and the family we would make. Strangely, I too have started visualising and anticipating a togetherness that is pre-destined and inseparable. Aniruddh has dismissed all my resistances and has planted into my private space some fantasies that would probably fill the days that follow. Surprisingly, I have accommodated him and many of his choices effortlessly, and I don't feel any of them as imposed! I have stopped protesting when he forces me to have fruits and almonds; I don't feel intruded when I am disconnected and he brings me back to the present with a loud snap of his finger or a bear hug from behind. There are times when I am doing my work, or scrolling through answer papers or reading a book; from the corner of my eye I find him engrossed with something on his laptop or reading fat books on art, culture or architecture or talking over phone with some professional associates with unbelievable politeness even when he doesn't approve whatever is coming from the other end! Quite unlike what I had expected, his presence does not threaten my space. Rather it fills me with the confidence of having someone around, who can support my vulnerabilities and for whose wellbeing I stand responsible! We usually meet a little late in the evening as per Santiniketan standards. Every time he comes, he hates to go back. I have to literally throw him out of the house. He waits till I have bolted the door.

The university closes for Durga Puja soon after. Santiniketan does not observe Durga Puja. Brahmo ideologies do not accommodate idol worship. Aniruddh wants to stay back and work on the finishing of his Kalindi. I offer that he comes to Kolkata and experience the best of Bengali celebrations. He agrees to stay at a friend's place and meet during the pujas. He would also meet my mother during these days. We travel back to Kolkata in his car on the Panchami day. The city is already decked up with lights and pandals; *dhakis* have arrived and are occasionally playing their *dhak* declaring that best days of a Bengali year have approached once again. Restaurants and shopping arcades are crowded and busy. *Shashti* morning, we witness the *Bodhan* and *Amantran*, inviting the holy mother's auspicious footsteps on earth. In the evening, when the city celebrates the homecoming of Durga ma with pomp and pleasure, a celebration of a different nature is on as my mother meets Aniruddh. She is happy that I have agreed to settle down. I am not sure whether I actually have agreed to that, but the way the old lady mingles with the handsome man and conspires together pulling my leg, I guess something good is happening. On Saptami morning, I open my eyes to the chants of Durga mantra being recited in the nearby pandal. Nabapatrika (nine plants) is given a pre-dawn bath and installed alongside lord Ganesha. Nabapatrika or *Kala bou* is believed to be his wife. This is an ancient ritual of worshipping nine types of plants representing nine gods. The banana plant represents Goddess Brahmani, colacasia plant represents Goddess Kalika, turmeric symbolises Devi Durga, jayanti denotes Devi Koumari, bel denotes Goddess Shivaa, pomegranate represents Devi Raktadantika, ashoka symbolises Shokrahita, arum represents Chamunda, rice plant is for Goddess Lakshmi. They are together worshipped as a consolidated symbol of the goddess. In the early hours of *Saptami*, the twigs of white *aparajita* plant along with nine bunches of yellow threads are used to tie the Nabapatrika. It is then bathed. All the nine goddesses representing nabapatrika are bathed with waters from eight different holy places. This bathing ritual is accompanied with varied mantras and diverse musical instruments for different goddesses. Thereafter starts the main Saptami puja of devi Durga.

In the evening, an elaborate dinner is arranged where the entire family comes together to meet the 'world-famous' sculptor and extends a heart-warming welcome. Aniruddh is ragged by my cousins and inducted into my extended family. Elders comment on how handsome the new addition to the clan is and shower praises on him. They voice just one demand: that he must learn Bengali! I am in splits watching his discomfort. They chide me scornfully reminding me that from now on, my abnormal whims need to be curbed. Dr Aniruddh passes amused looks. My cousins though make it difficult for him with their pranks and giggles. His sober nature takes a while to absorb all this initially, but soon after I find he has made friends with them and has bribed them with promises to take them for a movie and shopping and city touring! The madness continues till late in the night and everyone, including Aniruddh, sleeps at our place.

During pujas, I get up and go out early in the morning to pluck *shefali* flowers; these are beautifully fragranced small off-white seasonal blooms with a red base that holds the petals. It is *Ashtami*. Aniruddh wants to join me and my mother happily permits hiding a smile, much to my embarrassment. At 4:45 am when I come out of my bath, I find he is ready post a shower and has offered his puja to our family deities. My mother has no language to praise given that she has a disobedient daughter who needs to be specially invited to bow down before the shrines every day. We step out while everyone else is sleeping. We walk through the lanes from pandal to pandal; there is one at every corner. The pandits have already started warming up preparing for the day's activities; *dhakis* all geared playing the divine music; lamps in clay and brass are lit; each pandal smells of *agarbattis* and camphor burning to spread heavenly fragrance. I show him around the area. My school a few kilometres away; the old house where I stayed–it's almost a dilapidated broken down ruin now; the marketplace under it–people are washing the streets before they lay down their day's ware on display. Most of these people are very dear to us. They are old now and I too have grown; they take a while to remember as I stand in front of them. In my childhood when both my parents left for office, these were the people who guarded the entrance of the building keeping a keen eye on who entered it. I buy something or the other from them and they extend their blessings. We move across the neighbourhoods and I stretch myself to pluck the flowers; I store them in a clean basket that I am carrying. At times Aniruddh helps me. We are about to take the turn towards our lane when there's a shrill noise! My cousins, who have set out to find us have accomplished their goal. We are in for some lewd comments because 'the love-birds had fled early in the morning!' Pushpanjali at the local pandal starts at 10:00 am. We all wear white and rush there. Ma has gifted an off-white dhoti and *tussar* kurta to Aniruddh and I can't help stealing glances at him. He's looking innocently dishy in that dhoti. My cousin has helped him to wear it properly. Stiffly he stands fearing that the cloth might betray control anytime soon. He smiles looking away with the full knowledge that he has my undivided attention. Anjali starts; we take the flowers in our hands, close our eyes and recite the mantras as prompted by the pandit. From the right my cousin, Tia, nudges me with her elbow. I let my right eye loose and raise my eyebrows asking 'What?' 'Too smart I tell you!' She says shamelessly. I smile and close my eyes. An elbow again! 'What?' 'What makes you worship with such diligence suddenly?' She's pulling my leg. 'Practising,' I whisper back, 'These are the symptoms I have to exude to fit into the Rajasthani *gharana* of idol worship.' We chuckle. An elbow from the left this time. I turn with eyes wide open in astonishment. The male voice gestures with eyes shut but a mischievous smile on his lips, 'Quiet!' Tia and I giggle at each other and go back to the mantras, pretending absolute devotion.

After Anjali we return home and all the elderly women gather in the kitchen to prepare and serve *luchi* and *sooji halwa* made with ghee and dry fruits. For lunch, all cousins declare that we are going to prepare the Bengali *Khichdi* with *papad*, *alu bhaja* and *begun bhaja*. Aniruddh joins hands. All relatives come running protesting how can the would-be son-in-law be asked to work. We outshout them and send them off. While cooking and peeling vegetables I can hear that elders are discussing shopping for the upcoming marriage. Yesterday Ma has already had a word with his family without my knowledge. I am yet to take an update on that. My stomach curls thinking what rituals they'll expect me to follow! Will they ask me to wear elaborate jewellery twenty-four hours and cover my head with a veil? EEIKK! In a while I tame my wicked brain. Hasn't Aniruddh taken all the torture we have thrown at him? He has happily followed all our rituals, even wore a dhoti without complaint and has been behaving as if he knew this family since ages. And there he is, chopping cauliflower to help with the lunch preparations. I can't be that wicked.

Early in the afternoon all of us pack ourselves in two big cars and go out touring the city and visiting all big pandals. At some renowned ones there is a huge line. We are pre-decided that we'll not stand in lengthy queues and waste our time. But that doesn't mean we won't have fun. At every big line two of the cousins would step out amidst warnings of the elders, try to enter between the lines unqualified, have a fight and come back giggling. Once, Aniruddh volunteers to this activity, much to our surprise. Happily my cousins Roni and Tia escort him to the business. Politely he asks an elderly lady whether he can stand before her in the line. She looks at him for a while, looks around and stealthily gestures him in! They return laughing hysterically, pointing out that the new bro-in-law has an impact on all kinds of women and it is like 'age no bar' for him! We tour the city all night and at daybreak everyone is dropped off at their respective homes. Most of Navami goes in sleep. In the evening I meet Aniruddh at Dakshineshwar again, near the Ganges. 'Was it too taxing for you?' I ask. He is surprised at my question. 'No. With all this I was getting to know you better. These things make you happy, isn't it? These people, this fun, this chaos. But why then do you choose to remain in isolation?' I lean to half touch his hand with mine. 'I like optimum quantities of both. The silence and the chaos. The family is very dear to me. With them I am a different person. But I can't do this with everyone. I choose to retain myself for the more special ones in life.' His hands come round my waist and pull me in. 'This Diwali you'll meet my family. And don't worry. You will not have to do anything that you don't wish to. That's my promise.' I look up at him. 'Who told you I am worried about that?' He smiles down at me. 'Artists can read minds!' His hand caresses the back of my neck and the hair there. It slides down my back, holds my palm and puts something on my wrist. I whirl round to face him, objecting to the expensive gift. It's a gold bracelet. He stops me. 'Don't utter a word. This is my first gift to you. And Durga puja, I believe, is the right occasion to celebrate our togetherness.' His palm dangerously touches my hair. I smile and move back. People are watching!

Dashami comes with a subdued sound of the *dhak*. Married women pay tribute to the divine mother by smearing her with *sindoor* and sticking sweets on her lips. I watch them from a distance with a common sadness that engulfs every Bengali on this day. While no one is looking, I place a packet at her feet and beg for freedom from my past. All memories of Shekhar go down with her to the ever-welcoming Ganges. For the last time, I let my tears flow uninterrupted, as I seek permission from the departed soul to start my own departure from the self-imposed exile!

The Silence and the Chaos

Dr Aniruddh Jain Solanki
Santiniketan

I have observed that she hasn't, even for a day, removed the bracelet I gave her. In fact, I have caught her playing with it absent-mindedly when she is deep in thought. And she clutches it tight whenever she is nervous. These are simple gestures which mean an ocean to me. I found her clutch on to the bracelet many times when she met my family during Diwali. To keep the word from travelling, I had arranged this meeting at Delhi. We have a house at Green Park since my family keeps travelling to and from Delhi at frequent intervals for business. Also, people at home were not in favour of her staying in the ancestral haveli before marriage since it was considered inauspicious.

When I mention that I am going to fly her to Delhi for a few days, tension hovers over her face. But she doesn't protest. We decided that *Bhabhu* and Deivi ma would reach there with Jisa and Kaka sa, before us. I would introduce Sanghamitra to them first; rest of the family would join subsequently. She was very silent during the flight, almost non-responsive to the advances I made. Spending closely the last few months with her, I have known that the status of her mind never reflects on her face. More often than not, she exudes a strange expressionless facade. But that however does not mean she is bereft of emotions. When she is tensed, she rubs her fingers against her arms and crosses her hands in front. Of late, she clutches on to the bracelet, as if deriving strength from it. A frown with eyes downcast is a declaration of anger. Her eyes smile when she is amused. Since she is pre-occupied sitting in the adjacent seat, I spend some time studying her. A baby pink salwar-kameez, hair tied into a bun. Her ears have those ear-rings that Diya had got for her. An appreciation for her sweeps through my mind. It is nice of her to put these on and subtly express her acceptance, when she'll be meeting Diya for the first time.

However, other than those earrings, Sanghamitra wears no other jewellery. I know that the ladies in my house will frown upon her modest appearance and wrap gold around her neck, ears, ankles, wrists and nose. For a while I can't help wondering how she would look. But I don't wish to frighten her anymore than she already is. How much of the expectations she respects and whatever she chooses not to absorb, can be her sole decision, without my interference. I will definitely not impose anything on her. She can form her own bonds with the members of my family. I understand that Sanghamitra needs space beyond a limit. We'll see how to manage things in the days to come. I keep my eyes locked on her as these thoughts pass my mind. She turns and notices me; smiles and comes closer resting her head on my shoulder and interlocking her fingers with mine.

Jisa has come to receive us. He blesses her on meeting us at the airport; affection oozes out of his eyes. 'Mitra' as he calls her, responds with equal warmth. Deivi ma welcomes us as usual. *Bhabhu* stands beside her with a smile. Everyone is extremely cordial right now, but I know that the ladies are observing everything about Sanghamitra. As we enter the house, the shameless Diya appears and hugs her without even bothering to greet me. I am quite surprised that she is here already. The two older ladies smile at her excitement. 'She claims that you wouldn't have opened your mouth had she not spilled the beans. So it is her natural right to be the first one to greet and get to know Mitra.' I glance at the girls. Diya has already managed to break the ice with Sanghamitra. The two are softly talking about something and sharing naughty smiles. I leave her with the family and go upstairs to my room. Later in the day I meet *Bhabhu* when no one is around. 'Do you like her *Bhabhu*?' She responds with her usual dominance. 'How does it matter? Will it change anything?' I speak after a pause. 'Well. That means you didn't like her.' I turn to leave the room and she stops me. 'She is not as fair as you. I would have liked your wife to be fair and more beautiful. And why doesn't she wear jewellery? It is so inauspicious for a woman to keep her neck, hands or feet bare, without a gold ornament! Anyway, Diya has taken care of that! But I like her personality. She is calm and cordial; but I can also sense stubbornness in her. She doesn't protest if she is not approving something. Just, with a smile, she follows what is right for her. This attitude will help her carry on without offending. And she is following a noble profession. I hear that she is a gold medallist in Economics? That's what I love the most.' *Bhabhu* introspects and adds, 'Education is so important for a woman. All *shringaar* is incomplete without it.' I try to warn *Bhabhu* not to judge her solely based on those docile smiles and apparent quiet; she is quite rebellious and fiercely independent in her own way, I warn. She listens with patience, absorbing all information, as if with a purpose!

Delhi now is pleasant with an early November chill and warm clothes have started coming out. My cousins appear the very next day, eager to meet the new addition to the family. The second floor of the house is reserved for bachelors; first floor for unmarried girls. The ground floor is for the couples. Deivi ma has arranged it this way so that it is comfortable for everyone. In the ground floor, everyone is sitting together and talking to Sanghamitra. Her fingers are playing with the bracelet on her left wrist, as she talks. She looks at me, trying to convey something. Deivi ma must have taken her to the *puja-ghar*. There's vermillion and rice tika between her eyebrows. She brings her eyes together to look up at the tika of her forehead and makes a funny gesture at me; I look away trying to hide a smile. She is wearing some light gold chains and bangles, which Diya must have dug out from her collection. She is visibly uncomfortable with those. I find her unmindfully biting the gold chain hanging across her neck by lifting it between her teeth; at times she takes off the bangle and plays it like a disk making it go very fast around her first finger. At times Diya stops her; otherwise I nudge her on the ribs from behind if she is standing close. One evening when the elders are not around and we are spending some lazy times, Sanghamitra lets her hair loose, pulls out the bindi from her forehead and takes off all the ornaments to leave them on the table. A while later when we hear Deivi ma approaching, all cousins spring up to arrange her back with the hair and ornaments before she arrives. Whatever is left, Abhimanyu picks up in the last moment and hides them in his pocket. Everyone is in splits; Deivi ma raises a quizzical eyebrow in suspicion but lets it pass. Slowly other elders join us and home-made delicacies are being passed around. Diya snatches a cookie from Anish and feeds it to Sanghamitra; they laugh again while Anish looks with pretended disgust and complains as every time he is trying to grab something, it is being snatched away! I watch my family sitting and sharing their moments. Diya is sitting very close to Sanghamitra passing some remarks occasionally which no one else can hear. The elders are scolding her for this ill-mannered behaviour but with a half-concealed smile and no one is taking offence. The girls have bonded like two long lost friends and everyone appreciates that.

The next few days pass by rapidly. I hardly get to see her these days. She has been taken over completely by others. In the mornings she gets up very early and enters the *puja-ghar* with Deivi ma. She sits watching Deivi ma do her rituals and talks to her uninterrupted.

In fact, usual to her nature she sits there quietly helping out the old lady in her chores and listens to the stories that Deivi ma takes a lot of pleasure in telling her. I keep away from these sessions, allowing her to develop her own equation with my people. I am quite pleasantly surprised at her obedience and pliant compliance though. I had never hoped to experience this aspect of her being. She is trying to understand, absorb and learn, all with genuine sincerity. And then again, on the morning before Diwali when the elders are not around, she shocks me close to death.

I had been out for some meetings and return around noon. Right from the gate I can hear shill voices laughing out silly. I enter and walk till the garden and freeze. All my cousins and cousins-in-law are out in the garden, playing holi with mud! As I stand there hopelessly watching the mess, Sanghamitra comes running, chased by the giggling crowd and clashes with me, finally coming to a stop. The crowd stops behind her. My crisp formal shirt is mud-stained! Upset and disgusted, I prepare to offer a lecture on behaviour and etiquette. Much to my surprise, the whole group erupts into laughter even before I mention that I am not at all amused. They all run away leaving me foolishly pondering what to do next! Vainly I try to talk to them and restore peace. But they are driven by a strange madness. They pick up mud from the garden, create small balls and throw at each other. At times, they soak it in water so that the mud sticks to the skin of the victim! Getting hold of the youngest one here, I demand to know who started this. She elaborates, initially Sanghamitra and two others went gardening. In a while Diya teased her saying she's a novice and doesn't know anything about handling plants. Sanghamitra, in response, threw some mud at her to which she immediately reciprocated. Soon after, the rest of the clan joined in!!! I am yet to understand what to do about this when there's a honk of a car close by. Before I realise, laughter gets replaced by shrill warning calls and in no time everyone disappears inside. I am completely confused and turn around to understand what's happening. The car stops at the portico and the elders step out holding large packets in hand. They are returning from shopping. Suddenly their chatter comes to a stop as they find mud balls and mud stains splattered outside. Someone notices me standing with stains on my shirt and all desperate questions are hurled at me. They treat me like the prime suspect of the massacre around and start interrogating. I simply tell them not to ask me anything as I am an innocent victim and move away from there. I instruct the staff to clean up the mess and enter inside. I know the culprits are watching, lurking from multiple corners, and they are enjoying and softly chuckling at the trouble they had got me into by fleeing. I retain the grim look on my face till I reach my room where I let go of all inhibitions. As I laugh thinking about it, I realise that Sanghamitra has already bonded with my cousins and made friends and allies out of them. Also, she has successfully impressed the important people of the house, the decision-makers, the people who matter. Of course there are disagreements. I have seen some of my aunts whispering and gossiping, there are criticisms, but then it is all incomplete if that didn't happen.

On the morning of Diwali, Deivi ma calls me to her room. Kaka sa and my parents are also there. They had been out shopping the day before and want me to have a look at the stuff they have purchased. Quite surprised, I want to know why I am being dragged into all this. They exchange glances and ask me to comment on whether the purchases would match *Mitra's tastes*! I turn to leave, embarrassed, but Deivi ma calls out from behind. They show me the gold necklace they have bought from our ancestral jeweller in Jaipur. It is *shagun* for Sanghamitra. She asks me to wait; the others leave. She starts gathering things and putting them back in her almirah. Then she sits down with me. 'She is nice, and a quick learner. Many of our rituals I didn't even have to teach; she observed us and followed the pattern. Intelligent!'

'How is she with the morning puja?'

She smiles. 'Bad. But as I said, she's a quick learner.'

'I doubt if she'll ever learn, Deivi ma. She doesn't believe in all this. If she is doing something then it is to please you and the others in this house. But it doesn't come to her naturally. Can't we allow her to practise her own ways of worshipping?' I appeal earnestly. I dare to say these to her because Deivi ma is much more modern in her outlook and ideas. More importantly, she is flexible and open to change.

Deivi ma looks into my eyes. 'If this is not her choice then I have enough reason to be glad about her. She never gave me a chance to sense her disinterest! And she's doing all this so that you are not embarrassed in front of your kin and your choice is less questioned! The girl genuinely cares for you.'

I tell Deivi ma the life she leads in Santiniketan. This would be a diametric opposite to her system and lifestyle and I urge Deivi ma to keep it slow for Sanghamitra. I am afraid she'll be distressed if things are imposed on her against her choice. She is being civil and friendly, but is it correct to take her for granted? I have perceived Sanghamitra as a part of Nature. She comes to me in rhythms and alliterations like a beautiful, free-flowing poetry. I feel, there's a soft music about her presence. Disconnecting her with practices and expressions that come naturally, would mean stripping her considerably of the effect she stirs in a moment with her participation. I want her to remain the way she is; my inspiration and my creation; my Kalindi in anticipation of her lover.

Deivi ma takes out a bunch of silver keys and a Lakshmi-Narayan in gold and puts them on top of the red cloth that packed them. 'Do you recognise these?'

'Yes,' I smile and touch them, but don't lift them from where they are. 'The family deity and keys to the haveli. You inherited these from *Baa*, didn't you?'

'Yes. And who do you think would inherit these after me?'

I start wondering and mentally check on our family hierarchy. Slowly my eyes widen and I sit there thunder-struck! I am the eldest in my generation and my wife is meant to inherit those! Sanghamitra!! Her image from yesterday's mud-holi massacre swings across my mind like a pendulum. It can't be; there must be an alternative to this rule. What if I didn't marry? Bewildered I look at Deivi ma. 'Please don't pull her into all this,' I urge. 'She will not be able to do the job you had been doing. She is not meant for this. And if she gets to know that this is what's waiting for her post marriage, I'm sure she'll run away!'

Deivi ma laughs at my distraught face. Then she adds seriously, 'All of us were new to the system once. We had our own romantic dreams of survival. And slowly we experienced life in this family. Sanghamitra will *have* to take up this responsibility later in life. She is free to design her own pedagogy, but she can't escape this. By the time she takes it up, she'll be well trained into it. Your mother has always been ambitious about her would-be daughter-in-law. Because she knows that she has to play the king-maker as much as I, since she has mothered the eldest son of the family. I'm glad she likes Sanghamitra and approves of her.' She stops and looks at my face tensed with the sudden information and realisation. 'Don't think too much about it now. I know you have plans to go abroad and there are many more milestones you wish to cross. But trust me, once you have a child, you would come back home without being prompted. Children always remind you of your roots and you will be no different. And Sanghamitra too would change with time, not because we want her to, but because change is the norm of life. I'll have to do very less to groom her into this role. She will fall into it herself because such are the traits of this family. Expectations and responsibilities would mould her. She'll make mistakes and learn. And then there would be a time when she would not be allowed to make any further mistakes. Or rather, she'll stay prepared for things that go wrong with an overriding alternative. She'll learn to play the game her own way, the way my mother-in-law did, the way I do.' She pauses again and continues, 'I have observed her closely, Aniruddh. She is responsible and selfless in terms of materialistic acquisitions; both of these qualify her for an eventful future. I felt it was my duty to inform you about this before you got married. Everything will be fine, I assure you.' She smiles.

I let out a deep breath and look outside the door. A corner of the hall is visible where women are preparing clay lamps for Diwali. Someone is teaching Sanghamitra how to make those. The curtain on the door flies up and down, enabling and disabling vision. I look back at Deivi ma and manage a half smile. I am visibly worried. How will this carefree, fun-loving woman take up such grave responsibility in the days to come? It is not fair on her. There are so many rituals she'll have to absorb and learn in order to occupy that role! It won't be easy. I get up, take leave from Deivi ma and move out of the door. Standing on one corner of the hall I watch her from a distance. She turns and smiles. Whatever be the future, I can't let go of our present, I decide. I force myself to kill every thought that reminds me of Deivi ma's words. For the last few days I have hardly seen her. Most of the times she is fluttering around with my cousins, giggling with Diya or sitting with the elders. Leaning on the wall, I send her a text, 'Do you remotely remember when we last met? I mean just the two of us?' She reads and smiles. 'When are you free from all this nonsense?' She responds with a mischievous smile, but doesn't care to type on her mobile. 'Are you on Vipasana?' No answer, not even that irritating smile. I am seriously displeased now. No one has been so non-responsive towards me. I am telling her something and she confidently chooses to ignore! Almost determined to pull her out of the gathering, I approach and stop abruptly. She has applied *mehendi* on her hands and they are still wet. She realises I am standing behind and looks up; then raises her palms to show me the designs. I offer a casual glance at her palm and smile at her. So that's why she could not respond to my SMSes; her hands are occupied. It is her first Diwali with my family. God knows what all they'll subject her to. She doesn't show any dissatisfaction though. But who on earth has ever had access to what's going on inside this weird brain? Sanghamitra is responding with endless patience, to everything that she is experiencing, things that are in contradiction to her beliefs. She is not even voicing her thoughts on anything!

By evening, the house is all set for the Diwali celebrations. There's *rangoli* on every corner, women have lit earthen lamps all around and fireworks are ready to be set off. The kitchen smells of various delicious delicacies. My mother inducts Sanghamitra through the puja rituals. She looks confused but not unduly depressed. Neatly she prepares the ghee, sandalwood paste and vermillion in separate chambers of the puja *thali*, puts a gold coin in between, lights the lamp, keeps a gold chain beside, and looks at *Bhabhu* for approval. I remember one of those early days when this woman had told me that she is some kind of atheist! Holding the *thali* with both hands she does the *aarti*. Everyone follows suit. Men start with the fireworks soon after. Women also indulge in it. Those who are less interested serve the sweets and savouries. Another set plays cards in the hall. After so many years I am once again privileged to spend Diwali with my family. By next Diwali, this crazy girl serving fruit juice all around will be my wife. With a passionate longing I watch her move. A yellow *anarkali*, *jhumkas* in pearl, a *bindi* between her eyebrows, colourful bangles adorning her hands and anklets–I have never seen her dressed up so elaborately. She looks beautiful. I turn and face Diya standing right next to me. She just says, 'I chose the dress she is wearing,' and walks away. I can't help control a smile. 'Good job Diya!' I call after her.

I retreat early. Fireworks, dinner and card parties are still on in the ground floor. I can hear the laughter and shouts. But I need to sort out some papers by tomorrow morning before contracting the place where my upcoming exhibition will be held. I reach my room, get into my night clothes, climb on to the bed, pull the soft blanket over me and start reading with only a night lamp on. Almost an hour later, my ears are alerted by the sound of anklets and bangles jingling. Immediately I put off the light, jump out of bed, move to the window that faces the corridor and look through the curtain. My lady is walking in stealthily, clutching on to her bracelet yet again, not sure about which room to knock! She's got guts, I marvel, to take this plunge in a house full of people, all of whom are keeping a watchful eye on her conduct! Slowly I open the door and wait. As she passes my door, I pull her inside and bolt it. In the darkness she can see no more of me than a blurred outline. 'What brings you here? Aren't you scared of getting caught?' I demand to know. She fiddles with her bracelet for a while, then says, 'I thought you wanted me here but I guess I was wrong. I should be more mindful about how others react to me!' She turns to leave. I block the door. 'All these days you never felt like coming to me?' I ask. She is quiet. No answer. I can only hear her quickened breath. I pull her in for a long, passionate hug and dig my nose into her shoulder. Her skin is soft and warm; it rubs against the rough of my face. She exhales a hot breath; raises herself standing on her toes and kisses my chin. The dupatta hanging loose falls off. My body touches hers without any pretence. She doesn't move away but shivers like a rain-washed bird in adventure, resting finally on my bare chest!

The Diwali night did not put to rest, but ignited my desires further. Her submission to my lust was even more divine. I just did not want her to leave. Next morning, however, she is scheduled to travel back while I would return two days after. At a secluded corner of the airport I plant a prolonged kiss on her lips before she walks inside.

I return to Santiniketan in two days time. There is a lot that I need to wrap up here. My days are limited and I need to move out immediately to take charge of my exhibition and also plan the future. In retrospection, I find the time I have spent here has been eventful and fast. My world has taken a 360-degree turn. Nothing is the same as before! Just a year ago I was sitting with Krishna Uncle around this time around and discussing philosophy! And what had Sanghamitra been doing? Concentrating on the music that's audible even if you don't wish to listen? Chatting around with friends? Having tea at

Sukumar da's dhaba? She sits beside me wearing a plain white sari and a shawl that protects her from the winter winds. She turns and raises an eyebrow. This is the way I know her. And this is how I like her. Simple, true to Nature. I wonder why she put up with every demand of my family. Was it because of me? She giggles when I ask her. 'Mr Sculptor, the gods must be wondering above what's wrong with me. I could see them whispering to each other that I have lost it!' She adds after a moment of silence, 'For your family to come to terms with my practices, first I guess I'll have to come to terms with theirs. Otherwise they'll feel I am challenging their beliefs! End of the day, either I'll change or they'll evolve. And if neither of us mend our ways, then even better!' Profound, I admit. Many thoughts cross my mind. I'm not sure whether this marriage will give her the life she wants or deserves. Hope it won't clip the wings of a free bird! The role that she is expected to prepare for might just come in the way of those mischievous glances and naughty smiles. Will she change as a person? Will she stop loving me for pulling her into things that she did not believe in? I end up asking her, 'Sanghamitra, if you get to know that my cousins have planned a booze party on the terrace, which Deivi ma won't approve of, what would you do?' She blinks her eyelids for a while and says, 'I will insist that the women will also drink with them if there's a party in the house. What's in the house is for the entire house.' I take a while to absorb what she has just said and burst out laughing. Her madness might just be the perfect answer for our generation. Deivi ma was right. She'll probably take on the job with sensibilities specific and unique to herself! Or, she'll just let go and relax. I don't need to be so worried or concerned.

It is 23rd December today and Santiniketan celebrates its biggest festival. *Poush Mela.* Students have put up elaborate stalls showcasing their talent in the fair. Till late last night we were working to put things in place. I slept really late. When I got up, washed and came to Mrigaya, I was greeted with a big lock! Mobile switched off! For the next forty-five minutes I am running up and down to every possible place that the lady is expected to grace. Finally I find her in front of Uttarayan, walking towards Upasana Griha. With a wide grin she says that she had switched off her mobile during *Baitalik* and forgot to switch it on later. But I'm sure she has done it deliberately. This is her way of punishing me for not attending *Baitalik* with her. We walk into Sukumar da's dhaba for breakfast. It's pretty crowded here with locals and visitors who have come in to enjoy the fair. Known faces greet us from different directions. As we take our first bite into the alu paratha, we find Anusua walking in hurriedly. 'Sukumar da, tea,' she calls and turns to me. 'I heard you are leaving? Students told me last night!' I share a quick glance with Sanghamitra and nod in confirmation. 'But why? What's the point of joining and leaving so early?' she says loudly. I smile as I answer her. 'I was never a full-timer here, Anusua. Such was my arrangement with the department.' She looks sad. Sanghamitra tells me she always reacts like this when people leave Santiniketan. Soon we are joined in by the rest of the crowd. A quick breakfast and we are headed for the fair.

This place has magic. These crowds that shout and cheer and enjoy, elevate lost spirits. In chaos and silence, I have given my life a fresh start. All these people–who have loved me, hated me, praised me and have been indifferent towards me–hold a very important space in my heart. Because they have shared space with the most beautiful developments of my life. As I emotionally prepare myself for a transfer, I am at a loss for words. Seldom have I got an opportunity to thank life for whatever it has given me. Today, I live each achievement as if it is a blessing. And through my work, I offer life to my fantasies. It feels, I own both dreams and destiny!

The calm of Sanghamitra's home has witnessed my rare passion confronting the apparent restraint which was once my pride and strength. So easily have I slipped and transited from some age old habits. My body, mind and soul react to her mysterious attraction with an animal instinct and I find it to be my most sacred experience! One such evening when I was sitting next to her, imprisoning her tight between my hands into a close confinement and digging into her depths, Sanghamitra mischievously lifted my face with her hands and asked, 'What will you tell Sagnik about us?' For a moment I didn't know who she was referring to! Before I connected to it, pat came her next question, 'Did you ever feel jealous when he spoke to you about his romantic interests for me?' Intensely she looked into my eyes as my face stilled very close to her, waiting for her to stop so that I get back to what I was engaged in doing! The notorious smile in her eyes told me that she was challenging my restraint and was quizzing me with silly distractions only to further fuel my hunger! But there was impatience in her eyes too, as I wasted a few moments simply watching her. Finally I uttered, 'Keep quiet and concentrate on me; leave Sagnik to me, I'll handle him.' 'But did you feel jealous?' She repeated with melodramatic angst in her eyes. I clutched both her hands with mine so they couldn't stop me from getting back to her and terminated her immoderate vocal indulgences with my mouth!

Swagata, or Stuart, as they call him, is enjoying his smoke at one corner. I don't agree with most of what he has to say, but there is something that makes me like him. He is one of those who have known Sanghamitra for a very long time. A large part of her existence, without me, is captured somewhere in his brain. I walk up and stand next to him. The smoke irritates though! Without looking at me, he comments, 'You and Sam are having a scene, right? Decided anything yet?'

'Yes,' I say, 'marriage in two months!'

He drops his cigarette and enfolds me in a hug. Others come running unsure of what provoked two disagreeing particles to unite. We don't answer. The unruly crowd doesn't allow anyone to block space for too long, without a reason. From stall to stall we wander, voicing our good wishes to the students and professors in charge.

At one opportune moment Stuart again manages to share a word with me in isolation. Amidst smoke that emerges from his nostrils after inhaling the white butt, he asks, 'So, what's the last wish before you marry, bro?' I smile back at him. 'I wish that you'd stop smoking; I wish that you agree to vegetarian dishes being sacrosanct and being preferred over non-vegetarian meals; and I sincerely wish your Sam stops calling me Mr Sculptor!!'

Not very far away, Sanghamitra is busy with sweet nothings. Dark red flowers that locals call *rudrapalash* have changed the texture of the soil by covering it with their petals. Of and on, the tree disowns its over-mature blooms and they fall on the ground to be picked up by pedestrians. Sanghamitra is busy picking up the better ones among them to be kept in the vase of her living room. She calls them her Fall Winter Collections!

Acknowledgements

I never knew how to tell a story! I stop blank every time after I've said to my son, 'Once upon a time there was a king!' But when it comes to Santiniketan, I guess every soul has an exclusive, unparallel tale. For most of us, who have been there done that, our story remains embedded somewhere deep inside and never experiences daylight. However, spending days with my author husband probably made me treat the word file of my laptop with patience, a word that seldom defines me. I thank Tuhin A. Sinha for the positivity he brings to my life and the inspiration that led me to write down things without bothering about who will think what when they know what occupied my mind!

I can't ever thank enough Mrs Tultul Niyogi for accepting this manuscript and agreeing to work with me on this. And of course my editor, Gita Rajan. She helped transform some disconnected loose thoughts to bind into a complete novel. It was a delight working with both of you.

My friends Amit Sharma and Ranjan Pant, 'thanks' is a small word for the encouragement I have always received from you in everything I have ever done. Sanhita Banerjee, you were my Kala Bhavan connection and a lot of magnificence there I sensed and experienced through you. Dr Abhra Bose, Dr Sreela Bose, Supratim Pal, Nirmallya Mandal, Soma Chatterjee Mandal, I still cherish the fun that we had together and you guys never failed me. Prof. Dipankar Roy, thanks for those wonderful photographs that you have allowed me to use for the promotions of the book.

It took my mother, Ratna Dasgupta and father, Late Dhruba Ranjan Dasgupta quite some courage to let their only daughter leave the shelter of home and live elsewhere, in a hostel, though I already had admitted myself to a good college in Kolkata. They loved Santiniketan as much as I did, and stood by my happiness like they have always done. Nothing can begin or end, till I have remembered both of you.

Lastly, all those friends in Viswa Bharati who made my days vibrant and evenings fun-filled, with many of whom I have lost touch over time, this goes out as a pleasant recap and reunion for all of us.